J.C. HANNIGAN

collateral

BOOK THREE OF THE COLLIDE SERIES

J.C. HANNIGAN

COLLATERAL

acknowledgements

Thank you so much to Lisa Davall for editing, Nikki Colligan, for proofreading, Yosbe Designs for bringing Harlow to life again in another phenomenal cover, and Chelsea Barnes – for being the best Book Manager, encourager, and friend I could ask for, and my FANnigans; your belief in me makes me feel that I could move mountains, and your support has been unwavering.

When I started writing the story of Harlow Jones three years ago, I really had no idea that it would grow to what it has today. I can honestly say with upmost certainty that I wouldn't have made it this far without the consistent voices and honest input of Christina Harris, Kristen Johnson, and Lauren Jones. They made themselves readily available each and every time I needed to sort through character development and plot issues. They kept me going when I wanted to throw in the towel and quit.

I also wouldn't have gotten far without my hilarious chats with Whitney Barbetti, who understands how frustrating it can be to be so invested in characters. Elizabeth Barone also needs to be acknowledged and worshiped; that girl gets mad props for telling me to participate in NaNoWriMo in 2013...without her peer pressure, I never would have sat down and penned *Collide*.

Furthermore, it wouldn't have been possible for me to continue writing without the support and encouragement of my husband and our two boys.

J.C. HANNIGAN

COLLATERAL

dedication

This one is for those who stood by me. Thank you for believing in me; thank you for supporting me and thank you for making this dream worth having over and over again.

Love is friendship that has caught fire. It is quiet understanding, mutual confidence, sharing and forgiving. It is loyalty through good and bad times. It settles for less than perfection and makes allowances for human weaknesses.
-- Ann Landers

J.C. HANNIGAN

prologue

IF FEAR had a taste, it would be metallic, like blood and blades.

For the last several weeks, sleep came to me with great difficulty if at all. I usually awoke at the ungodly hour of three o'clock. I'd stay in bed, lying there in the dark of night, staring up at the ceiling while I tried to ease my racing heart. I always woke up feeling panicked, as if someone was lurking in the farthest corner of my bedroom…watching me.

I knew better than to give in to my paranoia and turn on the light. I knew nobody was in my room. Instead, I waited for the seconds to tick by, the minutes to fade away until it was a more appropriate time for me to get up.

The gym opened its doors at six o'clock sharp. I liked how peaceful and quiet it was at this time. Aside from one or two employees that left me alone, the place was mostly empty.

On that particular morning, I awoke from the same nightmare I always had, the terror clinging to my skin like the sheen of sweat that coated my body. I tried to fall back asleep, but it was pointless, so at five-thirty, I threw my hair up into a ponytail and made my way over to my own personal sanctuary.

Exercising had become my drug of choice to battle the demons in my head. It was here that I was *almost* able to disconnect from the fears that plagued me, but sometimes even the ferocious exertion wasn't enough to drive away the lingering terror.

An hour into my workout, I was feeling little to no respite. My fists pounded against the punching bag furiously in response to the memories that always seemed to come at me in a strangled rush—memories that made up the reoccurring nightmare. Sweat poured into my eyes, but I didn't pause on my enraged attack to dry my sweaty face. I blinked away the moisture, challenging all of my pent up frustration through my fists and into the burgundy punching bag.

When Andrew Cooper appeared in my bedroom holding a large hunting knife, intent on getting the revenge he felt he deserved, I hadn't thought the outcome would be very good for me. I knew by the twisted look of rage on his face that he wouldn't stop until he hurt me in all the ways he dreamed of for ruining his life…and Andrew Cooper had dreamt a lot about his moment of revenge.

At the beginning of twelfth grade, I walked in on him raping a girl at a party. I encouraged Jenna Burke (who later became my best friend) to press charges and I testified as an eyewitness. The trial brought up evidence that Carl Cooper, the Chief of the North Bay Police Department, had covered up several more sexual assault incidents to protect his son, as well as countless other dirty deeds. Andrew walked away with a slap on the wrist and a smear on his permanent record, but Carl Cooper had faced serious jail time.

Andrew blamed me for ruining his cushioned, carefree life and vowed to make me pay for it. His intention had been to maim me in unspeakable ways.

It was the most terrifying moment of my life. I attempted to run away, but Andrew caught me by my hair, pressing the cold steel of his knife against my throat. He dragged me back to my room, throwing me on the bed, and started talking about all the horrifying things he was going to do to me...with and without his weapon.

I put up a commendable fight when Andrew climbed on top of me. I kneed him hard in the balls, hoping to stun him enough to get away. Instead of the escape I had hoped for, Andrew cracked the butt of the hunting knife down hard against my cheekbone, breaking the skin and nearly the bone.

I remember the sensation of my blood dripping, wet and sticky, down my cheek and into my ear as Andrew struggled to get into position. I truly thought in that moment that I would die. I had almost *wanted* to die. It could have been worse—so much worse—than what it was had Jax Walker not come to the rescue when he did.

Jax had exploded into my room and thrown Andrew clean off me. His large, imposing size and his training in Mixed Martial Arts made him the stronger, faster fighter. But Jax suffered a stab wound when he turned to tell me to run.

I swung around, my foot connecting hard against the solid punching bag with a smart thump. I continued my assault, pounding my fists against it until a tear escaped, trailing along the same pathway of sweat droplets from my forehead. I finally stopped, my breathing labored. I hunched over with my hands on my knees, my eyes still focused on the punching bag.

Grabbing my hand towel and water bottle from the floor, I dried my face as I took a deep drink of cold water, finally beginning to feel at peace. I kept my eyes on the punching bag, not wanting to make eye contact with any of the few others working out.

I wanted to be normal; I wanted to be happy, but it was impossible to be happy with every subconscious thought drowning me in that night.

My chest heaved with frantic breaths—partly due to the exertion, but also due to the panic that the memories brought on. I placed the water bottle down slowly, keeping my eyes on that blasted punching bag as if it was to blame for all of the turmoil I felt.

I got into position again, taking a brief pause before I resumed the therapeutic thumping of my fists against the textured surface. The punching bag was anchored to the floor and the ceiling by a thick chain; it wasn't going anywhere, but I punched it like I could free it from the chains and send it flying across the gym. I punched it like I could unload every last negative, confusing thought that gripped my mind and soul and darkened it.

chapter ONE

I BALKED before the mirror hanging on the back of my bedroom door. I was dressed and ready for the day, but I hesitated in doing my usual final check. My reflection mocked me, showing a young woman that looked strong and resilient when I felt anything but. My body was beginning to reap the benefits of my new, vigorous gym schedule; my muscles were leaner and more toned than they had ever been before. My long, wavy dark hair and emerald green eyes were the same as ever, but my face had lost some of its roundness...its innocence.

Each time I looked in the mirror or any other reflective surface, my eyes would instantly find the only physical scar from that night.

I gingerly touched the three inch mark that cut across my left cheekbone. Three weeks ago, I was attacked. Three weeks ago, it was an angry reddish purple colour. Now, it was faded to a soft pink. The plastic surgeon that glued the split skin together on my cheek told me it would take time to heal, but would eventually fade.

It was unfathomable to me just how quickly my body healed in three weeks. My skin had meshed itself back together while my mind and soul remained tattered and torn. I couldn't help but feel as if the emotional scars of the trauma would never fade.

I was lucky. I knew that. I was *thankful* for that. I knew that it could have been a lot worse than it actually was; I could have walked away with worse than a mere cut on my cheek.

My body could have been mutilated. I could have been raped. I could have been killed. *I could have lost Jax.*

My hand trembled slightly, memories of that night resurfacing. I squeezed my eyes shut, gritting my teeth. Now was not the time for a trip down memory lane, especially not *that* part of my life, but I was powerless against the onslaught.

I shook as the memory of Andrew and Jax fighting exploded in my brain. The terror that gripped my heart as I watched the knife in Andrew's hand lash out against Jax was *still* very real to me, even though it was just a memory—even though Jax was fine.

I still shivered when I remembered the white bone when Jax had raised his hand to wipe the blood from my cheek wound away. He hadn't even realized that Andrew had cut him with the knife—at least not until I pointed it out before fainting in his arms.

Like I said, things could have been a lot worse than they were. Jax walked away with minimal damage. He had used his forearm to block the attack, and when the knife dropped down, it bounced off his rib cage.

Jax hadn't seemed bothered by the fact that he'd been sliced open because of me. He didn't blink before throwing himself at a knife-wielding maniac. If that wasn't romance, I didn't know what was.

I ran my brush through my long dark hair, working the tangles out. I was completely aware of the fact that I was procrastinating. Since the attack, I had strategically avoided almost everybody in my life. I didn't want to see the worry on their faces; I didn't want to hear the concern in their voices. I wanted to become a part of the background again. I didn't want the attention this stupid attack had brought me. I wanted the scar to hurry up and fade away, and most of all, I wanted the fear to go with it.

Unfortunately, it didn't look like the attention was going to go away any time soon. The university's newspaper and the city paper had both blown up with the "breaking news" of Andrew Cooper's attack. Naturally, some intelligent reporters had gotten the inside scoop on the North Bay drama too. Thankfully, the only dirt they managed to dig up was that I was involved in putting Carl Cooper behind bars. The stories ended up going viral on Facebook, much to my absolute horror and dismay.

It was hard to forget about it because I was not only haunted by memories, but because everyone around me constantly brought it up in some way. Maybe it was a comment, an attempt at causal indifference when they asked *"how are you doing?"* but the pity and the concern underlying that statement are always there.

My family and friends were absolutely horrified to hear that Andrew Cooper had been stalking me, biding his time for a while. He knew my every move, he was always watching in the shadows...*and I hadn't even known it.* That knowledge made me angry and anxious. What else was lurking, waiting to strike out when I was most vulnerable?

My cell phone started to ring, the shrill sound cutting through the silence of my bedroom and the hollow echoes of my thoughts. I picked it up and clicked answer without reading the caller ID. I instantly chided myself for my negligence when my mother's frantic voice filled my ears. "Hello? Harlow?"

"Hi, Mom," I sighed, sinking down onto my bed. I had a feeling this conversation was going to take a while. It was the first time in a week that Mom's attempts at getting me on the phone were successful. "How are you? How's Larry?"

"We're fine, honey," Mom said. "What about you? How's counseling going?"

I rolled my eyes, knowing that she couldn't see me. "It's going good, Mom. Really good, I'm great. Really, I am. And I'd totally appreciate it if everybody would stop acting like I'm made of glass now."

Mom chuckled sadly. "Oh, Harlow, nobody thinks you're made of glass. I'd be calling you anyway to check in. I miss you."

The resentment and anger still lingered beneath the surface, and the thick blanket of guilt just made me feel as if I was suffocating. "I miss you too, Mom. I'll get out there soon." It was a lie and she knew it. I hated going back to North Bay. North Bay had never felt like home to me, especially not after everything that happened there.

Andrew Cooper was well known in North Bay. He had been the town's golden boy, its pride and joy. His connections protected him from facing the law for years, and when I walked into town and blew apart the pretty little façade that was the Coopers, everything went to shit. I immortalized the Coopers in the biggest scandal the town had ever seen; I had also tarnished their name in the process.

Rightfully so, if you asked me and every last one of Andrew's many victims.

"Easter is around the corner!" she reminded me, cutting into my thoughts. The hope was evident in her voice. My eyes flickered over to the calendar pinned to the bulletin board hanging over my desk.

"Easter isn't for another two months," I pointed out. I'd forgotten to change the calendar, and December winked at me tauntingly. I stood up, stomping over to my desk so I could flip it to January.

"Well, time flies and I know you're going to be busy this semester. It's your last one, after all! Larry and I would really love it if you and Jax could book Easter weekend ahead of time. We'd love to see you both," Mom said, trying to be casual. I could hear the yearning in her voice from miles away.

"I'll ask him," I said, trying to pacify her even though I knew I'd likely forget all about it. "But look, I'm running late for class. I'll call you later."

"Okay, honey. I love you," Mom said.

"Love you too," I muttered, ending the call.

The sound of footsteps falling against the hallway floor made me take pause. Someone was approaching. Each footfall spoke of caution and determination.

I glanced up as Jenna came to a stop in the doorway of my bedroom.

Jenna's short blond hair was arranged perfectly under her dark purple knitted toque. She was dressed in skinny jeans and the adorable knitted sweater that I bought her for Christmas; it was a dark gray with a scooped neckline that rested against her thin shoulders. She'd matched a black belt with it, and she looked perfectly put together…like always.

I felt grungy next to her, wearing my favourite pair of jeans and a boring t-shirt. I'd done the same makeup regimen I'd done for years: cover up, mascara, and liquid-eyeliner "cat eyes". It was almost automatic to do my makeup that way; I didn't even think about it anymore.

"Are you ready to go?" she asked, almost seeming to steel herself against my response.

"Yeah," I responded, my tone void of any emotion. I brushed past her, making my way down the narrow hallway and through our apartment to the front door. I slid into my leather jacket and pulled my black knitted toque over my head, reaching over to grab my messenger bag from the hook by the front door.

She sighed quietly from behind me, defeated by my mood. I had been in quite the foul disposition lately. Jenna understood, but I could tell that she was beginning to get sick of my scowling, perpetually angry attitude. Jenna was trying to be there for me, but I was making it very difficult. Part of it had to do with the fact that I really hadn't been sleeping well. If I wasn't waking up in a cold sweat, convinced that I felt the metal of a hunting knife against my throat, then I was unable to shut off my mind.

I didn't really know *what* my deal was, but I knew if I didn't figure it out soon, I would push more than Jenna away.

Thoughts of my boyfriend, Jax, nearly took my breath away. Thinking about Jax was like a double edged sword. Thoughts of him made me happy, but they also made me feel incredibly guilty, considering I had locked lips with my ex-boyfriend.

Iain Bentley had been my twelfth grade English teacher, and in my final year of high school, I fell *hard* for him, and he had fallen for me too. I followed my desires and ignored the risks as they led me straight into Iain's arms. We carried on a relationship from September until February, when I received an envelope full of photos of the two of us.

The photos had been a warning, more or less, from Andrew Cooper's father, Carl. I was going to testify in court for Jenna—I had been the one to walk in on them that night. I heard Jenna sobbing hysterically, begging Andrew to stop. I went into the bedroom and found Jenna in tears with Andrew. It was obvious from the tears streaming down Jenna's face and the way Andrew had casually tucked himself back in his jeans that he had forced himself on her.

My testimony was important to the trial, and the pictures were a warning that if I spoke out, those photos would be brought to light. And Iain would get arrested.

Not testifying wasn't an option, though, and Iain knew that. He agreed completely with me, and...I would say that he sacrificed himself so that I could do the right thing and help Jenna attempt to get justice.

I foolishly thought that Carl Cooper wouldn't make good on his threat, and I was almost lulled into a false sense of security as the days passed after the trial without incident. I knew that I couldn't run back into Iain's arms, but I had started to believe that we would both escape unscathed.

Unfortunately, we weren't that lucky. Another envelope full of photos surfaced at the police station. Iain was arrested and served one year in jail for sexual exploitation of a minor. After his release, he didn't seek me out. I hadn't seen him until a few days before Andrew attacked me, when I randomly ran into him at the mall when I was shopping with Jenna for a Christmas present for Jax.

I hadn't *meant* to kiss Iain, but when he showed up on my doorstep shortly after the attack, it just sort of...happened. He saw my face, got super emotional over it, and before I could react he was kissing me. It hadn't lasted more than a moment, but for that brief fleeting instant, I kissed him back...and I liked it.

I kept no secrets from Jax though, not after my last secret nearly got us both killed. The very day it happened, I tearfully told him the truth about Iain.

It shocked the hell out of me when Jax didn't dump me as I expected him to. Most guys don't handle it well when their girlfriend tells them that she kissed an old flame that she still has lingering feelings for. He was hurt, but he also understood. He gave me a pass, more or less.

The kiss with Iain had come at a confusing, conflicting time. I'd just been released from the hospital after the attack and was still in shock over the whole thing. My mind wasn't moving at the pace that it usually moved.

Still, I couldn't help but overanalyze it. Did I kiss Iain back because I was in shock, or did I kiss him back because a part of me still wanted to be with him? My conflicting emotions about the whole thing were making it damn near impossible for me to get any sleep, even when Andrew wasn't haunting my dreams.

Jenna was scrutinizing me with a concerned frown on her face. I shook my head, realizing that I had zoned out and completely missed whatever she had said.

"Coffee?" I grumbled, trying to make amends. Jenna perked up, nodding. We headed out of our apartment.

"I heard you last night," Jenna said, eyeing me carefully as she paused to lock the apartment door behind us. Jenna and I lived in the second floor apartment in a beautifully renovated Victorian house. There was no elevator, but the house was full of charm and it was within walking distance of campus. It was the first place I'd ever really been in that had *felt* like home and I loved it. My hand reached out, touching the wooden railing while I waited for Jenna to pocket her keys.

"Sorry," I finally responded when Jenna fixed me with a penetrating stare. I guess the intense workout I'd had the night before hadn't succeeded in stomping out the nightmares.

"Don't be sorry. Have you spoken to Dr. Philips about it yet?" She took a moment to slide her hands into the matching purple mittens. I shoved mine in my jacket pockets, my teeth clenching together with aggravation. It was bad enough that I had to deal with my mom hovering over me, making sure I was speaking about my feelings to the shrink.

"No," I replied, starting down the stairs. Jenna was on my heels. I could hear her boots thudding against the wooden steps as she rushed to keep up with me, but I didn't slow my pace or look at her. I was trying to calm myself.

I hadn't told Jenna—or my mother—about bailing out on my appointments with Dr. Philips. I didn't want them to pressure me into going again. The only person who knew I'd stopped going was Jax, and he wasn't on my back about it. He just understood…silently.

"You've still been going to your appointments, haven't you?" Jenna scolded, her brow furrowing as she assessed me. She'd been a part of my life long enough to recognize when I was keeping something from her. "Harlow!"

"I've been busy," I argued, my voice rising a little in defense.

"Harlow, you really need to go," she said, her voice gentle and soft. "I think she could help you."

"Maybe," I sighed doubtfully, stepping out onto the stoop of our apartment. In the few appointments I had with Dr. Phillips, I hadn't let her get close. I'd been stubborn and closed off, tight lipped. I looked back at Jenna, who was keeping a careful distance from me as if she thought I would lash out and attack her. My shoulders slumped slightly and I frowned. "You know me, Jenna. I don't open up easily...especially not when I *know* the person just wants to crack open my head and fix what's broken."

"Don't you want that? To fix the broken parts?" Jenna whispered, her eyes wide.

"What if it's not that simple?" I murmured, averting my gaze. "I've seen psychiatrists before; they always want to prescribe something. I've had antidepressants and anti-anxiety medication. I don't need sleeping pills or anything else. I just want..." I trailed off, unable to put into words what I wanted.

I wanted my life to stop being so bloody complicated and confusing. I wanted one year to go by without something traumatic happening. I felt dangerously close to the edge and I hated it.

I used to be tough, untouchable, and almost ruthless. I used to wear armor; I used to keep myself so locked off from everyone else. After the trauma I had endured in my first year of high school, I never wanted to give anybody the opportunity to hurt me again.

Much like Jenna, I was also sexually assaulted. It happened at a party that I had gone to with my first boyfriend, Cole. Our relationship was still in the early stages—the one where you were so enthralled with one

21

another. Being with Cole felt like innocence and magic. It was exciting, dating a popular guy on the school basketball team. Cole was well known and well liked, and he chose *me*, the quiet girl that sat toward the back of the classroom.

I was elated to have Cole's attention, elated to have *anyone's* attention, really. My mom was constantly working and when she wasn't, she was dating. Making friends wasn't exactly a talent of mine even then. I was too solemn, too dark looking. I spent most of my time alone until Cole smiled his crooked grin at me and I felt like someone was actually *noticing* me.

We had only been dating for three months when we received an invitation to hang out at one of his friend's houses after a home game. Several of his other teammates were there, but I was the only girl. One teammate, Casey, put a roofie in my drink.

The details of that night were still fuzzy, but for the longest time afterwards, I believed the rumors I heard about me: that I had slept with the entire basketball team. My classmates turned against me for hurting Cole, the girls wrote terrible things on my lockers and the guys were forever making suggestive comments.

I couldn't handle it anymore; I switched schools and met Lauren. She became my first female friend ever, and the first person I ever truly connected with on a deeper level. We were fast friends, kindred spirits, spending all of our time together until she died in a car accident. I was with her, and I could still recall the horrible memories of that night...of her face lying against the dark pavement, blood seeping out from a wound in her head.

I felt responsible. It had been my boyfriend, high on drugs, behind the wheel. I walked away with barely a scratch, but my best friend—the first person to truly get me—was gone. Her absence was so notable that I couldn't escape it.

I relocated with my mom. I wasn't able to handle the ghost of Lauren. She was everywhere I looked in Toronto, or worse...her parents were. They had never forgiven me for the accident; I could feel their hatred rolling off their bodies in waves at the funeral.

I needed a fresh start where I could keep everyone at a distance until I graduated.

Then I met Iain. I fell in love and opened myself up to all the heartbreak that comes with it. Being with him was incredible. He filled the void in my heart that had been a constant companion since Lauren's death. But then I lost him, and the aftermath of that relationship was not pretty. I shut myself off and walked around in a numbed state until four months ago, when Jax Walker sauntered in to my life with his smooth smile and rugged good looks.

If Jax wasn't Jax, and if he didn't make me so happy, I could hate myself for being with him. I never wanted to be that flighty woman that fell in love every other year with someone new; I never wanted to be my mom, a serial dater who *needed* a man to feel complete. I didn't want to need *Jax*, but it was glaringly obvious that he *did* make me feel complete.

Jenna's hand on my arm brought me back to the present. "I'm not saying you need to go back to Dr. Philips and spill your guts, but you *need* to talk to someone. I'm worried about you, Harlow. I know that you can take a lot of punches, and you *have*...but you need to know that it's okay to ask for help. Don't keep closing yourself off from everyone; you'll never heal that way and you know it."

"I know," I sighed. I wasn't impervious to the fact that psychiatric help was a good thing—a necessary thing. I just didn't think that Dr. Philips could eliminate these particular demons. I had a feeling that they had more to do with my perception of love and my actual love life and less to do with the whole Andrew thing. Simply put: I needed to get over myself and deal with my shit.

Maybe Jenna was right. Maybe if I let her, Dr. Philips could help me sift through all the shit in my head and make sense of it.

"Good." Jenna sighed with relief and we started to walk along the sidewalk, our footsteps crunching patterns in the fresh snow and our breath escaping in puffs of clouds in front of our faces.

chapter TWO

WE MADE our way to *The Bean*, the coffee shop that we frequented more than I cared to admit, and not *just* because I worked there. *The Bean* was notorious for having the best coffee, sandwiches, and baked goods in town. It also had a comfortable, trendy environment that everybody loved. The owners, Jamie Hunter and Mark Judge, were personable and memorable. It was impossible not to like their outgoing personalities. They hired me on the spot when I brought in a resume shortly after moving to Ottawa.

Although I couldn't see myself slinging coffee for the rest of my life, I loved my job. I had quite a cushion put away in my savings account since my rent was so cheap. Jenna's father insisted on covering the cost of our cozy little apartment. He wanted Jenna to focus on school and he refused to accept my offers to pay even half.

He claimed he would have done it anyway for Jenna, and that he liked that I lived with her. Apparently, he worried less about her when I was around—or at least, he used to. I wasn't really sure if he still felt that way after the whole Andrew thing. I hadn't seen Mr. or Mrs. Burke since just after the attack, and they were shaken up.

When I entered the coffee shop, I was instantly greeted by the comfortable buzzing of conversation, the sweet, thick aroma of coffee, and the little chime from the bell that rang whenever someone opened it. The smell of coffee always made me relax a little.

The shop was surprisingly quiet at the usually busy hour of eight o'clock. A few customers were scattered throughout on comfortable arm chairs, sipping their caffeinated beverages as they stared at their cell phone screens with glazed eyes. I closed my own eyes, enjoying the fragrances and sounds of this familiar place. Coffee, fresh pastries, and the sound of spoons clinking against ceramic mugs. This place was more than just a paycheck to me; it was warm, it was home.

"Good morning, my beautiful darlings!" Jamie's sing-song voice rang out. I opened my eyes to Jamie's toothy grin as he stood behind the counter. He had recently gotten a haircut, and now wore his light hair in a Mohawk comb-over hybrid that would have looked ridiculous on anybody else but somehow suited him. Jamie's pale blue eyes assessed me with intelligence. He didn't miss a thing.

Jamie's buoyancy was sometimes a little much for me, but I loved him all the same. He had completely taken me under his wing and filled the supportive authority figure spot in my life. It didn't matter that Jamie was only twenty-seven, a mere six years older than me; he still fussed over me like a mother hen.

"Caffeine," I managed, hoping that I didn't look as exhausted as I felt.

Jamie was already preparing our drinks without asking us what we wanted. Jenna came in often enough that he'd memorized her order as effortlessly as he had memorized mine. He had taken her under his wing as well. My friends were always welcome around Jamie and Mark.

"How are you doing, Harlow?" Jamie asked, purposely keeping his voice light as he sent me another searching look over the coffee machine. The words he didn't say hung between us, thick and sticky.

After the attack, I took a couple of weeks off at the insistence of everyone around me, including Jamie and Mark. My bosses flat out refused to let me come back until I had a few weeks of rest. I personally thought it was more detrimental than helpful—I damn near went insane. I started to spend *a lot* more time at the gym, working my body in an attempt to distract my mind. I found working out was a rather good distraction...almost as good as the distraction Jax provided. After two weeks off, I finally went back to work a week ago, and I was thankful for the normalcy of it. But Jamie still worried and fretted over me. He still asked me if I was *okay* before each and every shift. He wanted me to talk to him; he wanted me to divulge how I was feeling and how I was handling things.

"I'm fine," I said honestly, meeting his inquisitive gaze with a determined one of my own. I was determined to not show how exhausted I was, how emotionally draining this entire thing had been.

"Okay." Jamie nodded, accepting my answer. I could tell he was a little disappointed, but he shrugged it off well enough. He placed a large green tea and a large coffee on the ledge and gave me another easy smile, his white teeth flashing against his tanned skin. "Lucas will be working with you tonight."

"Really, Jamie. I'm fine," I insisted again, rolling my eyes. Lucas was another employee at *The Bean*. I didn't need Lucas to keep an eye on me, and frankly, I didn't want him there. "Besides, I'm sure Jenna wants to hang out with Lucas," I added, nudging Jenna's arm with my elbow. She was dating Lucas.

Mark Judge pushed open the revolving door, carrying a tray of freshly baked croissants and scones. He whistled happily, sending a large wink Jenna's way. She smiled at him before answering.

"We're hanging out tomorrow," she said, forcing a smile. I took a moment to swallow the sudden rise of panic. Since the attack, my anxiety had worsened. It was another thing that I *probably* should admit to someone like Dr. Philips, but I was stubborn. I wanted to control my own reactions, and I couldn't shake the foolish and stupid notion that taking medication would mean that I was out of control...again.

I took a slow breath, forcing a smile to my face as I struggled to appear completely unaffected. I didn't want to give my friends anything else to worry about.

"Really, I'm fine," I said, keeping my voice even despite the panic and anger. Since my return, both Jamie and Mark had been tip-toeing around me. They scheduled me to work the day shifts, when either one of them or Lucas could be there. All I wanted was things to go back to the way that they were before. "You don't need to have Lucas babysit me. I can close by myself."

Mark paused, watching the interaction between Jamie and me. I could tell Jamie was about to argue. He opened his mouth, but Mark swiftly cut him off. "I think she can handle it."

"I know she can," Jamie agreed, his eyes falling on Mark's face. He smiled lovingly, an expression that would have made my heart ache with loneliness if the thought of Jax hadn't crept in.

Jamie and Mark had one of the most loving relationships that I had ever witnessed. They were affectionate with one another and had an easy banter about them. They almost seemed to speak their own language. Mark was completely tuned to Jamie, and vice versa. They were a unit, a team. They were a force to be reckoned with.

Seeing them together before I met Jax was so sweet that it stung. It made me ache for the same thing; someone that was just *home* to me no matter where we were.

They looked at each other for another moment, communicating with one another without words. Jamie nodded as if Mark had brought up an important point. "We're just looking out for you, honey. You look like you didn't sleep at all last night. Is Jax keeping you up too much? We need to have a chat with that boy!"

"I stayed up late studying last night," I responded. While that wasn't exactly true, Jax hadn't spent the night. I wish he had, though. I slept much better with him beside me.

Jamie sighed heavily, pressing his lips together while he considered me. "Fine, Lucas can get off at seven and you can close the store," he relented.

I felt the eely sensation of panic lessening slightly. I glanced at the clock over the counter. "We've got to go though. I'll be here at three."

"Have a good day, sweetie," Jamie said warmly. Mark put his hand on Jamie's shoulder and smiled at us as we turned to leave.

Jenna shook her head, smiling while she took a quick sip of her tea.

"What is it?" I frowned, pushing open the door and venturing outside. A gust of icy cold air made it feel as if my nostrils were frozen shut. It was unpleasant, and probably one of the things I liked least about winter.

"Oh, I was just thinking about Jamie," Jenna responded. "He cares about you…a lot. Mark too. You can see it in their eyes."

"I know," I grumbled. I desperately hoped that Jenna wasn't about to start an *'everybody cares about you'* spiel, I just didn't have time for it. Thankfully, she didn't and the rest of our walk to the campus was quiet, our boots crunching against the snow on the pavement the only accompanying sound.

"Looks like someone's been waiting for you," Jenna remarked, breaking the silence as we headed up the concrete steps, a genuine smile relaxing her lips as Jax Walker came into view. He was leaning against the doors of the lecture hall by my first class of the day.

An involuntary smile brought the corners of my lips up effortlessly. My heart rate jumped and began to race in my chest. Jax was one of those guys that radiated sex appeal and style in the delectable off-handed way that made any warm-blooded woman melt into putty. Jenna liked to describe him as a "barbarian." She claimed he was the kind of guy that could instantly make you feel both safe and in danger—or at least, in danger of getting pregnant.

Jax was tall—nearly six-foot-three inches—and he towered over me even when we were both sitting down. He had perpetually tanned skin, courtesy of his Hawaiian heritage. He wore his brown hair long, reaching just past his shoulders. It danced about in the wind, the majority of it held in place by a dark gray beanie. I'd even seen him toss it up in a bun while working out, and he *still* managed to pull it off and look like a certifiable sex god.

Shaving was never very high on Jax's priority list either, and he was currently rocking a three week old beard that did incredible things to my uterus. Jenna's earlier statements about being in danger of procreating with him were definitely viable. It was hard *not* to want to make babies with him, even if you definitely didn't want babies, which I didn't.

Or at least, I hadn't before…but Jax made me question that. Jax made me question *everything*. He was the total package: completely in shape, completely sexy, and completely loyal. The best part about him was his personality. He had a heart as gold as the rings encasing the pupils of those soft brown eyes. I'd never met anybody like him. He made me feel better from simply being in his company. Even just walking towards him had a lot of the tension and anxiety rolling away from me, and in its wake, a rising desire to get him alone and peel away those drool-worthy clothes that did little to hide how hard he worked in the gym.

I could practically feel the saliva pooling inside of my mouth, so I quickly took a sip of my coffee.

"Good morning, beautiful." Jax drawled, half of his mouth curling upward in a teasing smile that told me he knew *exactly* what I was thinking. He was dressed in his usual dark denim jeans that fit snugly around his muscular hips and waist and a charcoal thermal shirt beneath his open, black Northface jacket. Like I said, his outfit of choice did *little* to contain all that raw masculinity and really did make me want to hop on board the baby train.

"Dressed to kill today, aren't we?" I asked coyly, arching a brow. It was remarkable just how much better I felt in his presence. The tight grip of anxiety had lessened considerably, and it almost felt easier to breathe.

"You know it." Jax grinned, his arms opening for me. I walked into him, feeling them wrap around my body with a gentle strength that always made me sigh my complete surrender.

"You'll do awesome," I whispered, my cheek resting against his chest. I felt the rumble of his laughter just as I heard it.

"I know." He winked. Jax would be graduating in July with his Bachelors of Science in Psychology, and he was focused on his path of one day opening up a Mixed Martial Arts gym that specialized in helping troubled youths. He had a formal interview today at the gym he already worked at as a part-time personal trainer. He was hoping to introduce an official program for local youth as a part of his placement program. Jax pressed his lips to the top of my head in a tender kiss, his hands pressing against the small of my back and holding me to him. "Are we still on for tonight?" he asked.

"Of course." I grinned. I couldn't wait until tonight, when we would finally get to spend some time together.

My eyelashes fluttered against my cheek as Jax's hand gently came up to stroke the hair away from my face. His fingers lingered near the scar, and I felt him inhale deeply before his lips descended against mine. He kissed me softly at first, then followed my lead as I pressed harder against him. I was hungry for his touch, hungry to lose myself in him. He grinned against my lips a moment later, shaking his head.

"What are you doing to me?" he breathed out slowly. With those six words, I could tell that he was just as affected by our kiss as I had been.

"I guess the same thing that you're doing to me." I whispered, smirking. Jax grinned and kissed me once more before regretfully breaking away. He gave me a final longing look before turning around.

I bit down hard on my bottom lip the moment he started to walk away, trying to divert the focus from the pain in my chest. Whenever he left, my heart began to ache. Jax made me feel *whole* again, but that just meant that when he wasn't around, I felt everything full force. Unfortunately, I felt it full force a lot.

Jax was a busy man. In addition to attending university full time and his part time job at the gym, he worked at a local garage. It was hard for us to steal moments to be together, but he went out of his way to make sure it happened at least once a day.

Jax also frequented my bed quite often, although he was still officially living in the same student housing building that *Andrew* had lived in. He hated being there just as much as I hated him being there. I hadn't been able to go back there. Still, neither one of us had broached the idea of him moving in with Jenna and me. It hung between us like a heavy cloud.

It shouldn't be so difficult to ask him to move in, given that I missed him like crazy every minute he wasn't around, but it was. I was too afraid of my deep feelings for him; I was afraid that things would change if he moved in. It was a silly thing to fear, given everything we had been through together, but I wasn't exactly the best at the whole 'relationship' thing.

"See you later, Fabio," Jenna said dryly to his retreating back. I could hear Jax chuckle as he waved at her over his shoulder. Jenna gave me a scathing look, making me feel almost like a reprimanded child.

"What?" I demanded.

"You totally forgot I was standing *right here*, didn't you?" She arched a brow, shaking her head at me.

"No, I didn't forget...I just didn't care," I shot back, smirking. Jenna glanced in the direction Jax had just gone, a wistful smile on her lips as she softly shook her head. "What's up with you?" I asked, frowning with slight concern at the strange look on her face.

34

"What's up with *me*?" Jenna turned to look at me. She appeared bewildered by my question. "Is the queen of personal subject deflection really asking that?"

"Yeah, I am. Don't think I didn't notice the weird way you've been acting lately," I pointed out, referring to how quiet she'd been and the strange way she'd been acting whenever the subject of Lucas came up.

Jenna sighed. "How about I tell you what's going on with me *after* you tell me what's eating you, alright?" I arched a brow, almost surprised by Jenna's snappy behaviour. I'd known Jenna for just over three years now, and for the most part, she was a very happy, bubbly person. Although I'd been dealing with my own shit, I had definitely noticed the strange undercurrent to her smiles and laughter recently.

There was something going on with Jenna and I'd been too locked up in my own head to even ask what was going on with hers. I was a crappy friend, but I was going to change that.

No more living in the darkness; it was time to pull myself completely out again. Somehow.

"Fine, after I get home from work we'll get some Ryan Gosling therapy, and we'll babble on and on about our wounded hearts and souls while we eat straight out of the ice cream container...alright? But right now, we should probably both get to class before we're late."

"Fine." This time, the smile that touched Jenna's lips was almost real, but there was still a sadness and uncertainty in her eyes. "Have a good day, Harlow," she added as she walked off in the direction of her first class. I turned around, about to finally head inside. My toes were cold and I knew my coffee was beginning to drop in temperature too. January was a frigid bitch.

"Harlow! Harlow, wait up!" I almost cringed at the exuberantly familiar voice shouting my name at a pitch that even Mariah Carey would be envious of, but I refrained from doing so, knowing that it would only hurt her feelings. Instead, I turned around and forced a smile.

"Hey, Crimson. How was your break?" I asked. I hadn't had a chance to see Crimson since the incident, or at least...I'd been avoiding her since then. It was fairly easy, considering we didn't have any classes together this semester.

Crimson leaned forward, trying to catch her breath. It wasn't that I didn't like Crimson's company—I didn't mind it, actually. I genuinely liked her, but I just wasn't ready for her torrent of questions that I knew would undoubtedly come flying at me in rapid succession. She meant well, and I knew that, but she was a lot to handle; especially when my short term goal was to forget that it happened.

Crimson was still bent forward with her palms on her knees, her chest rising and falling rapidly. She brushed back her bright curly red hair and peered up at me with astonishment, her jaw practically hanging open.

"How was *my* break?" Crimson repeated, dumbfounded. Her eyes were as wide as her mouth. She almost looked comical. "I've been trying to get a hold of you forever. How are *you*?"

"Oh, you know, just dandy," I replied, shrugging.

Crimson stood up to her full height. Even then, she was still pretty short. She scrutinized me, zeroing in on the scar on my cheek. "I am so sorry," she said, almost whispering. Her eyes were full of sympathy and before I could react, she grabbed me in a hug so tight that I could scarcely breathe. It was surprising just how strong Crimson was—I would have never guessed that she could crush ribs with her small frame.

"It's alright," I said, awkwardly patting her back. I was not good at hugging people. I could only count three people who had made that kind of physical contact feel *normal* for me. Everyone else just made me feel like a gazelle in a canoe. I swallowed hard, trying to untangle myself from Crimson. Thankfully, she took the hint and gave me some space.

"It's not alright." Crimson shook her head. "Are you nuts? I can't believe that happened to you!"

"Well, you know, it's not the first time," I remarked. Crimson winced, taking it the wrong way. "I didn't mean..." I trailed off, feeling completely overwhelmed and a little bit aggravated.

"I know, it's just...yeah..." she trailed off as well, both of us at a loss as to how to continue this conversation.

Crimson was dating my ex-boyfriend, Cole. The same ex-boyfriend from high school that was involved in my sexual assault. I honestly thought for the longest time that Cole had participated—that *all* the guys had. I only recently found out that only one of the guys had raped me, that the rest had held Cole back and then blackmailed him into silence.

I mean, it still wasn't *good* by any means, but Cole also wasn't the total monster I had envisioned for years. He was just a coward, and a hurting one at that. He'd tried to apologize to me, but when I showed him the door and told him exactly where to take his fucked up apology, he tried to kill himself. He was found in time, and last I heard, he was receiving inpatient treatment for his depression.

"How is he?" I finally asked, the silence getting to me. I wasn't as cold and impervious as I liked people to think, and I did care that Cole had nearly taken his own life out of desperation. I hadn't known that he was suffering as bad as he was, and truthfully, I hadn't cared enough to listen to him until it was almost too late.

"He's...alright." Crimson's expression fell for a fraction of a second before she reined it in, focusing on my face intently. "But let's talk about *you*."

"I don't really want to talk about me," I responded shortly, turning around to head inside. I felt a smidgen of guilt over shutting Crimson down like that, but I was honestly sick of people pestering me about whether I was okay. Obviously, I wasn't fucking okay and I didn't particularly want to get into it with everyone and their mother.

I just wanted to live my life and be happy. I wanted to forget about it.

I paused by the door, turning back to face her. Although I didn't want to talk about the attack, I didn't want her to feel like I didn't want to talk to *her*. "Do you want to grab lunch tomorrow?"

Crimson's face split into a happy grin. "Yeah! Sure!"

chapter THREE

WITH MY shift at the coffee shop finally over, I locked up the store front and headed home. The walk was quick, but I was still on edge, still clenching the Kubotan pen that Jax had gifted me shortly after the attack within my coat pocket. It was an added sense of security for me, more of a comfort than anything, like walking around with a proverbial teddy bear.

I was no longer able to listen to music during my walks home, like I had for years. I was too paranoid now. I needed to hear every little sound in the night; I needed to see everything.

I let out a gentle exhale of relief as I thundered up the wooden stairs to the apartment I shared with Jenna. She was already in front of the TV, waiting for me with a Ryan Gosling movie on pause.

"Somebody's eager for some Gosling bod tonight." I snorted, kicking my boots off and discarding my jacket on the island stool before flopping down beside Jenna. She already had the ice cream carton out in front of her with two spoons. I snagged one up, wasting no time in diving in.

"Of course." Jenna grinned, grabbing the remote and hitting play. The volume was down low enough that it wouldn't distract us entirely, but there was something about Ryan Gosling that always instantly cheered Jenna up and made it easier for the both of us to talk.

Talking had never been my strong suit. Even though I had known Jenna for years now, even though she knew some of my darkest secrets...I still had a hard time letting her in. It wasn't easy for me like it was for most people.

Ryan Gosling was a tradition that started in high school, and it seemed to be the only time I could truly open up to Jenna.

"So, today fucking sucked," I remarked, brushing my hair behind my shoulders before taking another massive scoop.

"Why?" Jenna inquired, not looking at me. This was how our deeper conversations happened: the both of us staring at some weird romantic comedy while stuffing our face full of ice cream or Chinese food. Or on bad nights, all of the above.

"First off, Crimson cornered me after you left. She kept asking me if I was okay."

"And that's a problem because? She cares about you, she's worried about you," Jenna scolded. Jenna was quite fond of Crimson. Crimson was easy to like; she was sweet, happy and maybe a little naive. She almost made others want to protect her and shelter her from the world. She had this rare gift of seeing the good in absolutely *everybody*, including people who didn't deserve it. But she could also be overbearing and over excitable.

"I know." I rolled my eyes, sighing. I didn't need a lecture on how sweet Crimson was. It was one of the things about her that I liked. And hated. "It's just...hard. I just don't want to talk about the attack anymore."

I felt Jenna's eyes on my face, so I purposely stared ahead. "So tell her that. I'm sure she would respect it. She isn't one to poke at a sore spot."

"I know." I sighed again, knowing that Jenna was right. Crimson was just concerned about me. I couldn't be mad at her for it. If the roles were reversed, I suppose I would be just as worried about her.

"She's trying to be your friend. She hasn't really seen you since before Christmas break and I know she misses you," Jenna said.

"How do you know that?" I tilted my head, studying my friend carefully.

Jenna scooped up more ice cream, slowly eating it before she responded."I've been hanging out with her," she explained. "You've been so busy doing your own thing lately, and I've been so bored. I ran into her at the mall and she asked if I wanted to go out for lunch and catch a movie. I did. We've been hanging out a lot, and we talk on Facebook sometimes too." Jenna shrugged as if it was no big deal, and I knew it wasn't. I couldn't be mad at my friend for making friends with...my friends. "You should really stop pushing her away. Besides, I think she needs friends right now," Jenna added gently. "If you have a hard time letting *her* be there for *you*, why don't you let yourself be there for her?"

Jenna knew how I operated. I may not be able to let people fuss about me, but I certainly would put aside my own issues to be there for them. I'd done the same thing with Jenna in high school.

"Fine, let's all get mani-pedis and have a slumber party," I said dryly, rolling my eyes. It irked me that Jenna was right; I wanted to sulk about things for a while. I wanted to shut myself off from everyone, but she knew with that one comment that I *would* try and be there for Crimson. When I was irritated, my defense mechanism was sarcasm. Jenna pinned me with her gaze, unimpressed with my sarcastic wit. My shoulders slumped slightly, and I put on my best, most innocent looking smile. "I'll try to stop being a bitch, okay?"

"You know what? That's not a bad idea, actually," Jenna said thoughtfully. She assessed me carefully, a slow smile perking her up lips. The expression on her face reminded me of a cunning fox; Jenna was up to something.

"The whole 'stopping the bitch act' part?" I inquired.

"No, the slumber party…" She trailed off and I could practically hear the gears grinding in her head. Her eyes lit up like the Fourth of July and she twisted her body towards mine, her knee bashing off mine in her haste. "Let's do a girls' weekend!"

"You already know I don't do that spa shit," I argued crossly, scowling.

"Then we won't do spa shit." Jenna grinned. "I have something else in mind. But more about that later—I have to make some calls. For now, how about you tell me what's *really* bugging you."

"What are you talking about?" I tried to keep my voice passive, but Jenna saw through me and rolled her eyes.

"I'm talking about Iain," Jenna said slowly. She folded her legs beneath her body and shot me another one of her famous penetrating stares. I knew she was reading me like a book for my reactions. That was one of the setbacks to letting people in: they started to learn your unspoken language. "Have you seen him since?"

"No," I answered, my taste for ice cream evaporating. I stared ahead, but the TV seemed out of focus. All I could envision was Iain's face. The way he had looked standing in front of me in the moments before his hands had tangled gently in my hair, pulling my lips toward him. I closed my eyes, trying to drive that image from my mind as the guilt brewed.

I knew that I didn't want to be with Iain, but I still couldn't help but be haunted by the feel of his lips on me...and by the fact that I had kissed him back. I wanted to think that I had more self-control than that.

"Harlow." Jenna turned her body toward me; her eyes looked wounded. "You need to forgive yourself. Jax already has. That man doesn't have a question about you...and it's obvious how he makes you feel. The only times you smile lately are when he's around. Don't think I don't notice."

"Speaking of smiles." I looked at her hard. "What's with yours?"

"What about mine?" Jenna looked momentarily confused.

"There's something going on with you, and you said you'd spill so...spill."

Realization dawned on Jenna's features, and she smiled sadly. "I don't know, it's complicated."

"Right, I wouldn't get that at all," I pointed out. Jenna chuckled, shaking her head slightly. She bit her lip and stared at the TV again. "Is it Lucas?" I gently pressed. I wasn't just eager for the topic change; I wanted to know what was up with her. Absently, I picked up my spoon again. The ice cream was beginning to melt, and the spoon sank easily into the rocky road goodness.

Her eyes quickly snapped back to my face and I could see the guilt and confusion. She hesitated for a moment before she slowly exhaled. "Yeah."

"What's going on?" I set the spoon down, focusing my attention on her.

"I just...something is missing." Jenna bit her bottom lip, avoiding my gaze. "Like, I look at you and Jax and I see such passion and desire. And I just...I don't have that. I keep trying to, you know—*be intimate with him*—but..." She sighed again, tucking her hair behind her ear and raising her cornflower blue eyes to meet mine. They were watery with unshed tears. "I think I'm broken."

"You are *not* broken," I told her. The moment the words were out of my mouth, I paused. "Okay, maybe you are...just a little bit." Jenna snorted in response while I chewed on the inside of my cheek as I considered my words carefully. "Jenna, your *first* introduction to sex was...not good."

45

"Neither was yours, and you seem to be doing alright," Jenna countered, crossing her arms like a sullen teenager.

"Yes, but don't follow *my* example. Not everybody is the same. Besides, you went through it more recently too, and you had a hell of a lot more to deal with than I did," I reminded her gently.

Jenna ended up pregnant from her rapist. She hadn't been able to consider any other alternative, so she had carried the baby to term and put her up for adoption. We didn't talk about it often because Jenna didn't *want* to talk about it, but I knew her birth daughter was never far from her mind. Hell, Jenna's daughter was never far from *my* mind, either. I constantly thought about her, especially when I thought about Iain. Iain's sister was Jenna's daughter's adoptive mother, although Jenna didn't know that. It was yet another piece of the guilt I had, and each day it felt heavier and heavier. I knew I needed to tell my best friend, but I just didn't know how. The mere subject of her birth daughter sent her spiraling into depression every time. She fell into darkness whenever she received an update letter, and it took her weeks to pull herself out again.

I didn't want to put her through that. Maybe that was selfish of me, I didn't know. I just couldn't watch her heart break like that and know that I was the cause of it.

"So is this how it's going to be for the rest of my life?" Jenna asked, her question pulling me away from my thoughts. I looked up, watching the tears spilling down her cheeks. "Am I always going to flinch whenever a man touches me like that?"

I bit my lip, my own eyes watering at my best friend's pain. Like I said, I *hated* seeing Jenna in pain. She was too bubbly and sweet to feel pain like this. I put my arm over her shoulders, pulling her close to me. Jenna was one of the three people that I could hug. "I don't know," I admitted quietly. "Do you want to be intimate with him?"

"I think I do...but then when we start...I panic," Jenna whispered, resting her head against my shoulder.

"Maybe you're just not ready yet. Maybe you just need a little more time. Is Lucas being understanding?" I demanded, pulling away to search her eyes. "I swear to God, if he's pressuring you, I'll make him suffer."

Jenna furiously brushed away the tears from her eyes, but they kept coming. It was as if the floodgates had opened and stopping them wasn't happening any time soon. "No, he's fine. He gets it; he doesn't pressure me at all about it. Honestly, it's...me."

"Then stop pressuring yourself," I told her softly. "The worst thing you could do is rush it before you're ready," I added, thinking about the first time I was intimate after my rape. I had been so numb that I hadn't felt a thing...and that wasn't good.

Jenna's face broke into despair again and she tried to hide it in her hands. "God, I feel like fucking Claire Danes when I cry."

"You're more like Dawson," I joked, shoving my shoulder against her playfully. "Seriously, nobody cries pretty. Don't worry about it. I promise I won't take any photos and turn them into memes."

She laughed. "Gee, thanks, Harlow. That's *so* considerate of you."

"I know." I smirked. "Now, let's watch this part. Ryan's about to take off his shirt," I added, turning up the volume.

* * *

Jax knocked on our door just as the credits started to roll. A small smile spread to my lips, and Jenna grinned in response, shaking her head.

"I'll make myself scarce," she promised, standing to tidy our mess as I jumped up.

"Don't worry about that." I rolled my eyes, starting towards the door.

"Trust me, it's not for your benefit...it's for mine. I'm going to drown out all sounds with my new *Autumn Fields* CD." Jenna's eyes glazed over momentarily.

"Still got a thing for that guy, huh?" I asked, looking back at her and smirking at the tell-tale smile on her face.

"Very funny." It was Jenna's turn to roll her shining eyes at me. "It's just a crush. Like my crush on Ryan Gosling."

"Okay, whatever. But Ryan Gosling doesn't follow you on Twitter, Instagram, *and* have you as a friend on Facebook," I said.

Autumn Fields was an up-and-coming Canadian band that was quickly making waves in the music industry. The folksy vocals and the way they harmonized together made them instantly popular. We saw them perform at a fundraiser several months back, during the beginning of their Canada-wide tour.

Jenna had a huge thing for Kyle Russell. He was one half of the amazing singing duet, along with a girl whose voice could bring tears even to *my* eyes, not that I'd admit that to Jenna. They had good music, and Kyle *was* Hollywood handsome, so I could see Jenna's appeal for him.

I personally delighted in her online friendship with Kyle. It was fun watching her melt over him when he'd reply to her comments or like her photos. Social media was such a strange place—one that I didn't comprehend and rarely used. I didn't have an Instagram account, I wasn't signed up for Twitter and I very rarely used my Facebook. Jenna was obsessed with social media; and with Kyle. Each time he liked a photo or commented on something, Jenna would freak out and dance around the room like God Himself had clicked the thumbs up button.

"You're such a fan-girl," I joked, laughing again at the guilty look on her face before I turned my attention to the door to open it. My laughter faded quickly, and I couldn't stop the sharp intake of breath as my eyes hungrily lapped up the tall hunk of man standing before me.

Pretty sure I was also incredibly guilty of fan-girling over Jax.

Jax's head was tilted down, but he lifted his eyes when he heard the door open. They landed on my face, and my breath caught in my throat. His serious look quickly faded to one of rolling desire and amusement.

"Hmm, looks like I'm just in time for dessert," he said softly, his eyes dropping down to my lips. "Rocky Road this time?"

I quickly wiped my lips with the back of my hand, a faint blush dusting my cheeks as Jax laughed.

"You didn't have to do that. I would have licked it off," he almost growled. My skin burned at the delightful suggestion; I knew he meant every word.

"And...that's my cue to leave!" Jenna called out from the kitchen, closing the refrigerator door. Jax chuckled again, and I stood aside to let him in.

He was carrying his backpack with him, likely stuffed with clothes for tomorrow. I didn't comment on the bag as I closed the door; I was glad he was planning on spending the night. I locked up, driving the deadbolt home and making sure the chain was safely in place.

Needless to say, since the whole Andrew thing, I'd gotten even more obsessive with my locking ritual. Jenna was forever complaining about all the different keys she had to use to get in.

Jax arched a brow but wisely didn't comment on the obsessive way I double checked the door. He dropped his bag down on the ground and stalked toward me, the golden rim that lined his pupils almost sparking with his desire.

His eyes were incredible. Jax's whole damn package was incredible; he could completely derail any thoughts in my mind with his rugged handsomeness.

He caged me against the door, and my hand came up to grip his coat, the material cold from the subzero temperature outside; but Jax's body heat radiated from beneath it. His scent invaded my nostrils and made my mouth water. Amber with hints of sandalwood and spice mixed perfectly with his pheromones to make a combination that was a deadly assault on the senses. I felt my knees weaken and the desire pooling between my legs; I ached for him in a way I had never ached for anyone. Nothing I had ever felt before came close to what I felt for Jax.

My desire for him was insatiable.

Jax knew the effect he had on me, and he couldn't help but grin before his lips descended on mine.

Every time Jax kissed me, it was like the very first time. He made all the chaos and noise fade away to nothing; he drove out every insecurity, every fear. He made my skin hum; he made me feel alive in a way that I'd never experienced before. I came close once, but not like this. Jax brought out the good in me. I knew he'd always have my back; I knew I could count on him just as surely as I could count on the seasons changing. But Jax refused to be a Band-Aid. He wouldn't let me bury my problems. He urged me to face them head on.

Jax's teeth nipped my lips, tugging gently. My body buzzed with desire for him, and he chuckled again at my willingness to completely surrender to him. It was so easy to surrender to him.

"What would your roommate say?" he whispered against my earlobe.

"Nothing. She's made herself scarce for tonight," I replied coyly, tugging on Jax's coat in an attempt to free him from it.

Jax grinned, stepping back to take his coat off and hang it on the rack. He turned to face me, arching a brow with that delicious smile still on his face. "So, I picked up a movie and thought we could watch it toni—"

I didn't let him finish what he was about to say before I launched myself into his arms. I didn't want to watch a movie, and I didn't want to talk. Not yet, anyway. I wanted to lose myself in Jax.

He kissed me back with fervor, effortlessly picking me up. I tightened my thighs around his hips and allowed him to carry me down the hallway, to the bedroom where I'd been attacked a little over a month ago. I wasn't even thinking about that. In fact, none of the memories that usually crashed into me the moment I stepped foot in my bedroom were in my mind. The only thing I could think about was Jax's hands on my body, his lips on my lips, the way his tongue danced with mine. His entire being consumed me; made me burn with fire and that emotion that both terrified and thrilled me: *love*.

Jax gently shut my bedroom door with his foot without pausing as he continued walking toward my bed. He deposited me on top of my unmade mattress. The look in his eyes promised I was about to receive the very work out I craved, the very thing that would drive the demons away.

* * *

For the first time in over a week, I slept peacefully. No nightmares haunted my subconscious mind, no anxiety gripped my heart, making falling asleep and staying asleep impossible.

I awoke feeling well rested. I blinked the sleep from my eyes, taking a moment to adjust to the soft sunlight streaming in from my partially closed blinds. I stretched my legs out, my toes barely brushing against the warm body of the man sleeping beside me.

Jax's thick lashes rested against his perpetually tanned skin. A soft smile played against those full lips. His breathing was slow and steady with sleep.

I took a moment to study him, biting my lip as I attempted to ignore the onset of heady emotions.

I couldn't deny the fact that on the nights I slept without the anxiety and nightmares, Jax was with me. It sort of pissed me off—mainly because it scared me. I had never needed anybody the way that I needed him, and that was a terrifying feeling. I couldn't help but be left wondering what would happen to me if he ever left, but I also didn't *want* to need him to the extent that I did.

Jax stirred, his eyes slowly opening and immediately seeking out my face. The smile on his lips remained, but the easy lightness behind his eyes changed slightly as he assessed me.

One brow arching high in unspoken question, Jax pulled me closer to him, his arms locking around me.

The warmth radiated off his naked body, heating the chill from my skin.

"What's got you all twisted?" he murmured, his voice vibrating through my very being.

"Nothing," I said, smiling at him. I didn't have to force a smile with Jax, and in that moment, I was happy. I didn't want to ruin our time together with my insecurities, with my darkness and confusion. I just wanted to enjoy the light he brought.

I curled my body even closer to his, using my hands to explore the hard muscles of his defined chest and abdomen. The muscles clenched beneath my fingertips, the desire as evident on his face as it was beneath the blanket.

I pressed my lips against his, wanting to kiss him good morning. Jax didn't let me pull away, though, despite my protests and worries of morning breath. Jax didn't seem to care in the slightest. He slowed the kiss, rolling so that he was positioned over top of me. His strong arms were on either side of my body to hold his weight. His abdomen pressed against mine, his length pressing against my inner thigh, but he made no move to take it further. He looked down at me, his long hair falling around us like a curtain, obscuring us from the world.

I always thought it would be a turn off to date a man whose hair was better than mine, but it was impossible not to love Jax's hair. It was thick and soft, and I knew he took pride in caring for it. Jax rocked the long hair and still managed to ooze sexual appeal in the most annoying ways.

Jax inclined his head slightly, and the strands of his hair tickled my neck and face. A strange sound escaped my lips and he grinned. "Was that a giggle?" he asked, deeply amused.

"Definitely not," I said, quickly schooling my features. "I *don't* giggle."

Jax snorted in disagreement, lowering his face closer to mine. I bit my lip, trying to hold in the secondary giggle that threatened to erupt at the sensation of his beard against my cheek and neck.

"That's not fair. You're purposely using your furriness to tickle me." I almost pouted.

Jax lifted his head up again, his face aglow with amusement."My furriness? What am I, a dog?"

"Or a bear." I shrugged. "You're hairy, and you're using it against me."

"Should I shave?" he contemplated, bringing his hand up to rub the scruff on his jaw.

"No. If you shave, you have less time to spend with me," I pointed out, lifting my own hands to brush against Jax's chest. They trailed lower still, to the legendary V muscle that *still* made me swoon, despite the fact I was lying down. The playful glint disappeared from Jax's eyes, completely consumed by his passion for me. He shivered as my hands traveled even lower, his lashes brushing against the tops of his cheeks again as I gripped his thick, long length in my hand. "Don't you enjoy spending time with me?" I inquired coyly, arching a brow.

He opened his eyes, smirking at me."I think you know the answer to that," he said before lowering his lips to mine again.

Jax focused on lavishing my lips slowly, as if we had all the time in the world. I was withering beneath him, almost panting and arching my body against his impatiently when he finally slid inside me without breaking the kiss.

chapter FOUR

JAX MADE love to me slowly and thoroughly, bringing me to several orgasms before he finished. Sex with Jax was always incredible; the man *really* knew how to read me, and he had the moves. This knowledge coupled with his sex appeal made it virtually impossible for me *not* to be in the mood around him, so our sex life was active…very active. Even after the attack. Most girls would have been traumatized of a male's touch after the things I'd been through, but Jax's touch calmed me.

My thirst for him was insatiable; my stomach swirled and danced with desire as Jax's thumb brushed across my lower lip.

As I looked into those brown eyes so full of promise, I wanted to tell him to stay, to move in with us. I wanted to wake up every morning like this; I wanted to *sleep*, to feel at peace all the time, but the words remained lodged in my throat. I couldn't get them out. It seemed wrong to ask Jax to move in just because I felt better when he was around. Naturally, I wanted him around because I enjoyed being with him, but the mere fact that I seemed to *need* him just made me all that more stubborn and determined *not* to ask.

"I have some news," Jax said. "I wanted to tell you last night...but you distracted me."

"Oh? Sorry about that." I smirked. He knew I wasn't sorry.

"I can go ahead and start the program next month." Jax grinned, his eyes lighting up with excitement.

"Oh my God, Jax," I exclaimed, my eyes widening. "That's huge!"

"I know." He exhaled, his eyes roaming my face. I don't think I'd ever get used to the way he looked at me; each time it was as if he was seeing me for the first time. It was as if he was content to just *look* at me. "I'm going to start advertising for it next week. I need to come up with flyers. I'm going to put them around high schools and group homes."

"That's an awesome idea." I smiled, completely excited for him.

"There's another thing too," Jax warned, his expression becoming serious and brooding. He hesitated for a long moment and my heart jumped with fear. *This is it*, I thought. *He's going to break up with me.* The thought came out of nowhere, and my stomach twisted with anxiety and fear. I tried to rein it all in and tell myself I could survive if that was the case, but I honestly didn't know if I could. I felt all panicked simply *thinking* about it.

"I'm moving," he finally said. "I can't stand living in that...place anymore. I've been looking for a while now, and I actually found an apartment."

"Where?" I couldn't ignore the sadness that washed over me. It almost consumed me completely. I felt heavy with sorrow that I desperately tried to ignore and push away. I was naturally assuming that Jax was leaving me when that likely wasn't the case. I didn't even recognize myself anymore.

"Actually," Jax's dazzling grin eased the sorrow and dread, "it's an apartment really close to you. In fact, it's here."

Aside from the two bedroom unit I shared with Jenna, there were four other units in the converted Victorian house. The house had been sliced in half and sectioned off. The main floor had two apartments, the east and west side. Mrs. Smith lived in the west side apartment, and across the hall from her was our landlord, Richard.

Stairs from the main foyer lead up to the second floor to two more units. Our apartment was above Mrs. Smith's on the west side of the house, and a smaller one bedroom apartment rented out by a timid librarian and her painter boyfriend that had only just moved in a week ago. They had a Scottish Terrier that yipped a lot when they weren't home, but aside from that, they seemed friendly enough. Jenna had spoken to them on several occasions, apparently. That's how I knew she was a librarian and he was a painter.

"The owner is renovating the attic unit. It's pretty small, but it's actually really nice. Beats trying to make breakfast on a hot plate, and it's cheap too." Jax twirled my hair around his large hand, grinning. "And maybe...if you're ready...you could move in with me there." He winked. His suggestion made my stomach do summersaults.

I allowed myself a moment where I freely pictured what Jax was offering. Living with him in a place of our own. Falling asleep in his arms every night and waking up there in the morning. Sharing meals together. Building a life together. I wanted it so badly that I could taste it. I imagined myself able to jump into something like that without feeling afraid.

But the reality was that I *was* afraid. I was already scared of how intensely I felt for Jax; I was already overwhelmed. The mere idea of him leaving twisted me up hard; I couldn't imagine starting to build a life with him only to have him leave me—because everybody leaves, in the end. Or at least, that's what I'd been conditioned to feel.

I felt more at peace around Jax than ever before, and I desperately wanted to cling to that, but I was also scared of things changing between us. My thoughts were going around in circles and Jax was watching me expectantly, waiting for me to answer him. "Jenna needs me," I said softly. And it was true; Jenna *did* need me. She hated being alone.

Jax's expression was easy to read. I always knew where I stood with him; he didn't mask anything. I knew he could—I knew he could hide every emotion. I'd seen that talent come into play a few times before, usually when he spoke about his family when anybody else was in ear shot. But Jax chose to let me in. He chose to let me see it all.

So I saw the patience, the understanding and desire on his face as if he'd spoken the words, naming the emotions. His thumb brushed across my lip again. "The

60

offer still stands whenever you want to take me up on it...whenever you—or Jenna—are ready."

"When do you move?" I asked.

"It's mine as of the first of March, so you've got plenty of time to decide what you want to do. If you choose to move in with me, you'd obviously still be near work and Jenna. I just got the call with my approval yesterday. I signed the lease last night before I came over," Jax answered as he absently played with my hair, twisting it around his fingers.

"Yeah…" I trailed off. I was having a difficult time coming to terms with what I was feeling. Things between Jax and me just felt...serious. They felt right, of course, but the seriousness of them unnerved me a little. The fact that I could *see* a future with him unnerved me. I'd never had that before, not even when I was with Iain. When I was with Iain, it was all about living in the moment. It was as if I knew our time would come to end, and I wanted to enjoy whatever happiness while I could.

Jax's brown eyes locked on mine, his gaze full of sincerity. "I want this, Harlow," he said, his hands roaming the length of my body. "I want to wake up to your beautiful face every single day. I want to build a future with you...if you'll let me."

"Woah," I exhaled, feeling dizzy. "That's a pretty heavy sentiment."

Jax's lips pressed against the nape of my neck and I squirmed, his beard tickling my skin. "Is it?" he murmured, his warm lips buzzing against my skin pleasantly. My stomach rolled with desire and my eyes suddenly felt heavy. I struggled to keep them open and focused on him. It wasn't the time to drift off into euphoria with him; he'd just asked me to move in.

My throat felt tight, as if all the words I wanted to say were just...stuck. "Jax...I don't know. It feels like it'd be too soon, and I don't want to move too quickly. I want it all to be for the right reasons." I choked on the last of the words as they spilled from my mouth. I was exposing my tattered heart to him, and it was a scary experience.

Jax nodded, his eyes full of understanding. I knew it wasn't a show with him, either. "Whatever you need, Harlow. If time is what you need, I'll give you all the time in the world," he whispered, and I knew he meant it.

* * *

I had to rush to make it to my first period class. By the time I fell into my seat, I was completely out of breath.

My hair was tossed back into a messy, careless braid and I hadn't had time to put any makeup on, but I still felt the incredible aftershocks of being with Jax and I couldn't fight the smile as thoughts of our goodbye replayed in my mind throughout class over and over again.

Jax had gently grabbed my hand and tugged me against him. His other hand came up to grip the braid gently, directing my lips to his. Before he kissed me, he looked at me and told me I was the most beautiful woman he'd ever laid eyes upon.

"We'll talk tonight," he promised, his eyes flicking across my face a final time.

Looking into his honest, warm eyes, I couldn't help but feel like a model on a runway, and it felt incredible.

He had definitely given me a lot to think about during class. I could barely focus on the professor's lecture. In fact, I didn't register a single thing. I kept looking at my phone, watching the time and replying to Crimson's quick messages about our upcoming lunch date. It was a good thing she reminded me; Jax had me so distracted that I likely wouldn't have remembered on my own.

"Hey!" Crimson said with a toothy grin as I approached her after class. She was waiting for me by Tabaret Lawn. She looked cozy and warm with her huge, thick royal blue scarf wrapped twice around her neck and over her head. I shivered, regretting my decision to not bring a hat.

"Hey. Did you decide where you want to go?" I asked, coming to a stop in front of her. I shoved my hands in my pockets, trying to warm them up a little and seriously hoping that wherever she wanted to go was close.

"I really don't care." Crimson shrugged, rubbing her belly. "Somewhere near, because I'm famished!"

"Well, *The Bean* is like five minutes away," I suggested, eager to get out of the bitingly cold wind. We started walking, Crimson filling the silence with small talk about her classes so far this semester and other random things she thought of. There wasn't such a thing as a quiet moment with Crimson, and if there was it didn't feel normal. I hummed and nodded in all the right places, and aside from that, Crimson didn't really need my input to carry on a conversation.

I pushed open the door, sending her a quick, tight-lipped smile.

"You really need a hobby, girl," Jamie said, clucking his tongue as I approached the counter.

"If you keep saying that every time I come to visit, I'm going to stop visiting. You're giving me a complex," I retorted, pretending to pout. "Besides, it's not *my fault* Mark makes incredible sandwiches or that you're placed conveniently close to campus."

Jamie laughed, rolling his eyes at me. "I suppose that *is* true," he allowed. "What can I get you?"

"A sundried tomato pesto panini and a vitamin water."

Jamie typed it in to the cash register without looking down. "Sure thing, my sweet." Jamie winked. "And who's this lovely lady with the radiant hair?" he added, accepting my money while he studied Crimson with open interest.

"Hi! I'm Crimson," she responded, stepping up toward the till. Her eyes fluttered back to the menu, taking in all of the different sandwiches. She chewed on her bottom lip thoughtfully. "Actually, could I just have the same thing as Harlow? It sounds delicious, and there are *way* too many options! I'll be here all day!"

"That's how we lure you in." Jamie grinned, his white teeth flashing. Crimson paid for her order and Jamie handed us both our waters. "I'll bring your paninis over once they're made. Go have a seat!"

Crimson's eyes were wide while she took in the comfortable atmosphere of the cafe. It was bustling; several university students occupied the comfortable chairs, typing away on their laptops, chatting and drinking specialty coffees.

"This place is incredible," she remarked, sliding into a vacant booth. I sat down across from her, twisting the cap off my vitamin water and taking a sip.

A few moments of silence passed, both of us busy drinking our waters and not looking at one another. The tension between us was heavy and awkward, and I knew I had myself to blame. Crimson had only ever tried to be my friend. She'd only ever tried to be her genuine self and I'd been shutting her out ever since the whole thing with Cole went down.

Crimson hadn't known about my past with Cole. How could she? She had only just met me in September, and our friendship was in the very early stages when the opportunity to meet her boyfriend had arisen. We'd all gone to a party at a classmate's house, and he was supposed to meet us there.

When I turned around and saw Cole standing beside her, I lost my shit. All the rage I'd felt towards the boy who had been my first boyfriend—the boy who had led me to the lion's den—rushed out. Crimson hadn't even known what was happening.

At the time, I didn't know the truth. I only knew the rumors I had heard about myself, about how I'd slept with Cole and all his friends. All I had from that night were broken wisps of memory: Cole kissing me, his hands unbuttoning my pants, his friends cheering him on, pain as I was penetrated and lots of darkness.

I didn't know that Cole had tried to stop everything when he realized how out of it I was. I didn't know that two of the other guys held Cole back and made him watch while the ring leader, Casey, raped me.

I didn't know that Casey had threatened Cole with the photos he'd taken of Cole kissing me and doing things to me while I'd been unconscious. Cole was trapped. If he spoke a word of the truth, Casey would go to the police with the photos and the other guys would back him.

But there was really no reason for me to remain angry with Crimson about it. Her only crime had been asking me to hear Cole out, and it turns out that wasn't really a crime. She just wanted me to know the truth about what happened, and she wanted Cole to find redemption.

Crimson cleared her throat, drawing my attention away from the label on the water bottle my fingers were carefully shredding apart. The usually cheerful look on her face was replaced with a serious one with a thick underlying sadness beneath it.

I sighed. "Look, Crimson, I'm sorry for being a shitty friend. I'm really not good at this kind of thing..." I trailed off, trying to figure out where I was headed with this.

Crimson turned her head to the left and watched my lips as I spoke. She only had 55% hearing in her left ear, and 30% in her right. She relied on turning her better ear to the speaker and reading their lips to understand what people were saying. "You don't need to apologize, Harlow," she said gently. "You've been through a lot the last few months. I completely get it."

I shifted awkwardly in my seat. Crimson didn't even know the half of it. All she knew about was the thing with Cole and the attack by Andrew.

"I guess," I finally managed, my eyes dropping back down to the shredded label in my hands. "But I'm sorry regardless, and I'll try to not be such a bitch."

"Is Harlow actually apologizing for something?" Jamie's musical voice interrupted our conversation as he came to a stop beside our table carrying two white plates. He had a mischievous smile on his face, and his dark green eyes glinted with trouble. He looked over his shoulder toward the counter, where Mark was carefully placing several freshly baked desserts on the display. "Mark! This one is for the scrapbook!" He laughed, winking at me.

Mark chuckled, shaking his head at Jamie's antics.

"Ha ha," I said dryly. "Very funny."

Jamie's slender hand reached out and gently squeezed my shoulder. "You know I'm just playing, honey. Enjoy your sandwiches, girls!"

"*Paninis!*" Mark corrected, scowling at Jamie from across the room.

"That man always gets his panties in a bunch over the silliest things." Jamie sighed, rolling his eyes. There wasn't a trace of annoyance on him as he smiled lovingly at Mark. "Enjoy your *paninis*, ladies!" he added, bowing for emphasis.

J.C. HANNIGAN

Crimson giggled, watching as Jamie took off back to his place behind the counter to serve another slew of customers.

"Your bosses are seriously the coolest," she finally said, pulling her plate closer towards her. She picked up the panini, pausing with it halfway to her mouth. "My boss kind of sucks," she added, a sad look settling in her eyes.

"How so?" I asked before taking a bite of my own panini. It was delicious, the perfect ratio of cheese, sun dried tomatoes, and pesto.

Crimson sighed. "It's no big deal. I guess I don't have to worry about it anymore anyway," she said darkly.

I tilted my head, chewing as I studied her. I didn't know Crimson as well as I knew Jenna, but I could tell that something was upsetting her.

Crimson was usually a happy person, and it wasn't that she wasn't happy now...she just seemed troubled.

I swallowed and took a slow sip of vitamin water before fixing my no bullshit stare on Crimson. "I know this is going to sound very hypocritical, but if you want to talk about it, I'm here."

Crimson laughed. "You're right, that *is* hypocritical," she agreed. She still had yet to take a bite of her panini, and went to raise it to her mouth. She paused again, staring at it for a moment. Then she sighed and set it back down on the plate. "Well, I'd like to talk about it if you don't mind. I really don't have anybody else..."

I tried to ignore the stab of guilt I felt at Crimson's words. "Go for it. I'm all ears."

"Ha, funny." Crimson snorted. She absently tucked a strand of her unruly hair behind her ear, her hearing aid glinting in the bright afternoon sunlight that streamed in through the front windows of the cafe. "Okay, well..." she took a deep breath, exhaling slowly. "I lost my job at the body shop because I missed too much time after the whole Cole thing."

"I'm sorry to hear that." I frowned. It didn't seem fair that you could lose your job when someone you cared about was hospitalized after trying to kill themselves.

"Yeah, it's not a huge deal though. My scholarships cover my living expenses and school expenses, but I do need to find a new job soon. My savings account is getting pretty sparse."

"I could talk to Jamie and see if we're still looking for another barista," I found myself offering. "Jamie and Mark are great. They'll work with school schedules and everything."

"You'd do that?" Crimson asked, her eyes widening. I nodded and she smiled. "Thanks! That would be awesome!"

I took another sip of my water, waiting for her to continue. I had a feeling the whole job situation wasn't the only thing on the list of things bothering her. She noticed me waiting and sighed, biting her bottom lip. "Is that all?" I encouraged, arching a brow.

"I can't really talk about the rest," she muttered, looking away from me quickly.

"It's okay," I assured her. "It doesn't bother me..." I trailed off. "Well, it doesn't bother me *anymore*," I added, hoping it was true.

In hindsight, I had bigger fish to fry. Cole was a blip on the radar of fucked up things that had happened to me. I didn't think I had any energy left to be mad at him now.

Crimson's eyes turned back to mine, searching to make sure I was sincere. She wasn't very good at detecting lies, though. That, or I was a skilled actress in the art of deception. "Okay...well, it's just been really hard with everything with Cole. Since it all happened, he hasn't really been talking to me. I've only seen him a handful of times since the hospital, and each time I saw him, he wouldn't look at me." The hurt Crimson felt was written all over her face.

"How's he doing?" I asked.

"He's back home with his parents now, on a new medication. He's taking some time off work still, but he won't take my calls anymore. He only texts me two-word replies." She bit her lip again, as if trying to keep the pain inside. Her eyes started to water.

"Maybe he just needs time to process and adjust," I supplied, shrugging.

"I know. That's probably it," Crimson said doubtfully. "But I just feel like it's something more than that—like he doesn't want to be with me anymore. I'm trying to be there for him, I'm trying to understand and be sensitive to what he's going through, but I won't lie. It hurts that he's shutting me out," she added, her shoulders dropping in defeat.

I took a deep breath, considering the situation. Normally, I'd blurt out the first thought that came to mind, but this was different. This was Crimson, and this was the guy I'd thought for the longest time had taken part in my rape, and I suppose in a way he had. I had to tread carefully, or I'd hurt Crimson...or myself.

"I can see you have something to say." Crimson smiled sadly. "Go on, say it. I'm a big girl."

"Well..." I sighed. "I can't speak for Cole because I'm *not* him, but it's obvious that he's going through a lot right now. Maybe he just needs to focus on himself. Maybe he feels ashamed about what happened. Maybe he feels weak and he doesn't want you to see that...but you should tell him you care and you'll be there for him, but that you understand he may need the space. You've got to be okay with that, though."

Crimson slumped even further down in her seat. A tear escaped and rolled down her cheek. "I know. It's just hard to let go. Cole has always been there for me, and I can't describe it, but he's always made me feel like this incredibly gorgeous woman. He was the first person to ever make me feel desirable."

My heart ached for Crimson in that moment, in the raw way that only one who has experienced heartbreak and insecurity could feel.

"Crimson, you *are* incredibly gorgeous—inside *and* out. You don't need Cole to make you feel that way," I told her, willing her to believe it. "Besides, you may not *have* to let him go. And if you do, it might just be for a little while until he heals a little."

Crimson's genuine smile was back and she shook her head, almost with disbelief. "Thank you, Harlow. I know Cole is probably the last person you want to discuss right now, but thank you for listening anyway."

"It's okay," I answered, waving away her concern. I was surprised to feel that it *was* okay. Maybe I was right; maybe I just didn't have any energy left. Maybe I was simply dissociating myself from the situation, or perhaps Crimson's heartache helped me get over myself a little. "We'd better hurry up and eat; I've only got twenty minutes before my next class."

* * *

I encouraged Crimson to talk to Jamie before we left, telling her that I'd meet her outside. My phone chimed in my pocket, and I quickly fished it out as I started walking towards the door, opening the message with a swipe of my finger.

Can't wait for our session tonight, beautiful. Miss you, the text read. I smiled, quickly typing my reply as I pushed open the doors to the street. Before I could send the text message, I walked into someone and dropped my phone against the icy sidewalk. I was more concerned with the massive cracks down the middle of my iPhone than I was with whoever I'd run into. "Sorry," I muttered, not looking up as I bent over to grab my phone. It had landed beside the person's brown Doc Martens in an icy puddle. They crouched down at the same time I did, attempting to help me pick up my shattered phone. We bumped heads.

72

"Fuck!" I swore, standing up at the same time he apologized.

I glanced up and nearly swallowed my damn tongue. Iain Bentley was standing in front of me, his hand rubbing his temple and a sheepish look on his face. His Caribbean blue eyes were fixated on my face, and he ran a hand through his dirty blonde hair.

"Harlow, I—"

"What the fuck are you doing here?" I interrupted. My palms were sweaty and my hands were trembling. He was the last person I wanted to see right now, and I think he knew it too. He cleared his throat, shoving his hands into the pockets of his brown jacket.

"Well, I do live in Ottawa…and sometimes I walk down the street." Iain smiled wryly.

"Very funny," I remarked, rolling my eyes. "What are you doing here, on this street, right now?"

"I'm meeting with someone?" Iain responded, his answer sounding more like a question. I felt a swell of curiosity at his words, wondering just who he was meeting with, but I pushed it aside with a frown. Iain arched a brow, seemingly amused by my behaviour. "But now that I've run in to you…do you think we could talk for a minute?" he added uneasily.

I wanted to storm off, to leave him standing there with that bewildered look on his face, but the pain behind those eyes kept me rooted to the spot. It was hard to be unaffected by someone you once thought you were in love with.

I could still remember the day that I'd met him, the day that I'd walked into that classroom. It felt like time stood still when those deep teal eyes locked with mine. My stomach had instantly started clenching with pleasure, and I'd *felt* something. For the first time in years, I had felt something *wonderful* and I hadn't wanted to let that feeling go. I'd wanted to pursue it, to bask in it.

It hadn't mattered that he was my English teacher; I went for that good feeling anyway. I honestly hadn't expected him to return the feelings of attraction and longing, and I certainly hadn't expected anything to come of it.

It was one of those relationships that had marked me in so many ways. He taught me how to open myself up again. I still wasn't the best at it, but at least I tried now.

At the time, our relationship had felt right. And it was; it had been everything I needed and more at that time. The only thing I regretted was that we'd gotten caught, and Iain had served jail time for our relationship. He'd lost his job, the majority of his friends, and his dignity and pride over me. And I had repaid him by moving on and falling for someone else.

The guilt I carried was why I couldn't exactly storm away from him, leaving him there with that pained look and no answers to any of the questions he probably had for me.

I had only seen him twice since high school, and I hadn't been able to tell him I'd moved on either time because a part of me was still stuck in the past. I didn't know if I was trapped there because I still had feelings for him, or if I was stuck there because of all the guilt I felt over everything. It was impossible to tell, but the one thing I was certain of was that I didn't want to find out either way.

A desire to rip those roots up from the ground took over me, giving me strength and resolve. I didn't know what my lingering feelings for Iain meant, but I did know that I was in love with Jax. I hadn't been able to admit it to myself until the day I risked losing him, and I didn't want to lose Jax.

Iain sighed lightly, the pain and regret that swirled in his eyes evident in the soft exhale of breath as he quickly bent over to pick up my forgotten iPhone. He handed it to me, and I pocketed it before I crossed my arms. I sighed, rolling my eyes at him. "Fine, what is it, Iain? I swear to God, if you try to kiss me again, I'll knee you in the balls."

He winced at my words, wounded by them. "I'm sorry, Harlow. I should've never done that...given what you were going through."

I opened my mouth, about to tell him he shouldn't have done it because I was with someone else, but before I could respond, Crimson was bouncing outside. She grabbed my arms with excitement, her eyes dancing happily.

"He said if you vouched for me, the job was as good as mine! Thank you so much, Harlow!" she squealed, completely unaware at what she'd just walked into.

"No problem, of course I'll vouch for you..." I trailed off, awkwardly glancing from Crimson to Iain.

Crimson finally took notice of the man standing in front of me."Oh! Sorry, I didn't realize you were..." She tilted her head as if she could taste the strange heaviness between Iain and me.

"I'm not. I was just leaving," I murmured, avoiding the particular way Iain was studying me. "Sorry, Iain. I really do need to go. I'm late for class..."

"Yeah, of course," Iain said grimly, nodding once. The pain that still remained behind those blue eyes made my heart hurt, but I couldn't do anything about it. I couldn't even tell him about Jax—not with Crimson standing there. I didn't want to have to explain the complicated history.

Crimson and I took off down the street, and I couldn't help but glance once over my shoulder. Iain remained standing outside of *The Bean*, watching me with a broken, wistful expression on his face. I had to turn away.

"Tell me, what's the scoop with *that* stunning man?" Crimson asked, peering back over her shoulder for a third time despite my previous warnings not to.

"An ex," I responded, my brow furrowing.

"God, Harlow." Crimson's jaw dropped. "Where do you find these guys?"

In classroom settings, I wanted to reply. Instead, I bit back a smile and said, "You have no idea."

chapter FIVE

MY LAST class of the day was Creative Writing. I sat in the lecture hall, trying to calm my frazzled nerves after seeing Iain. It was going to take a lot of concentration to ease my thoughts away from wondering what Iain wanted.

Out of all of this semester's classes, this one was my favourite because it gave me an excuse to write. The professor was forever assigning us the kind of homework I actually didn't mind doing. We had to dissect books that landed on the bestsellers list and write why we thought they made it, as well as the multiple writing projects he assigned. Most recently, he'd had us all write out a novel outline using a variation of different methods.

Despite how captivated I was by the subject matter, the professor intimidated me. He was an attractive man in his early thirties named Professor Sharpe. He had dark wavy hair cut close to his head, and a thick beard he kept in pristine condition. He was the personification of lumber-sexual, with nary a hair out of place on his head or beard.

Most of the girls in the room had a difficult time putting their pouty, flirtatious lips away long enough to focus on the things he said, which was a shame because he was very intelligent. A self-published author of six novels, four of which hit the bestsellers list—he could certainly open doors for anyone, and he'd mentioned that at the beginning of the term when he told us to take his assignments seriously.

He was nice enough, but I still kept my distance, choosing to sit towards the back of the room. I kept my head down, even if everything Professor Sharpe said interested me. I couldn't help but be wary of him. And myself. While I thought he was attractive, it was merely a passing reflection on his appearance; I didn't harbor any feelings of attraction towards him, but I still hid in his classes. He was the only attractive male teacher I had since high school. Naturally, that made my mind reflect back to Iain, even without my consent.

Professor Sharpe cleared his throat, capturing our attention. He was standing before the podium, his black eyes sweeping over each of us carefully, as if gauging whether enough of us were listening.

Although there were nearly two-hundred students in this particular class, Professor Sharpe always seemed to pierce each and every one of us with his intelligent eyes. "Some writers write by the seat of their pants," he explained with a serious edge to his husky voice. "But it takes discipline to sit out and write an entire outline—to know the direction things are going to go before you get there. Now that's not to say you won't get surprises along the way, of course. But this will also help me get a feel for the kind of writers you are, and to see how far you've come from the outline to the first draft."

Murmurs exploded from those students who were surprised by the mention of a first draft. If they'd read their itinerary, they would have seen that Professor Sharpe intended for us to write a novel. The first draft was due towards the end of the semester. Once he read through them, he'd hand them back out to us—only we wouldn't get our first drafts back, we'd get someone else's and we'd have to edit their novel in order to get a complete grade.

I was excited for it. Writing my outline had been easy, and I'd already started on the manuscript.

Professor Sharpe cleared his throat again, this time in a subtle attempt of getting the class to fall silent. "There were a lot of interesting outlines. I am incredibly excited to see them turn into novels, but I'm especially excited for one in particular." Professor Sharpe glanced towards the area where I was sitting and winked with a grin before quickly turning his gaze to the other side of the room. I couldn't be sure that he'd been winking at me, but I still sat a little lower in my seat.

The girl sitting beside me sat up straighter, thrusting her chest out proudly. "I bet he's talking about mine," she whispered, a seductive smile on her lips as she stared hungrily at him. A moment later, she looked at me with an inquisitive gaze, as if wondering why I hadn't seconded her sentiments.

"Yeah, maybe." I shrugged, feeling a little twitchy and annoyed. I didn't know which one of us he was looking at, and frankly, I found her remark a little pretentious. Her appearance was almost exotic; she had beautiful olive skin, hazel eyes and coffee coloured hair. I wasn't sure what her ethnic makeup was, but she was stunning and she was one of those girls that just knew it. She was also intelligent, haughty and sophisticated, and it was obvious from the way she focused 100% of her attention on Professor Sharpe that she was striving to be his next prodigy.

"My name is Delilah," she said, thrusting her slender hand towards me.

"Um…Harlow," I muttered, taking her hand and awkwardly shaking it. I wasn't even aware that introductions required handshakes anymore—at least not with our generation.

"What happened to your face?" Delilah asked, her eyes honing in on the scar on my cheek with mild surprise. I guess it was the first time she actually looked at me long enough to notice it.

I pulled my hand away from hers as if her touched burned me. "What happened to your manners?" I retorted.

Delilah laughed as if my answer pleased her. "I'm sorry, you're right. That was rude. I'm just very curious. Blame it on my journalistic tendencies," she apologized, but her voice held no remorse. She was still assessing me like I was a puzzle she was trying to piece together. I didn't like it. I bristled, my eyes narrowing at her.

That moment, Professor Sharpe started to speak again. Delilah's mouth clamped shut and she turned to face the front of the room, her chest thrusting out again like a bloody peacock. I shook my head in wonderment, barely catching the tail end of Professor Sharpe's lecture.

"Your marks will be posted on the student portal by eight o'clock this evening." The rustling of papers and feet roused me to stand as well, joining my classmates in their preparation to leave.

Delilah packed up delicately, placing all of her books in her shiny L.L. Bean bag, and gave me another one of her calculating smiles. "What's your novel going to be about?" she asked, watching as I swept my things into my beat up messenger bag.

I straightened, brushing my hair back from my face. "Um…" I frowned. I didn't feel comfortable sharing my novel idea with anyone else, especially someone like Delilah.

She assessed me quietly for a moment, her eyes full of intelligence. "Ah, I see. You're like me — very possessive of your ideas. Don't worry, I won't steal yours, but I get it if you don't want to share," she said, shrugging. "I'm mostly making conversation."

"Why?" I blurted out, my brow creasing as I met her gaze.

"I don't know," Delilah said thoughtfully, tilting her head. "You seem…interesting. I like interesting people."

I bit back my reply that she didn't seem interesting at all; there was a vast difference between interesting and lofty. Her egotistic air made me not want to be around her at all, and she was kind of rude. Instead, I forced a tight smile and shrugged. "Interesting is one way to describe me."

We began to walk down the stairs, towards the exit doors to the lecture hall. We were nearly there when Professor Sharpe's voice rang out. "Harlow, could I speak to you for a moment?" he asked.

I froze, turning around slowly. I tried to keep my expression open and neutral. Professor Sharpe had a gentle smile on his face. He was standing in front of the desk at the head of the classroom. He motioned for me to come closer, and I did. I could feel Delilah's eyes boring a hole into my back. "See you next week, Miss. Moreno," he added, glancing over my shoulder at Delilah while she stood watching by the doors. I heard the door close, and the sudden silence overwhelmed me.

"Yes?" I came to a stop before him, waiting expectantly as I kept as much distance between us as possible.

"I was completely blown away by your outline." Professor Sharpe's dark eyes sparkled, and an impressed smile lifted his thin lips. "It has true potential and I can't wait to see where you take it."

"Thanks…" I brushed a strand of hair out of my eyes, discomfort rolling off me in waves.

"I strongly suggest that you attempt to publish this book when it's completed." Professor Sharpe leaned casually against the desk where his laptop and an assortment of papers rested. His hands gripped the desk on either side of his body, the muscles taunt. His eyes were focused intently on me, watching my reaction. "I could help you edit it, and I know many people in the industry. Or, if you choose to go the self-publishing route, I could help you along the way."

"Oh." I cleared my throat, searching for something to say as my heart raced out of control. "Thank you," I finally finished weakly, giving him a tiny smile.

"It's my pleasure. I know a bestseller when I read it." He winked. "This already feels like a bestseller. Have you started writing it yet?"

"Yes, I have," I answered, dropping my gaze. I was uncomfortable with the fact that my nerves were on edge.

Truthfully, this is how it had been since the whole Iain thing. Each time a teacher pulled me aside to talk to me about my assignments, I shot back like a boomerang to that day in English class, Iain's words washing over me as if he stood before me instead of Professor Sharpe. Only the desire, the need to connect was gone. In its place was hesitation and wariness.

"I wanted to tell you that you write beautifully and articulately. You have a real talent and I'm looking forward to reading more of your work. Have you thought about a career in writing?"

"I'm sorry, what was that?" I asked, paling. Professor Sharpe was looking at me with curious concern, his mouth agape as he awaited my return from my trip down memory lane.

"I said if you ever want any extra pointers, or if you want me to just take a look at it if you're stuck, please let me know. I'd be happy to meet with you to discuss it." Professor Sharpe's smile seemed a little too gentle, as if he was aware of my discomfort. His head was tilted slightly, and I knew he was studying each and every one of my movements with a calculating eye.

"Thank you," I muttered, beginning to back up. "I'm going to be late for my next class…"

Professor Sharpe nodded. "See you next week, Harlow."

I didn't have another class. I just needed to get out of there. My chest was constricting; it was getting harder to breathe.

Seeing Delilah waiting in the hallway outside of the classroom, I came to a sudden stop. She had a pinched look about her face. "What was that about?" she asked; I could tell she was straining to keep the animosity from her voice.

"Nothing," I answered, blowing past her and bullying my way through the students crowding the halls. The last thing I wanted to do was talk to her.

The sharp bite of winter air invaded my lungs as I pushed open the doors and stepped outside, but I welcomed it. I drew in strangled breaths, adjusting to the bitter cold and trying to steady the erratic thumping of my heart and organize my thoughts.

It took nearly fifteen minutes for my heart rate to recover to a normal speed. As soon as I could breathe without choking, I made my way to the gym. I needed a workout like I needed food and water; the workout would drive out the panic, the memories, and the feelings from that encounter with Professor Sharpe.

Professor Sharpe hadn't done anything wrong at all—he often reached out to students he felt had potential. It was a known fact within the English

84

department. Last year, he helped a student named Brimley Stevenson with his novel. Brimley became a bestseller too, because of Mr. Sharpe's suggestions and connections.

It wasn't Professor Sharpe's fault that I was haunted by my past and my own decisions. My reaction to him was completely my fault.

chapter SIX

JAX WORKED part time as a personal trainer at the same gym I'd been frequenting a lot lately, and I knew he had a client to see before me. Still, I headed to the gym early. I'd slept so well the night before and with Jax in my bed, I certainly hadn't wanted to go in the morning.

I wanted to get in a good warm up before seeing Jax for my mixed martial arts lesson. It would be an added bonus to work out some of the frustration and guilt I felt over briefly seeing Iain and the way it profoundly affected me.

Changing into my workout clothes and tying up my Nike Freeze shoes, I fished my shattered iPhone out of my jacket pocket. I swore, studying the several cracks splayed about the screen. I'd completely forgotten it had cracked when it fell to the sidewalk. After seeing Iain, I walked through the remainder of a day in a conflicted haze, my thoughts racing around from Jax inviting me to move in with him to seeing Iain again. I kept wondering what it was that Iain wanted to tell me, as he hadn't gotten around to saying it. Then I had feel an intense wave of guilt for even *caring* about what it was that Iain wanted to tell me.

I shouldn't care what my ex-boyfriend had to say when I was with someone else.

I started fiddling with it and by some stroke of magic, my music icon was between two of the many cracks and I was able to click on it. The only thing I couldn't do was scroll to select music. I'd have to let whatever wanted to play, play.

Satisfied that I wouldn't be completely without music, I left the locker room and started my regular stretching exercises. I ignored the people around me, blasting the volume on my shattered iPhone.

Once I stretched thoroughly, I approached a few of my favourite machines. I worked the muscles in my legs and thighs on one, then my shoulders and biceps on another until all my muscles burned with exertion. I listened to my music loudly, losing myself completely in it while I did my best to sweat away my guilt and confusion.

I was lifting weights when I felt his presence. The air became denser, my heart rate jumped. It was as if my body was so completely wired to him that I could sense him before I even saw him. I raised my eyes to the mirror, seeing Jax exiting the private training room with a client. I couldn't fight the annoying jealousy that rose up when his client brushed her fingers against his arm...especially when I saw who his client was.

It was Delilah Moreno from my creative writing class. The same girl that I'd fled from a few hours beforehand. And gauging by the way she flirtatiously batted her thick lashes at Jax, she wasn't just here to get in shape. She had a thing for him—it was obvious in the way she bit her lower lip and gazed up at him through heavy lids.

My eyes narrowed as I watched them in the mirror. As if he could feel the daggers I was aiming at them, Jax's head lifted up. His eyes found me as if drawn to me like a magnet to metal and he grinned. He removed his arm from her touch for a second time, muttered a goodbye and sauntered over to me. His eyes held my gaze in the mirror; his smile warmed every cold part of my heart.

I knew I had nothing to worry about where Jax was concerned. He wasn't flirtatious, his eyes always sought out mine, and I knew it wasn't his fault that the majority of his clients were females that really wanted a different kind of workout than the one he offered.

Jealousy is a twisted, crazy bitch, and no matter how many times I told myself that Jax was mine, I still couldn't completely make those feelings go away. Still, I forced the displeased look from my face as he approached. If I couldn't make the jealous feelings go away, I could at least hide them from him.

"You ready?" Jax asked, pausing several feet behind me. He crossed his muscular arms, his eyes still fixated on mine in the mirror. The entire gym was lined with mirrors from the ceiling to the floor; muscle heads loved watching themselves. I avoided the mirror at all costs…unless I was looking at Jax in it.

"Yeah, give me a minute." I finished my reps and put away the weights, grabbing my water bottle before I turned to approach him.

Twice a week, Jax taught me mixed martial arts in the private training room at the gym where he would soon be hosting the same class for troubled youth. My heart swelled with pride every time I thought about Jax's class. I knew the kids would benefit from it; I certainly had.

Now if someone attacked me in my own home, I'd at least be able to do some serious damage.

Jax grinned at me, those thick lips widening to reveal white teeth that flashed against his copper skin. "Come on then." He nodded, placing his hand on the small of my back and leading me towards the private training room.

Delilah was still in the gym, her gaze focused on Jax and me. I narrowed my eyes at her. She had the decency to finally look away and I smirked.

"What?" Jax demanded, catching my reaction.

"Nothing," I said, schooling my features. I didn't want to admit how irrationally angry this girl was making me—between dealing with her in class today and seeing her practically panting like a dog in heat over *my* boyfriend. Yeah, I definitely wasn't a fan of Delilah.

I didn't trust her as far as I could throw her, and judging by her height, I couldn't throw her very far, but it sure would be fun to try…

* * *

Jax's warm, large hands gripped my hips from behind. He carefully adjusted my body, using my hips to guide me into the stance he wanted me in. He pressed down gently, forcing me to bend my knees and gain surer footing on the blue mat.

I swallowed hard, my blood feeling hot and thick beneath my skin. Jax's touch was making it difficult to concentrate. He raised his hand to brush back the sweaty hair that had fallen loose from my sloppy ponytail, his fingers grazing the nape of my neck.

I closed my eyes against the sensation of his fingers against my skin. It was impossible to ignore the fact that the gym was empty; we'd completely lost track of time. Most of the lights were off, and Jax and I were the only ones who remained. My skin erupted in goose bumps as Jax's warm breath breezed across the back of my neck. I could sense him standing directly behind me, my body completely aware of how close we were.

"I'm going to keep knocking you on your ass if you don't keep your stance." I could hear him smiling; I didn't need to see it. His hand gently squeezed my hip once more before he slowly walked around me and turned to face me.

His large hands were wrapped in tensor tape, and his long hair was piled up in a sloppy bun that made him somehow appear even more imposing. I never thought I'd use that word to describe a man rocking a sloppy bun, but it was true. Jax rolled his head, cracking the kinks in his neck. His white tank was drenched in sweat and his workout shorts hung loose against his muscular legs.

There was no doubt about it: my attraction to Jax completely melted my brain. He was distracting me, making me lose my focus. All I could think about was his hands and lips on my skin. I lost the urge to work out.

Seeing the distracted look on my face, Jax tilted his head and grinned, slowly standing up to his full height of 6 foot 2. "It seems I've lost you again, young grasshopper," he remarked.

I smirked. "Maybe I need a different kind of distraction tonight," I replied coyly.

Jax grinned, taking one huge step towards me. His hand came up to the back of my head before his lips leisurely set me on fire."It's about time we called it a night."

"Is the gym totally empty?" I asked, arching a brow. "I need a shower..."

Jax's face lit up. "Are you inviting me to join you?"

"That depends. Are you coming back to my place tonight?" I smiled mischievously. His hands felt incredible on me, and I didn't want to step away. I didn't even have time to feel self-conscious about the sweat trailing down the middle of my spine.

"Well I *could* be persuaded, I think…" Jax trailed off, eyeing me hungrily.

"I'm sure you could," I said, allowing my finger to trail down the middle of Jax's broad chest. He inhaled deeply, a slow smile teasing his thick lips upward.

"Meet back here in ten," he said quickly. "Then we'll head to your place."

It was the fastest shower I'd ever had; I barely let the water heat before I jumped in and washed the sweat off. It was freezing out, so I begrudgingly had to take a little time to blow dry my hair. The last thing I wanted was to get a cold from heading outside in subzero temperatures with wet hair.

Jax was waiting for me by the door. His hand found the small of my back, and he guided me out to the parking lot where he'd parked his truck. We barely spoke on the short drive, the electricity between us zapping and sizzling. My skin was prickled pleasantly with goose bumps, and I knew it had little to do with the weather outside.

Jax parked in the small parking lot behind the house. We quickly walked up the steps to my apartment, holding hands. "It's surreal that you're going to be right here in a couple months," I commented, looking toward the set of stairs that led up to the apartment that Jax would soon be living in.

He grinned at me, his eyes dancing. "How will I ever keep you out of my bed now?"

"Guess you won't." I shrugged.

"Does that mean you're going to move in with me?" Jax inquired, perking up.

I slid the key into the lock of my door, sending him a wary look. "I haven't even mentioned it to Jenna yet," I told him, opening the door. I withheld admitting the other part of the problem: that I wasn't entirely sure if I was ready to move in with him. I hurried into the warmth of my cozy apartment, coming to a sudden stop as I took in the extremely clean space.

Our apartment was usually neat and tidy, but it downright *sparkled* now. Every surface glistened, every framed photo or decorative piece was arranged just so.

It smelled of lemon cleaner and air freshener. The floor shined and even the coat and shoe racks were organized and neat.

In short, something wasn't right.

I could hear the distant sound of scrubbing coming from down the hallway where the bathroom was. "Jenna?" my voice started in low and then rose with alarm.

The scrubbing stopped and after a moment of silence, the toilet flushed and the sink taps started to run. A minute later, the running water ceased and Jenna stepped out into the hallway.

She was dressed in a pair of yoga pants and a ratty old t-shirt. Her eyes were red rimmed, as if she had spent the better part of the evening crying. She smiled at Jax and me in greeting, but it looked forced.

"Oh, hey. I didn't hear you guys pull up," Jenna said, fighting to keep her tone cheerful and relaxed.

"I'll see you later," Jax whispered, his lips catching mine quickly. I loved that he picked up on everything and he never took anything personally.

"Okay, I'll call you," I told him.

He nodded, smiling warmly at Jenna. "Have a good night, Jenna," he said before disappearing out the door.

I locked up before I turned to face Jenna. "So, what's up? Why are you obsessively cleaning?" I asked.

"I'm not obsessively cleaning," Jenna argued, folding her arms across her chest.

I gestured to the entire apartment. "You could have fooled me."

Jenna's shoulders sagged. "Fine. I broke up with Lucas," she said, her voice shaking.

"I'm so sorry, Jenna…what happened?" I asked, concerned. Jenna didn't reply at first. She made her way over to the freshly vacuumed and plumped couch and sat down heavily, grabbing the throw pillow and desperately hugging it to her chest as if it were a childhood teddy bear.

"Well, I just…I don't know." She sighed. "I'm okay with it…I initiated it, but…I just feel guilty."

"Was Lucas pressuring you?" I demanded. My eyes hardened at the thought. I sat down beside her, tucking my legs underneath me.

"No, it wasn't that…" Jenna considered her words. "I just got tired of it. There were no sparks, and I can't wait around for sparks, Harlow. I want a love like you and Jax have."

I swallowed hard. It wasn't uncommon for Jenna to make a statement like that, but I still wasn't used to it. "The right guy is out there somewhere," I told her instead of addressing her comment. "You'll feel sparks with him," I added, sure of it.

Lucas was a nice enough guy, but I could see why sparks and chemistry would be missing with him.

"I think I already found him," Jenna muttered, catching me by surprise. Her cheeks reddened and she dropped her gaze to the throw pillow in her arms, suddenly deeply interested in a thread that had come loose.

My eyebrows rose so high with surprise that they almost disappeared in my hairline. "You're giving me half-answers, and that's not cool. You *hate* when I do that to you," I said, calling her out on her shady behaviour.

She smiled apologetically. "I'm sorry." She shrugged. "It's just so...weird." She frowned. "I don't know how to say it without feeling like a total dork, and I really don't want you to judge me..."

"The only 'weird' thing right now is your behaviour. I'm not going to judge you, Jenna...just tell me who it is. You're making me nervous."

"It's Kyle Russell. I feel the sparks with Kyle Russell," Jenna blurted before hiding her face in her hands. Her complexion was a strange reddish purple. She was mortified.

I blinked at her slowly, not comprehending what she was attempting to tell me. "Are you sure you aren't just reacting to his celebrity status?"

Jenna's head rose ever so slowly, and she pinned me with a scathing gaze. "No, Harlow. I'm not reacting to his celebrity status."

"I didn't realize you guys spoke regularly, aside from the Facebook comments." I shrugged, still grinning. Truthfully, the whole social media thing escaped me—I didn't know what constituted as flirting and what didn't.

"He asked for my number last week," Jenna whispered. "We've been texting and he asked if he could call me."

"Did he?"

"Yeah." Jenna swallowed. "And I swear to God, I've never felt that many butterflies in my life. And it was over a phone call, just hearing his voice." Jenna appeared to be bewildered; her eyes were wide and innocent and full of hope.

I couldn't help but wonder if Jenna was placing all of her attraction on an unattainable guy simply because it was the safer bet. I knew she was still hurting after everything she'd been through, and I knew that she feared that she would never have a normal physical relationship again. It seemed perfectly logical to me why she'd cling to this notion, but I didn't want to rain on her parade or make her feel foolish.

"Realistically," I sighed, leaning back against the couch, "what are your expectations?"

"I don't have any." Jenna shook her head quickly. "I'm just saying…I felt butterflies with someone, they do exist. I just don't have them with Lucas."

I was silent for a few moments, digesting her words. A part of me wanted to lecture Jenna about it. Kyle was a flirt and according to every gossip magazine and website that mentioned him (more and more every passing day), he was in a relationship with his bandmate. But I wisely kept my mouth shut: this wasn't about Jenna's crush on Kyle; this was about her needing to justify her breakup with Lucas. She hadn't felt sparks with him and that was the important part, not her new crush.

"Makes sense," I replied. "So…you're sure you're okay? About the Lucas thing?"

"Yeah." Jenna exhaled. "I just feel guilty, you know? Lucas was pretty hurt."

"I don't blame him. You're a catch. He'd be a fool to not be upset over it."

"Thanks, Harlow." Jenna gave me a tiny smile. "I hope I didn't ruin your night."

"It's nearly midnight." I shrugged. "We were just going to crash." Well, *after* I worked out more frustration. But still, Jenna didn't need to hear that.

"Aside from my meltdown, how was your day today?" Jenna's question prompted the day's events to wash back over me. I thought about my lunch with Crimson, running into Iain, meeting Delilah, the encounter with Mr. Sharpe...and Jax. Everything that he'd said, everything that I was feeling. Jenna watched the subtle changes in my expression. "Your turn—spill."

"Well," I huffed, pursing my lips for a moment. "I had a lovely lunch with Crimson." I paused, noting Jenna's skeptical look. My use of 'lovely' was usually sarcastic, but in this instance it wasn't. "No, I mean that. We talked, cleared the air, and I may have gotten her a job at *The Bean*."

"That's great! I'm happy to hear that. Maybe you could mention the girls' weekend?" Jenna asked hopefully. "Crimson could use a little trip too. I think she needs a distraction."

"Girls' weekend..." I trailed off, confused as I tried to recall a hazy memory.

"Yes, the girls' weekend we talked about last Ben, Jerry and Ryan night," Jenna patiently reminded me. "I've planned it for two weekends from now."

"Oh, right." I'd nearly forgotten about it. "And…um…what are we doing?"

"We're going out of town." Jenna grinned, leaning forward. Her blue eyes glittered with excitement. "My dad is driving my car up this weekend. I'm sort of sick of cabbing it everywhere and it'd be nice to actually *leave* Ottawa at my own will. I think I can finish up my university experience without having to take a bus to the mall…"

I grunted in agreement. I missed the freedom having a vehicle brought. I sold my car when we moved to Ottawa, knowing that the insurance and the parking pass for our building would take up a hefty chunk of my monthly income. It seemed foolish to keep it around, especially when the university offered a free bus pass to students. Jenna had left her car at home, deciding to try and live like an authentically struggling university student. At the time, I'd found it a little amusing—Jenna's family had a lot of money, and I doubted she was getting the full taste of what a struggling university student dealt with. Her attempt was admirable, though.

"We need to get away for a weekend," Jenna pleaded, sensing my hesitation. "After everything you've been through—everything *we've* been through— we need this. Plus you didn't let me make a big fuss for your birthday, so consider this a birthday present."

"Consider *what* a birthday present?" I asked cautiously. It was true, I had animatedly told both Jenna *and* Jax that I didn't want any birthday festivities. Jenna had listened to me simply to appease me, but naturally,

Jax ignored me to an extent. He didn't make a huge fuss about it, but he did bring me a cupcake and a gift (boxing mitts, so I couldn't *really* be mad at him).

"We're going to Toronto!" Jenna squealed. I tried to ignore the sensation of my stomach dropping at the mention of the city I once lived in. "The hotel is already booked, and I've already snagged up the tickets for our Saturday night entertainment."

"*Which is?*" Jenna's secretive behaviour was beginning to put me on edge. I closed my eyes, the panic bubbling in the back of my throat.

"We're going to see *Autumn Fields* at Massey Hall." Jenna grinned. "Crimson loves them just as much as I do, and you don't mind them. I figured it'd be a happy medium for us."

Jenna looked so hopeful, and I didn't want to stomp on her excitement by telling her that the last thing I wanted to do was go to Toronto. I didn't want to tell her that the thought of going back there twisted my stomach and made me want to breathe into a paper bag with my head between my legs.

But I hadn't been back to Toronto since I'd left for North Bay.

"I think that's a great idea," I finally said, forcing the words out. We were silent for several moments, both of us locked in our own heads. *It's one weekend,* I told myself. *I won't even see anybody I know.*

"What are you thinking about?" Jenna demanded, pulling me away from my memories. I looked up at her to see that she was frowning. "Are you not excited about the trip? You don't have to freak out about taking the time off. I already spoke to Jamie about it."

"It's not that." I bit my lip. I'd told Jenna a little bit about Lauren at the end of high school, but I didn't go into detail about it. I couldn't talk to anybody about Lauren. Instead, I latched on to the first topic that came into my head that *wasn't* Lauren. "I just…I ran into Iain again."

The atmosphere changed, and suddenly I had Jenna's undivided attention. The happy, excited look on her face had been replaced with a serious, concerned expression. "What?"

"Yeah, when I was leaving *The Bean* after lunch, I ran into him outside. Like, literally. I dropped my phone and it shattered and everything," I added, pulling my phone out of my back pocket to show her.

Jenna's worry lines were back. "What did he say?"

"He wanted to tell me something, only he didn't get around to telling me whatever it was. Crimson came out and we left. I was kind of pissed off to see him, and I didn't want to hear him out, but now…"

"You want to hear him out," Jenna finished, sighing. She wasn't impressed with me. I had heard her opinion on Iain Bentley several times over the last few years, more so now that I was with Jax. In high school, when Jenna found out that my boyfriend, "Ben", was really our twelfth grade English teacher, she had romanticized it, looking at the whole relationship as a Romeo and Juliet type story.

Then Iain got arrested and several female classmates came forward to testify that he'd been inappropriate with them. I *knew* that wasn't true in my heart of hearts, but I had a feeling that Jenna wasn't so sure. She never said as much, but her frigid attitude towards him could only mean so many things.

"Yes and no," I replied. I lifted my hand to push my hair out of my face, my fingertips gently touching the edge of my scar. I dropped it quickly back into my lap, taking a deep breath to steady myself. "I appear to have a hard time letting go of the past, but I don't want to revisit it. I guess I just feel guilty."

Jenna didn't respond at first; she listened to me and then thought about what I said. I knew she understood. She wanted to break up with Lucas, knew it was the best thing for her, and she still felt guilty about it.

"I guess I don't like how he's just suddenly...back. Like, he went to jail and didn't bother trying to contact you. He supposedly was here the whole time, and again...didn't bother trying to contact you until we accidentally ran into him. Now he wants to talk? What's his angle?"

"Maybe he doesn't have one." I shrugged, uncertain.

"Or maybe he does," Jenna countered, arching a slender brow.

I exhaled deeply. I couldn't argue with Jenna about that. She was likely right. "Maybe," I said noncommittally. "But back to the girls' weekend...we'll talk to Crimson about it."

"Awesome." Jenna grinned. "I can text her right now." She pulled out her phone, firing off a text message with rapid precision that I envied. Jenna's device typing was ridiculously fast.

"Also, please make sure your parents don't mention coming up here to *my* mom, then she'll want to come with Larry," I pleaded, shivering. I didn't want to deal with Larry's over-bearing attitude or my mother's excessive fawning.

"Fine," Jenna rolled her eyes, pursing her lips like a sullen teenager. I knew she didn't agree with the distance I was forcefully putting between my mother and me.

"I appreciate it," I told her. I leaned back against the back of the sofa. "Just so you know, Jax is moving out of student housing. As of the first of March, he'll be our new neighbor," I said as casually as I could. I felt the urge to change the subject, not wanting Jenna to lecture me about my mom again.

"You asked him to move in?" Jenna couldn't mask her surprise.

"No, he'll be renting the upstairs apartment here," I quickly corrected. "But..." I added, hesitating. "He did ask me if I wanted to move in with him."

"Do you?" Jenna tilted her head, studying me with her cornflower blue eyes full of curiosity.

"Yes and no," I answered honestly. "I'm not the kind of girl that can jump into that...I feel like it's too soon. But I love how he makes me feel." I couldn't tell her that I was scared. Moving in with Jax seemed so permanent, and while I wanted that permanency with him, it still frightened the daylights out of me.

"You're scared and hesitating because of it," Jenna accused, crossing her arms and glaring at me. "You're holding yourself back. Why are you holding yourself back? Is it because you saw Iain today?"

"No! I would have felt the same way regardless. Not everything is about him, you know. And I'm not holding myself back," I argued, sure of it. My reservations started the moment Jax told me, not the moment I saw Iain. After all I had been through, I was scared to let myself believe in a happily ever after. "I just...I don't know. I don't want to leave you hanging. And besides, I like it here."

"First off, you *are* holding yourself back. Second, you wouldn't leave me hanging. I could find another roommate if I needed to. Third, you wouldn't be moving far away, just up the stairs. We could still have our Ryan Gosling, Ben and Jerry dates," Jenna pointed out. "Unless Iain really *is* a reason why you're hesitating. I mean, he's got to be! You're afraid to move forward and I think it's because you still have feelings for him."

I got the impression that Jenna really wanted me to dive into this, and that if I didn't, she'd assume that I still had feelings for Iain. I was admittedly growing a little bit aggravated. I didn't want to be pressured into making a decision about moving just to prove I didn't still have feelings for my ex.

"We'll just see how things go..." I sighed. It irked me that my thoughts did drift to Iain, just for a moment. I had a dark feeling that whatever Iain had to tell me would change things.

J.C. HANNIGAN

What they'd change, I wasn't exactly sure.

chapter SEVEN

"SO, YOU'RE getting trained by that yummy personal trainer at the gym too, huh?" Delilah's voice startled me and I lost the grip on my pen. I had written some notes for my novel before class started. Nothing major, just a couple of ideas I'd been tossing around that I didn't want to forget.

Scowling, I closed my notebook and bent over to pick up the pen as she dropped down into the free seat beside me. I really needed to make some friends, if only to fill up the chairs around me so I wouldn't have to interact with people I didn't want to talk to. The only problem was there wasn't anybody I really wanted to talk to—excluding my very small, selective circle of friends, none of which were in Creative Writing with me. "Actually, he's more than my personal trainer. He's my boyfriend."

"Oh my *God*, you lucky bitch," Delilah said, her eyes widening with astonishment. She considered me for a moment and then shrugged a shoulder. "I was going to ask how you managed that, but it makes sense."

I frowned. "What's that supposed to mean?"

Delilah flipped her coffee coloured hair over her shoulder and gave me a knowing smile. "You're hot.

He's hot. It's really not all that shocking. It's just a bummer he's off the market," Delilah remarked almost sadly. She pouted. "I was going to make him my next conquest. There are limited guys of interest in Ottawa, unfortunately. Not like back home. The selection there is far more…exotic."

"Where is home, anyway?" I asked, adding *and could you return there promptly* in my head.

"Portugal, originally," Delilah responded. "My parents and I moved to Canada when I was four. We travel home every summer to see family; I always have the best time. Portugal is full of rich culture and sexy men."

"Cool." I really wasn't interested in Delilah's personal life. In fact, I really wasn't interested in Delilah at all. I wished she'd stop trying to befriend me—if that's what she was even doing. Hell, even *my* friendship-making skills were more refined, and that was definitely saying something.

Delilah didn't seem put off by my lack of interest. "Well, I promise to not have *too* many naughty thoughts about him during my sessions," she said, giving me a coy smile.

I gritted my teeth, resisting the urge to slap her. It was better *not* to show someone they were getting under your skin.

Luckily, Professor Sharpe walked in and spared me the need to answer. He walked up to the podium and peered around the room, his eyes coming to rest in our direction. Delilah sat up even straighter, her regular seductive smile back on her face.

106

I sighed. It was going to be a long class.

* * *

I was right: it was a long class. Sitting beside Delilah was more exhausting than dealing with seven hundred children hopped up on sugar. I darted out of class quickly, trying to avoid spending any more time than required near her.

As luck would have it, I caught sight of both Jenna and Crimson walking down Taberet Lawn. I let out a sigh of relief and jogged towards them, catching up with ease. They were in the middle of a conversation — or rather, Crimson was in the middle of a lengthy story and Jenna was nodding and humming her responses. Jenna smiled at me in greeting, unwilling to interrupt Crimson.

"Hey!" I said, finally catching a break in Crimson's steady flow of words.

Crimson startled, my sudden appearance catching her by surprise, then she broke into a huge grin. "Harlow! Hey! We're on our way over to *The Bean*! I work in half an hour, and we figured we'd grab a coffee first."

"Awesome. I'll walk with you guys," I told her, glancing over my shoulder. I could see Delilah in the distance, heading in the same direction. I wasn't sure if she was trying to reach us — or me — but I didn't particularly want to find out. I'd had enough of her "friendliness" for one day.

"I was just telling Crimson about girls' weekend," Jenna filled me in with a gentle smile.

"Oh my God! I'm so excited!" Crimson squealed, her eyes shining. "I so need this. You don't even know!"

I looked over my shoulder again, seeing Delilah still walking in the same direction a couple yards behind us. I gritted my teeth with aggravation. We were almost at *The Bean*, and I just hoped we reached it before she caught up or saw where we went.

"Who are you looking at?" Jenna frowned, trying to follow my gaze.

I sighed. "Just this bitchy girl from my Creative Writing class. She won't leave me alone," I answered, my brow furrowing. Jenna arched a brow, and I could tell she was wondering if I was just being cold, like I'd been with Crimson in the beginning. "Trust me, Jenna, she's a bitch. She's conceited and her friendship-making skills are worse than mine. She's literally worse than Callie because she's actually intelligent."

Jenna pursed her lips, understanding the comparison. Callie used to be Jenna's best friend back in high school. Callie was also one of the main people who tormented Jenna throughout her pregnancy and sided with Andrew Cooper.

We pushed open the door to *The Bean* and walked inside, both of us lost in our own thoughts.

* * *

Between work, school, and exercising, I was busy over the next week. After my shift on Saturday, I all but ran home. The sooner I showered, the sooner Jax was going to pick me up for our date. I had no idea where he was taking me, but I was excited.

I pushed open the door quickly, coming to an abrupt stop as I stared at the full couch. I didn't expect to see my mom sitting timidly beside Mrs. Burke on our living room sofa, sipping from one of our mugs.

Her face split into an ecstatic grin when she saw me, and she quickly set her mug down on the coffee table before she rushed at me for a hug. Her thin arms wrapped around me, pulling me tightly to her body. "Harlow! Honey! I missed you so much!" she said, her voice wavering with emotion.

I looked up at Jenna, who was still sitting on the couch beside her mother, wearing a very guilty look on her face. *"I tried to text you,"* she mouthed, shrugging.

Even though I'd gotten the screen fixed and technically had no reason not to check my phone, I naturally hadn't the one day when checking my phone *probably* would have been useful.

"Hey, Mom," I said, trying to keep my voice light. "I missed you too."

"You look good," Mom remarked, backing up to inspect me carefully. Her eyes lingered on my scar for a fraction of a minute before moving on. "A little too skinny, maybe. Have you been eating?"

"Yes, Mom." I sighed, shrugging out of my coat. "Hi, Mrs. Burke," I added, smiling tightly at Jenna's mother.

"Hello, Harlow," Mrs. Burke said warmly. She was an older copy of Jenna; all legs and blonde hair. She was dressed in expensive-looking trousers and a blouse. Matching, naturally. I liked Mrs. Burke, even if she was a little too polished and Stepford-wifeish to me.

"Jenna was just telling us about your plans for next weekend," Mom said, smiling the same, tight smile I wore when uncomfortable or displeased. I could tell she wasn't ecstatic that I was making plans to head out of town with the girls when I claimed to be far too busy to visit her and Larry up north.

"Oh? Then she probably told you it was completely her idea. She even spoke to my bosses to make sure I could get the time off," I answered.

I couldn't help but feel amused by my reaction to my mother's unexpected visit. It was almost like each time I saw her, I instantly went back to the rebellious teenager I once was. Even at twenty-two, I still wanted to stick my lip out and pout and defy everything that she said just because she was my mother.

"Maybe I should start doing that," she joked, trying to ease the tension.

"Maybe." I smiled a small, yet genuine smile. It wasn't lost on me that Mom was trying, that she loved me and just wanted what was best for me. I put my rebellious teen self to rest. "Do you mind if I make a phone call then hop in the shower? Jax is supposed to come over. I didn't know you were coming, but maybe we could all go out for dinner?" my voice sounded strange to me—hesitant, vulnerable, and unsure.

I looked a lot like my mom had when she was younger; I had her features, her thick lashes and dark

110

hair. Mom was beautiful, but she carried worry on her shoulders and it had aged her. I was likely to blame for that. But when she smiled, it was radiant; it lit up her entire face and made her look ten years younger. "That sounds like a lovely idea, Harlow."

"Okay, great. I'll...be right back," I promised, edging my way down the hallway to the bathroom. I pulled my phone out of my back pocket, where I'd slipped it in after taking my jacket off. I sent a quick text message to Jax, explaining the change of plans and asking if he wanted to join us. Then I turned on the shower and undressed quickly, stepping under the steady flow of hot water.

I showered in record time, wrapping a towel around my body and sneaking to my bedroom while the sounds of conversation floated down the hall from the living room. Our moms were discussing their drive. Mom had driven Jenna's car, following Mrs. Burke. Apparently, she'd accidentally taken a wrong turn and ended up lost. Mrs. Burke had to back track to find her then put the address into the GPS so it wouldn't happen again. I closed my door to Jenna's laughter, shaking my head. It was just like my mom to get lost on a highway that traveled east and sliced right through Ottawa.

I dressed in fleece-lined tights and a sweater dress. I French-braided my long hair and applied my go-to look for makeup. In between getting dressed and doing my makeup, I checked my phone to find that Jax had texted me.

Hey babe…you should go to dinner with your mom. I'll pick you up in the morning for breakfast.

A small bubble of disappointment popped, but I shrugged it off. Jax likely didn't want to sit through an awkward dinner with us and our mothers. I could understand that, although it saddened me that I was losing time spent with him.

Plus, if I was being perfectly honest, a swell of insecurity had washed over me and I couldn't help but wonder if there was something else Jax would rather be doing.

Like Delilah.

I couldn't get her words out of my head, the way she openly admitted to wanting Jax. Nor could I get the image of her laying it on thick for him that day at the gym. He had pulled away from her touch, and he hadn't even looked at her with interest…but still.

Jealousy was a stupid bitch.

I knew I should just talk to Jax about it, but I couldn't admit my insecurity. How hypocritical would that be?

I responded to his text before I left my room, telling him I'd see him tomorrow.

"Are you guys ready?" I asked, joining them in the living room.

"Sure are," Mom declared, smiling. "You look lovely! Is Jax joining us?"

"Thanks…and no, something came up." I shrugged, trying to feign indifference. "Let's hit up Johnny's."

Jenna clapped her hands with delight. "Oooh! Let's! I'm dying for their pizza. I'll drive!"

We put our coats and boots on and headed down to Jenna's car. Mrs. Burke sat shotgun while Mom and I crawled into the backseat. Jenna obsessively ran her hands along her steering wheel, almost purring. "I've missed you baby!"

"Oh Jenna." Mrs. Burke chuckled, shaking her head as Jenna reversed out of her parking spot. It took less than seven minutes to drive to the restaurant and find parking.

We ordered bruschetta and wood-oven flat bread for an appetizer and a large Greco pizza for our main course. We sipped on red wine while Jenna and I took turns talking about our classes and what was happening in our lives.

"How's Lucas?" Mrs. Burke asked, pausing to take a sip from her wine glass. Her eyes were light and warm.

"Oh, we um...we broke up." Jenna flushed, avoiding looking at her mother.

"Really?" Mrs. Burke sounded surprised. "Why? He was such a nice boy."

"It just wasn't working," Jenna dismissed, shrugging. "Besides, I want to focus on finishing school and finding a job."

"Exactly what you should be focusing on anyway," Mrs. Burke said after some thought. She smiled warmly at her daughter and reached out to touch her hand. "You've got *plenty* of time to find the one, Jenna."

"I know." Jenna smiled.

113

"What about you, Harlow? You're still seeing Jax, right?" Mom asked, arching a brow.

"Yes," I mumbled, feeling uncomfortable. I shot Jenna a warning glance, pleading with her to not mention the whole *moving* thing.

She nodded curtly with acknowledgment before changing the subject. "How's Daddy?"

The small talk continued, and when dinner was over a scramble to pay for the bill ensued. Mom insisted on at least covering for our half, while Jenna's mom tried to insist it was okay. Eventually, she gave in to my mom's insistence. Maybe my stubborn streak could have been influenced by her, too.

"Well, we should probably get back to your place and grab my car." Jenna's mom sighed as we walked out of the restaurant.

"Are you sure you're okay to drive, Mom?" Jenna unlocked the doors and I crawled in.

"Of course. I only had one glass of wine. We'll hit up Tim Hortons before we leave town." Mrs. Burke winked. Jenna nodded, accepting this answer. She started her car and drove us back to our apartment. After hugging our moms goodbye, we watched while they drove off before heading inside.

"See? That wasn't so bad," Jenna remarked. She unlocked our door while I gave her a steady gaze.

"Did you know that was going to happen all week?"

"Nope," she responded, pushing open the door and flicking the light on. "I thought my dad was coming up, but he got held up at work or something. I didn't know about it until they showed up."

"Probably because my mom told your mom not to tell you. She knew I'd find out about it and probably thought I'd make myself scarce."

"Why would she think that?" Jenna frowned, unzipping her knee high boots. "I thought you said things were getting better with her."

"That was before the whole...thing...in December. Now she's back to frantically worrying and constantly fawning over me, so I've been avoiding her calls."

"Harlow!" Jenna scolded as she straightened up. "She's your mother. She loves you and she's worried about you—rightfully so. I can't imagine how I'd feel if my daughter was..." Jenna trailed off suddenly, her face paling and then turning a shade of green. She looked close to fainting.

"Jenna, are you okay?" I demanded, gripping her around her arms. She swayed a little, her eyes momentarily clouded as she was lost in her own personal hell.

The cloudiness cleared at my firm touch, and she shook her head. "Yeah, I'm fine," she muttered, brushing back a strand of her hair. I released her, giving her space that I thought she needed. "I'm just not feeling well...I'm going to go lie down."

"Okay..." I said warily, watching as Jenna shuffled down the hall to her room. She quietly closed the door, leaving me in our quiet apartment with my concerned thoughts.

* * *

I didn't sleep well that night; for a rare change, it wasn't because of nightmares. I tossed and turned, my thoughts gripping tight onto the look on Jenna's face when she'd mentioned her daughter. Even if she had said it without thinking, meaning for it to be hypothetical, she'd triggered herself. I knew she'd spend the next few days locked in that darkness and it only reminded me about the secret I carried.

I was torn. I knew I should tell her, rip the Band-Aid off and just get it out, but I couldn't imagine doing that to her. Besides, I wasn't entirely sure if it even mattered. Yeah, she wasn't Iain's biggest fan, but it wasn't like *Iain* adopted the baby. His sister did. She seemed capable and loving and kind, so why cause an issue out of something that was potentially a non-issue?

But keeping a secret from Jenna just felt…wrong. After everything that she had been through, and after everything that we'd been through together, it felt wrong to keep this from her.

My cell phone chirped from my bedside table. I rolled over, snatching it and unlocking it as I pulled it towards me. Jax had texted me.

Hey, I know it's early…but I know you sometimes can't sleep. Did you want to go for breakfast now?

I glanced at the time. It was four o'clock. The prospect of seeing Jax made me feel lighter already, and I quickly texted him that I would be ready in twenty minutes or less.

I was careful not to make any noise so I wouldn't disturb Jenna. I went to the bathroom and washed my face and brushed my teeth. Then I crept back to my room quickly, easing my door shut before I flicked on my overhead light.

I don't know why I was so worried about waking her up; Jenna usually slept like a log, and the rare occasions that she didn't were few and far between, especially when she was in her current mind-set.

I dressed in a casual pair of jeans and a long sleeved shirt, leaving my hair down. I didn't feel like 'putting my face on', as Jenna would say, so I settled for a little mascara. Once satisfied, I slipped into my jacket and headed out of our apartment.

Jax was waiting for me in his truck by the curb. He gave me a delectable grin when I opened the passenger door and climbed in. "Hey, gorgeous," he breathed, leaning over to kiss me hello. His breath tasted minty and sweet, and I kissed him back eagerly. I'd missed his touch the last few days, especially after being denied it yesterday.

"Hi," I responded, smiling.

"How was dinner with your mom?" he asked. He shifted his truck into gear and pulled away from the curb. He kept his left hand on the steering wheel and reached his other hand across the bed of the truck to rest against my thigh. Little gestures like this always made my breath hitch. Jax would search out any reason to touch me, even subtly. I hadn't realized how starved I was for that kind of connection until I met him.

"It was fine," I answered, forcing to keep the smile in place as his question prompted the memory of Jenna's face after we returned home, and with it, my dilemma.

"Good, sorry I bailed," he said, his thumb tracing slow and gentle patterns on the side of my hand. It was disconcerting how this simple gesture sparked such strong urges in me, and not just a physical craving to be taken by him either. The explosion of love within my chest, the desire to spend my life with him completely blindsided me even still, even with my fears sitting dormant. "I got held up at the gym. Besides, I figured you needed some time alone with her," he finished, glancing at me to make sure I was okay with that.

"That's alright, although Jenna and her mom were there too." I smiled lightly before I had to turn my gaze away from those intense brown eyes of his. I didn't want to unload on him about my stupid feelings of insecurity and guilt. But if he kept looking at me like that, I knew I would.

"What's that look for?" Jax inquired, not missing the tightness around my lips. Inwardly, I cursed myself. Jax was skilled at seeing through my deflective bullshit.

"Oh…nothing. I guess I was wondering what held you up at the gym," I responded. Although I fought to keep the disdain from my voice, I knew Jax could detect it. He shot a curious look at me from across the cab.

"My client was running a little late, then I had a meeting with my boss after," Jax answered. He caught the ever-subtle drop of my shoulders and squeezed my thigh.

"That client wouldn't have happened to be Delilah, would it?" I asked before I could prevent the words from spilling out.

Jax looked at me with surprise and caution. "You know Delilah?"

"She's in my Creative Writing class," I answered through clenched teeth.

"Ahh." Jax nodded slowly, checking the road before his eyes landed back on my face. "I'm sensing some friction there. Care to fill me in?"

"Not really, no," I answered honestly. I didn't want to sound like the jealous girlfriend. "Where are we going?" I asked, attempting to change the subject. I'd already made a fool of myself enough for one day.

Jax went with it, of course. "We're heading to a diner that's open twenty-four hours," he answered, making a left. The streets were mostly empty at this hour. "It's got good food," he promised, winking at me.

The diner ended up being just off the highway, a popular stop for truckers and weary long distance travelers. It was long and rectangular, with vinyl booths lining the straight wall of windows. I could see a counter with stools and the kitchen just behind that.

This diner was vastly different from the flashy one I'd once worked at. There were no decorative flashing neon signs (save for the open sign that hung beside the door), and no vinyl records or other various fifties memorabilia mounted to the walls. This place was simple and aged. Despite the sheen of grease that seemed to cling to every surface, it seemed clean and charming.

For five thirty in the morning, it was pretty full. An older gentleman sat at the counter, sipping a coffee and slowly eating a piece of blueberry pie. Every so often, he would stop and gaze off into the distance, as if remembering some fond memory from his past.

A trucker sat in one booth, drinking coffee and eating a heart-attack worthy plate of sausage, eggs and home fries. His focus was completely zeroed in on the food in front of him as if he was strategically avoiding conversation. A middle aged couple enjoyed two heaping plates of pancakes and spoke softly to each other with comfortable smiles.

The clink and clang of cutlery on plates and the comfortable buzz of conversation created a relaxing atmosphere for me, and the coiled nerves in my belly started to ease up as I slid down in the seat across from Jax. He grinned at me from across the table, his eyes setting a slow burn of desire rolling through me.

We hadn't even sat down before the waitress was standing beside our elbows with her notepad poised in her hands and a seductive smile on her face as she eyed Jax. Our waitress (Lindy, or so said the name plate pinned to her left breast) was a bold one, with dark hair trapped in a perm from the eighties and red framed glasses. She appeared to be in her late forties, but the obvious age difference between she and Jax didn't seem to bother her in the slightest as she shamelessly eyed him up. "What can I get you to start?" she drawled.

"Coffee," I grumbled.

"Coffee for me too." Jax grinned at me and just as surely as that smile turned my insides to liquid, I knew it was doing the same thing to our waitress, Lindy. "We'll also have the Ultimate Special."

"Of course. I'll be right back with your coffees," Lindy eagerly responded as she quickly wrote down our orders without once looking down at the page. Her eyes hungrily swept across Jax's broad chest, and I knew exactly what she was thinking. I couldn't help but snicker as she walked away.

"What's so funny?" Jax's brown eyes were full of amusement and a love for me that always knocked me off my feet.

I fought to catch my breath before answering. "The way anyone with a uterus practically squirts when they look at you," I responded finally, smirking.

"Oh, whatever." Jax rolled his eyes. "You should see how the guys eye you up. I constantly have to keep myself in check before I hulk out on them."

"I'm sure." I laughed once, quickly, and it faded away. I glanced down at the table, sensing that Jax's eyes were still on me.

"So…" Jax tilted his head ever so slightly. "Do you mind telling me what's putting a shadow behind those gorgeous eyes of yours?"

Jax bled beautiful words; it was one of the things that I loved about him. He always knew just what to say. I sighed, feeling my resolve to keep the whole Jenna-problem-secret slipping away. I had no secrets with Jax. That was the one thing that I'd promised him—and myself.

"Part of it is Delilah," I admitted. Jax nodded without surprise, his brow arching slightly in unspoken encouragement for me to continue. I took a deep breath. "I don't like her. There's something off about her."

"If it's any consolation," Jax told me, leaning forward, "I don't like her either. She's snotty and annoying. Trust me, Harlow, I'd rather spend every minute of the day with *you*."

I eased up even more at his words and gave him a small smile. "Well, she's only a small part of it. Mostly…it's Jenna," I explained, my eyes drifting to look out the window. The world outside was still dark, but the sky was slowly turning grey as dawn crept closer. "She triggered herself again."

"Did she get another letter?" Jax asked, his tone full of empathy and understanding. He knew how much the adoption update letters upset Jenna.

I shook my head. "No, it was…something she said. After dinner, we came home and she was lecturing me about avoiding my mom's calls, and she said something like 'if my daughter was –' and immediately turned green after. I thought she was going to faint."

Jax exhaled heavily, nodding once. "Yeah, I can see how that would do it."

I picked up the set of cutlery in front of me, gently tugging the corner of the napkin off. "Yeah. I couldn't sleep. I kept thinking about…" I trailed off again, sighing. I hadn't told *anybody* about what Iain had to do with Jenna's birth daughter, but the secret was consuming me. I took a deep breath, steeling myself.

"So, you know how I sort of dated my English teacher, right?"

"Yeah." Jax exhaled, the lines around his eyes hardening slightly at the reminder. I ignored it, knowing that it was the typical way anyone reacted to a girlfriend bringing up an ex.

"Well, he mentioned that if Jenna couldn't get an...*abortion*," I almost spat the word out, tripping over it, "that she should consider adoption. So, I suggested it to Jenna and obviously she did that."

"Yeah, and?" Jax was clearly confused; he had no idea where I was going with this.

"Iain only knew so much about adoption because his sister was going through it. She and her husband couldn't conceive and wanted to adopt. Well, it turns out that the birth parents that Jenna chose for her daughter were actually Iain's sister and brother-in-law. Jenna didn't know this because Iain's sister goes by her married name."

Jax was silent, absorbing my words thoughtfully. "So, Iain's the uncle."

Before I could respond, Lindy came over with our coffees and a bowl of creamers. "Sugar is right there, *sugar*," she purred to Jax before sauntering off. I couldn't even drum up the effort to be angry with her for the way she was blatantly flirting with Jax. Lindy had a ring on her finger and a bad perm. Lindy wasn't *Delilah*. I swallowed back the distaste and focused on my current, more prominent issue: Jenna. Delilah be damned.

"Yes," I responded once Lindy had disappeared again. I fixed my coffee silently, ripping open three packets of sugar and three creamers. Jax put one of each in his coffee.

"And Jenna doesn't know that."

"Ding, ding, ding." I sighed, looking up at him with tired eyes. "At first, I was in shock over...well, everything. The arrest, the media shit storm. Then my brain shut down for a bit. Then when I realized I hadn't yet told Jenna, six months had gone by and she was receiving her first adoption update and breaking down in the worst way over it. I couldn't bear to add on to her pain, and I didn't know if telling her would be harmful or not. I mean, Sarah—the adoptive mother—is really sweet. I met her at the hospital when Jenna gave birth. The way she looked at that baby girl...I just *knew* that they should be together, you know?"

"Yeah," Jax commented, frowning into his cup.

"What are you thinking?" I asked, panic fluttering in my heart. "Do you think I'm a terrible person for not telling her?"

Jax looked up quickly with shock in his eyes, as if the thought hadn't even occurred to him. He swallowed hard, shaking his head. "No, that's not it."

"What is it then?"

Jax sighed again, leaning back. He rested his arms on the back of the booth casually, a move only made possible by his height. He studied me quietly for a few moments before speaking. "I don't know what to think, to be honest. I obviously don't know the guy, and I don't respect him at all for what he did. I don't care

124

how fucking sexy you are—if I was your teacher, I would never consider…" He shook his head. "Anyway. You know how I feel about *that*. But hearing that the adoption thing was technically his idea, and hearing about how Jenna eventually chose *his* sister to be the birth mom…yeah. That makes me think he steered you in that direction purposely."

My stomach sank at his words. I wanted to believe that Iain Bentley was good, that his intentions had been pure, but having my deepest fears voiced by Jax of all people was unsettling. I opened and closed my mouth, searching for something to say.

"I don't think he did that intentionally," I finally said, my brow creasing.

"Then why didn't he mention it to you? Or better yet, his sister. Why not tell his sister that it was a conflict of interest?" Jax demanded gently.

"We weren't exactly talking at the time," I shot back, defensive. Still, I knew Jax's concerns were valid. I sighed, massaging my temple with my forefinger and thumb. "I'm sorry, Jax. I'm tired and cranky and I really don't know what to do about this."

"What are you so afraid of?" Jax asked, leaning forward to catch my hands in his. His eyes searched into my soul, looking for answers I couldn't find words for.

I swallowed. My brain was spinning and whirling with pictures and thoughts. "I'm worried that Jenna will freak out and hate me forever. I'm worried that she'll decide to somehow unpick Sarah and her husband as the adoptive parents."

"I don't think that will happen," Jax said, his eyes full of compassion. "Do I think Jenna will be mad about it? Absolutely. Will it hurt her? Probably. But the adoption is final, right?" I nodded in response. "There isn't anything she can do, arguably. No judge would undo an adoption that's been finalized unless there was just cause to do so. Iain's sister wouldn't pay the price for his actions."

I sighed again, looking out the window while I considered Jax's words. The sky had lightened to a pale grey, the first lines of pink dotting the horizon. What Jax was saying made sense—a lot of it. I just somehow had to get over this hurdle of terror and tell Jenna the truth.

chapter EIGHT

IT WAS Crimson's second day on the job, and she was a natural. She struggled with learning how to use the cash register at first, but by the end of her first shift, she got it. She did occasionally confuse an order, but she picked things up a lot quicker than most. Her hearing impairment barely seemed to hinder her, although I knew she occasionally struggled to hear the customers.

Thursdays were usually pretty busy at the café and we saw a steady flow of traffic from when our shift first started at 3 p.m. It was the first week of February, and it was coming in like a lamb with a high of 2 degrees Celsius. It was sunny, and more people seemed to be out and about.

It had been just over two weeks since Jenna broke up with Lucas, and he hadn't exactly taken the break up well. He stopped talking to Jenna and refused to acknowledge me. He showed up for his shifts, but I'd caught him a few times when I stopped in for a coffee break and either he was miserable in general, or he just really didn't like me anymore.

I couldn't bother to feel bad about it; after all, I was never really friends with Lucas. I disliked that it made things a little awkward at work, and I knew Jamie was dying for the inside scoop. He was invested in Lucas's happiness, but he also adored Jenna. Thankfully, with tax season around the corner, he was occupied with the business accounts and spent more time locked away in his office muttering about numbers than he did fishing for details.

My shift was almost up. I was scheduled to get off at 5 p.m. to allow Crimson a chance to close up shop on her own (with Jamie lingering in the background). Tomorrow morning, we were heading to Toronto for our girls' weekend. I found myself actually looking forward to it—almost. If I pretended that our destination wasn't the city I'd left a bunch of baggage in.

Crimson was vibrating with excitement over our girls' weekend trip. She'd confessed that this was the first time she had been invited to do anything like this before. She was ecstatic to be included, and I knew that she was looking forward to a little break from studying and worrying about Cole.

Shortly after our heart-to-heart, Crimson spoke to Cole. He finally told her that he needed space and she was doing her best to give it to him—or at least as much as Crimson could; space wasn't really in her vocabulary. I had to delete his number from her phone for her, just so the temptation to text him would ease. I told her that when (and if) he was ready, he'd reach out to her. Begrudgingly, she accepted it and did her best to keep distracted and busy.

There was a lull in customers and I'd just finished making a fresh pot of coffee. Crimson was kneeling on the ground, restocking paper cups. She stood up and brushed the dust off of her knees, meeting my gaze with an excited grin. "I can't wait for this weekend!" she squealed for the fifth time since our shift started. "I need to get out of this town for a little bit."

"How's the Cole thing?" I asked, knowing my question was awkward and rather brash.

"Same old story there." She sighed, her grin fading. Sadness edged her eyes, but she struggled to shake it off. "I'm trying to get over it...but..." She gazed toward the door.

"It's hard," I told her empathetically. "But who knows, maybe you'll meet a hot guy at the concert."

"Maybe," Crimson responded half-heartedly, sounding unconvinced.

"No maybe about it. I'm sure hot guys listen to folky music," I joked, giving her an encouraging smile. "Or at least hot hipster guys do."

Crimson snorted. "I need a rebound. I don't care if it *is* a hipster. I'd be all over his square beard and glasses like a fat kid on cake."

"Glasses and cake? Why are you discussing my early adolescence?" Jamie's lilting tone drifted over to us before he pushed the swinging door open with gusto. His hand prevented the door from swinging back, and he fixed his pale blue eyes on us with a forlorn stare. "I told my mother to burn those horrid pictures because I never wanted to see them again. How did you know about those painful, painful memories?" Jamie placed his hand over his heart as if he was wounded. The comical smile he was working hard to conceal gave him away.

"Easy, killer." I grinned. "We were talking about hot guys at the concert and how Crimson doesn't care if they have square beards or square glasses."

"Oh, in *that* case, I completely endorse you jumping all up on those hotties like my former fat-kid self on cake." Jamie winked. The door chimed, alerting us to the arrival of a new customer. "Speaking of fat kids and cake…looks like your preferred dessert of tall, dark and sexy is waltzing up, Harlow."

"I knew you liked me." Jax grinned at Jamie, ruefully shaking his head. He came to a stop in front of the counter.

My smile changed to the dopey one I always seemed to have around Jax. It had been a busy week again, between our individual studies, work and Jax disappearing to help the landlord with renovations, we hadn't really had time to hang out. He had crashed at my place several times, but we were too hungry for each other to really talk and hang out. We devoured each other before passing out from exhaustion only to rise again in the morning and repeat the whole thing.

Jax had booked off the rest of today and tomorrow morning so that we could spend time together before I left with Jenna and Crimson. I didn't really know what was on the agenda, nor did I care. Spending time with Jax was a pleasure no matter what we were doing, and I'd be lying to myself if I said I wasn't excited for it.

"Hey." I grinned. "I've still got twenty minutes," I told him, gesturing toward the clock that hung on the wall behind me.

"I know, I'm a little early." Jax winked. "Figured I could grab a coffee and stare at your beautiful face with adoration for a bit."

"Barf," Jamie joked. "You two make me ill with your lovey-dovey gooeyness. Harlow, get out of here. Consider yourself off early today, for the good of the customers. I don't want *them* to feel ill too."

"Gee, thanks, Jamie," I replied dryly, rolling my eyes while I hid a smile. I didn't know how to feel about Jamie sending me home early. I normally would have been a little irked—I liked money, I liked earning it and I liked saving it. But I also *really* liked spending time with Jax, and I hadn't had an opportunity to do that this week.

Shrugging, I stepped away from the front counter and headed to the staff room to grab my things, the sound of their casual conversation following me until the staff room door swung shut. I could listen to Jax talk for hours. He was one of those people that could talk to just about anyone. He was warm, friendly, and genuine. He was like Crimson in that regard, only he wasn't as enthusiastic. He was more laid back; most things rolled off Jax's shoulders.

I'd only ever witnessed Jax lose his laid back demeanor a handful of times. The night I told him about Cole and what had happened to me, the night that Andrew had attacked me, and the day I told him I'd just locked lips with my ex-boyfriend.

Forcing those thoughts from my mind, I continued to the task at hand: getting my stuff so I could get home for a quick shower. I needed to wash the smell of coffee and pastries off my skin and hair. My purse and jacket were stuffed into the lone locker in the staff room. I had to be careful not to knock any of Crimson's things out. I walked back out of the staff room, seeing that Jax was still standing at the counter chatting with Jamie and Crimson. Only, the three of them were not alone.

Standing beside Jax was Iain Bentley.

My heart felt like it was going to drop straight out of my chest cavity and fall into the pit of my stomach. I forgot how to breathe for a moment, my eyes widening at the sight before me. All the sound around me seemed to fall away for several moments before it came rushing back with an intensity that made me sway on my feet.

Jamie was gesturing animatedly at Iain, a huge grin on his face. "This is my brother. He's extremely handsome and talented and single," Jamie said. He sent a secret wink to Crimson. "He's no hipster, but he does write! Don't you, big bro? He's released his debut novel two months ago, and he's asked if he could do a book signing here next week for two days!"

Jax spotted me and the easy smile faded from his lips as he took in my pallor and the look on my face. "Are you okay, Harlow?"

The moment my name tumbled from his lips, Iain's head snapped from Jax to me. His eyes widened at the sight of me. "Harlow?" he said with surprise. He wasn't expecting me here, which meant he hadn't known I worked here when he ran into me a few weeks back. Still, it wasn't a welcoming thought.

I swallowed hard, my throat suddenly as dry as sandpaper, my heartbeat thudding loudly in my chest.

Did Jamie say that Iain was his *brother*? Suddenly, a memory from the time Iain and I escaped to Ottawa came back: when we laid in bed and Iain told me *you can't help who you love,* and explained how his family had accepted his gay brother without any hesitation so he had no doubt that they'd eventually accept the unconventional way we met.

Jamie couldn't be his brother. There was absolutely *no way* that the universe was that fucked up.

"Oh! You know each other?" Jamie said with an equal amount of surprise.

My eyes sought out Jax's. I could tell he was slowly putting two and two together. His jaw clenched and he exhaled through his nose.

"Yeah, okay. So, I need to go…" I said, backing away from them all and looking at Jax pleadingly. He read between the lines, grabbing his coffee off the counter before stalking over to me. His free hand was clenched at his side, and his eyes were burning with emotion. I didn't know what the cause behind all the turmoil rolling around in him was, but if I had to guess, it was my former lover and teacher.

I needed to escape this fucked up situation before I said or did something I regretted. Like start screaming at Iain, demanding to know why he kept popping up *everywhere* in my life, for example.

Somehow, I didn't think Jamie would be okay with that.

I grabbed Jax's hand and his fingers entwined with mine the moment our flesh touched. He relaxed a little, eased by the contact, and allowed me to lead him out the door. We didn't speak for several long, agonizing minutes. I finally looked at him, tugging his arm slightly to pull his attention back to me. "I swear to you Jax, I had no idea Iain was related to Jamie."

"I gathered that." Jax sighed, the tension releasing from his jaw.

The rest of our walk was silent, neither of us knowing what to say. We walked up to my apartment. I had to let go of Jax's hand to unlock and open the door. Jenna's boots and jacket were gone, meaning we had the apartment to ourselves. I closed the door behind Jax, locking it.

Jax stepped up behind me, wrapping his arms around my chest and pulling me back against him. He rested his head on top of mine after he kissed it. "Just so you know, I'm not mad at you. I think that you think I'm mad at you, but I'm not…not at you."

"But you *are* mad," I pointed out, melting back into him.

He chuckled lowly. "Of course I'm mad. I just exchanged pleasantries with someone I didn't even know I hated that much. The urge to rearrange his face when I finally clued in was difficult to ignore."

"Such a guy response." I sighed. "Angry. Must. Hit."

"Hey, that's basically your response too," Jax said, referring to my tendency to unleash all my fury on the gym's punching bags.

"Basically." I turned to face him. Jax looped his arms around my hips, letting his hands fall to cup my ass. "Now, back to what's important…" I said slowly, my hands settling on the back of Jax's strong neck and urging his face down to meet mine.

I kissed him slowly at first, lavishing his mouth with the attention I was just as desperate for. Jax changed the angle of the kiss, driving it deeper and faster. He cornered me against the door, feeding into the desire we both felt. I could feel him against my thigh, hard and completely at attention. Jax's responses to me always made me feel like a goddess.

I attempted to undo his belt without breaking the kiss. His hand stilled me and he regretfully broke the kiss to look at me with longing and mischief. "You know, if we lived together, I wouldn't have to worry about your roommate walking in on us. We could do it anywhere…"

I arched a brow. "Well, that just about sells it for me," I joked playfully. Jax growled, his lips finding mine again. Nipping, tugging, biting and pulling while his large hands roamed my body with promise.

Pulling myself up using Jax's neck, I tightened my legs around his hips. He carried me to my room.

* * *

Afterwards, we lay in my bed together, my head resting on his chest, his arm wrapped around my body while his other hand continued to roam and touch. Jax was always touching me; he never missed an opportunity.

I was struck with just how peaceful I felt when I was near him. He made the numbness go away; he made me want to embrace the good and the light. He made me feel warm and alive in a different way than I'd experienced before. With Iain, there had been an urgency to connect: everything was rushed. He was like a drug that I couldn't get enough of; a drug that made me high and left me feeling strung out.

This thing with Jax was different. He made me feel warm and alive, but it was more like the way sunlight helps a plant grow and flourish. Jax was my sunlight.

There was still an urgency to be with him, a desire that consumed me more so than anything I'd felt before, but this was better. *More*. It felt healthier, it felt right.

And yet...I still hesitated with him because losing people was all I'd known. Granted, sometimes I chose that. I chose to burn bridges, I chose to disconnect myself from people because I knew it would hurt less. My dad, Lauren, Iain—they'd all been taken from me before I was ready to say goodbye.

I knew I had an entire storage unit of baggage to sift through before I could allow myself to truly move forward with Jax, and that was a scary thought. I didn't know where to start.

"Penny for your thoughts?" Jax asked, his voice gravelly from our previous activities. He peered down at me with those eyes that I could lose my soul to willingly.

"I don't know," I answered.

"That's a lie." Jax's lips curved with the hint of a smile. "You do know...you just don't want to say it."

I didn't want Jax to assume I had regrets, or was thinking about my past in the way he probably thought

I was thinking about it. "I was just thinking…" I started. "About how in love I am with you."

"And the frown is for…?"

"Fear," I whispered, keeping my gaze on him. "The frown is for fear."

"You're afraid of your feelings for me still." He didn't say it in an accusatory way. He was simply stating a fact. A fact that may bother him a little bit, but I knew he understood it completely.

"Everything good in my life blows up in my face," I told him. "Everyone I let in, everyone that I care about…they always end up leaving in some way…or causing me harm."

"That won't happen," Jax said with determination. "Not with me. I already told you, I'll give you whatever you need. If you need time, I've got plenty of it. If you need space, I'll hate it but I'll give it to you. If you need me to walk away, I'll do it…even if it kills me. But only if you want that. Otherwise, I'm completely yours. You're it for me, Harlow. I've never felt this way about anyone before."

Jax's words unlocked something in me, and the fear seemed to disappear. In that moment, I was unafraid of being in love with him. In that moment, I was able to envision a proper future with him, and I liked what I saw. I smiled. "I don't think I need time," I confessed, lifting my head so that I could kiss him.

"Does this mean what I think it means?" Jax asked.

I pretended to think about it. "Yeah, it does. I guess I'll move in with you," I joked. The words felt right. "I'll tell Jenna this weekend."

* * *

Jenna's driving made me a little nervous, or maybe it was the fact that we were going to a city I hated. Either way, I was relieved that we made it safely to the hotel by four o'clock.

"The concert starts at eight, but we need to get in early to avoid the lines," Jenna instructed as we boarded the elevator up to our room on the fifth floor. She clutched the room card in her hand tightly.

"Just how do you suppose we avoid the lines?" I asked. "Isn't the show sold out? Meaning, won't it be busting at the seams?"

"Pretty much yes." Jenna shrugged, unconcerned. "But I have VIP passes!" she added, wiggling her brows.

"OH MY GOD!" Crimson screamed shrilly. "How on EARTH did you score those?" she demanded.

"Jenna has a thing with the lead singer," I told Crimson, smirking at the scathing look on Jenna's face.

"We don't have a thing," she said, frowning. "You can buy VIP passes."

"Yeah, but you didn't," I guessed. Judging by the pink tint to Jenna's face, I was exactly right.

"Whatever," Jenna said as the elevator dinged and opened. She stalked out quickly, leading the way to our room.

The hotel room was a little cramped. The door opened up to a quick little half wall that blocked the bedroom area. The bedroom had two queen sized beds and a huge dresser and two chairs, one on either side of the room. A flatscreen TV sat on top of the dresser, and the bathroom was directly across from the door.

"Let's get this party started!" Crimson declared before kicking off her shoes and instantly climbing up on one of the beds. She started to jump, motioning at us to join her. Jenna laughed, shaking her head as she took off her own shoes. She climbed up on the bed with Crimson and started to jump as well. "Why are you just standing there?" Crimson demanded.

"I don't really jump on beds," I said. "At least not like that."

"Harlow is allergic to having fun," Jenna joked, blowing me a kiss.

"That's not true." I frowned. "I just don't think 'fun' constitutes as jumping on a bed."

"Are you still wigged out about the whole Iain thing?" Crimson asked. She stopped jumping and sat on the edge of the bed. Jenna stopped as well, remaining standing up.

"What Iain thing?" Jenna demanded, her eyes narrowing.

I shifted uncomfortably on my feet, sending Crimson a displeased look. "He was at *The Bean* yesterday."

"Why?"

"Because apparently he's Jamie's brother," I grumbled.

Jenna was still for a moment, shock widening her blue eyes. "Holy shit," she said.

"Yup, and we're going to see a lot more of him," Crimson said gleefully. "He's doing a book signing for his novel next week."

"Wait, back the bus up." Jenna held her hand up to Crimson. "Why does she look excited about that?" she asked me directly. "Does she not know who Iain is?"

"Not entirely…" I trailed off, feeling guilty. I'd never gotten around to telling the awkward story, and I wasn't planning on it.

"What? What's going on?" Crimson looked back and forth between Jenna and I.

"You can go ahead and tell her." I sighed. "I need to go to the bathroom."

"The hell you do." Jenna snorted. "Get over here and sit down." She pointed to the opposite bed. I sat, crossing my arms. "Iain Bentley was our grade twelve English teacher," Jenna told Crimson.

Crimson was silent for a minute, then she whistled lowly. "Woah. I wouldn't have guessed that. I mean, he looks older, but not like…teacher older."

"Yup, there's the sordid details," I said, attempting to stand up again.

"Not done yet." Jenna waved her finger at me. "So, Harlow and Iain carry on this secret relationship. He gets caught, and he ends up going to jail. Then when he's released, he doesn't once reach out to Harlow to let her know how he is or what's going on. I watched this girl pine over him for nearly two years. She finally finds Jax and starts to move on, *and he comes back*. Now he's everywhere. Coincidence? I think not."

"Are you finished yet?" I asked her, sounding bored. Jenna nodded solemnly. "I don't think that Iain knew I worked for Jamie. I certainly didn't know they were related, and Jamie certainly didn't know that Iain and I knew each other. I do think that it was a whole fucked up coincidence."

"As for him showing up on our doorstep and sticking his tongue down your throat?" Jenna asked innocently. I glared at her, resenting the fact that she was all but forcing me to open up to Crimson.

"He showed up to tell me something after Andrew attacked me. He saw my face and when I told him who did it, he got all emotional. He was there when that shit with Andrew went down in North Bay. The kiss just…happened. I pushed him away. Jax knows," I added, for Crimson's benefit.

"Weird, isn't it?" Jenna remarked, also looking at Crimson.

"What happened in North Bay with Andrew?" Crimson inquired, looking back and forth between Jenna and me. Her head was rotating so quickly, trying to keep up with the conversation.

"See, unlike Jenna, I won't force her to talk about her past," I commented, giving Jenna a small smile to let her know I was kidding. "That isn't the point, anyway. The point is Jenna thinks my ex is stalking me."

"What do you think?" Crimson questioned.

"I think that the universe loves to fuck with me," I responded, shrugging. There was no other excuse.

Jenna was playing on her phone, seemingly ignoring the conversation. "Have you even checked out what his book is about, Harlow?"

"No…" I trailed off, the prickly sensation of unease exploding beneath my skin.

"Apparently it's about *you*," Jenna told me, shoving her phone at me. I took it. She'd opened up a web page, likely Iain's website. On the web page was a cover image of Iain's book and a blurb. The book was called *Circumstance*, and the blurb instantly chilled my blood.

Circumstance by Iain Bentley

They say that love knows no colour, no race, no age.

All of David Young's morals and ideals are questioned when he finds himself falling desperately in love with the beautiful and mysterious 17-year-old Leah Decker. Leah is other-worldly to David. She is as intelligent as she is beautiful, strong as she is vulnerable, brave as she is scared, and dark as she is light. She is a contradiction of everything he thought he knew of the world.

Marred by death and tragedy, Leah has not had an easy life. Her flame is close to flickering out, but it sparks when she's around David, the flames of her inner light catching and pulling him in. He watches her come back to life before his eyes, he watches her see her own potential.

But David is Leah's teacher, and Leah is his student. Can true love overcome circumstance?

My mouth felt like cotton balls as I handed Jenna her phone back. She handed it to Crimson so Crimson could have a read.

"Well then," I said. I really didn't know what to think about the whole situation. I wanted to talk to Jax about it, to see his take on it. My feeble mind latched on to the thought of Jax. "So, I guess now is as good a time as ever to mention that I've decided to move in with Jax."

Jenna's head snapped up, her eyes brightening with excitement. "Really, Harlow? That's incredible!" she all but squealed before racing over to me and throwing her arms around me.

"Oh my God." Crimson handed Jenna her phone, seeming a little shell shocked. I bet she wasn't counting on this kind of excitement during our girls' weekend. It was the first time Crimson had really hung out with both Jenna and me since that one party ages ago.

Jenna had fallen silent, her eyes clouded with thought. "What's wrong with you?" I demanded, stirring her away from whatever was consuming her.

"I was just thinking isn't it kind of fucked up that your ex-boyfriends keep popping up?" Jenna answered. She cast an apologetic look to Crimson. "No offense."

"None taken. It *is* kind of messed up. I mean, it's not like you live in the same towns where those relationships even happened…Cole was from Toronto, originally."

"Toronto?" Jenna looked at me, tilting her head. "You never said you lived in Toronto."

"Well, I did." I shrugged, uncomfortable. "But we should really start getting ready and maybe go get some food. I'm hungry."

Jenna gave me a look that read *we are not through talking about this*, but nodded in agreement. "Alright, let's get this show on the road," she said, rubbing her hands together.

chapter NINE

THREE HOURS later, we were piling out of the
hotel restaurant and into a cab, ready to head over to
Massey Hall for the concert. Jenna and Crimson had
both spent a ridiculous amount of time changing
clothes several times to find the proper outfits and
obsessing over their hair and makeup. In the end, their
fussing was worth it. They both looked stunning.

Jenna looked edgy in her grey skin-tight mini dress,
black quilted leather jacket, and black heels. She'd used
a black and grey palate to create a smoky look over her
lids, and her cornflower blue eyes were intense. Jenna
looked hotter than hell, but I couldn't help but tease her
that she was going to freeze her ass off.

Crimson was wearing cream fleece-lined leggings
and a gorgeous, chocolate brown, long-sleeved knitted
top. She had tamed her wild curls with some kind of
product, and the result was polished, tight curls. Her
hair, even when tightly curled to her head, was halfway
down her back. She was even wearing makeup: a
natural, subtle look that still made her eyes pop in a
demure yet enticing way.

I dressed in my tight black jeans with rips in the
knees, my shit-kicker boots and an old band t-shirt with
the sleeves ripped off. My long hair was down, but I'd

changed the look of my go-to black liquid eyeliner. I'd used a style called 'drop eye', where the eyeliner followed both the upper lid much like a cat-eye, but it also swooped down to follow the lower lid, creating a more dramatic look. My red lipstick was back full tilt, and I felt hot. Hot enough to send Jax a picture text.

"We look *smoking*," Jenna declared, satisfied. "Ugh…tonight is going to be amazing!" she added, practically squealing with excitement. I smiled, her happy energy affecting mine, lifting it up just enough for me to push thoughts of Iain—and his book—from my mind.

"Yeah, we do," I agreed, thinking about Jax's response to my photo text.

You and me, the second you get home. Wear that.

"We're here!" Jenna sang, leaning forward to pay and tip the cab driver. He'd parked right out front of the Massey Hall. We stood on the road for a minute, looking at the lineup that already stretched halfway down the road.

"Shit," I said, frowning. "Guess we should have gotten here earlier." Jenna didn't respond, she was busy texting on her phone. "Hey, I thought we said no phones this weekend."

"Trust me," Jenna said, looking up briefly. "This will just take a minute and it will save us an hour." She waited until her phone dinged, read the response then quickly smiled. "Alright, follow me, ladies," she said, leading the way to an alley beside Massey Hall. I didn't like it one bit, but I followed her, sure that Jenna wouldn't lead us into harm's way.

There was a metal door at the side of the building, held open by a large, very *bald* security guard. "Are you Jenna Burke?" he asked.

"Yes," she answered, flashing her VIP card and ID at him. He stood aside, letting us in. I almost swallowed my tongue when I saw Kyle Russell casually leaning against the wall in the narrow hall.

"Hey," he said, a dimple flashing on the side of his mouth. Kyle was just shy of six feet tall. His light hair brushed against his shirt collar and was carelessly styled. He was dressed in dark grey jeans, a black v-neck t-shirt and a leather jacket. He was the epitome of a celebrity: put together, sexy, and reeking of high maintenance.

His light eyes brushed over Crimson and me and came to rest on Jenna. He stepped forward, his arms wrapping around Jenna's body in greeting.

"Hey, Kyle." Jenna flushed, stepping back when he released her. "These are my friends, Harlow Jones and Crimson Stewart."

"Hey," Kyle said again with a curt nod to both Crimson and I, and I vaguely wondered if any other words graced his vocabulary. "Come on back. Your VIP passes grant you access to backstage, which is where we're hanging out until it's time for the show. Then Creed here will accompany you to the front row." Kyle motioned to the large security guard that had granted us entrance into the side door.

Creed grunted in acknowledgement, his tan face transforming to a friendly grin as I met his eyes.

Kyle led the way down the narrow hallway to another door and opened it. Voices spilled out from inside, and I felt my heart beating loudly in my chest. This was my first time meeting anyone who was considered famous. At first, I was a little star struck. I didn't know what was on the other side of that door.

My dad had been in a band, back in the days before I was born. That's how my parents had met. It was at one of his smoky bar shows in Toronto a lifetime ago: *my* lifetime ago. But he was never famous like the people in *Autumn Fields*. I could already hear the buzz of the audience, although we must have been separated by a wall or two. My dad played at small venues, and he barely made any money off those shows. He did, however, develop a coke habit.

I glanced at Kyle again, my eyes narrowing as I searched for outward signs of him being high. With fame and money came vices like drugs and booze. Kyle seemed fine though. His eyes weren't glassy and he was alert, charming even. The way he kept glancing at Jenna with the secret, adorable lopsided grin almost made *me* want to smile.

Jenna walked in with confidence, Crimson trailed behind her with wonderment, and I stalked in like it was the last place on earth I wanted to be. And it was, sort of. Once the initial *oh my God I'm meeting celebrities* wore off (which was pretty quickly for me), I was just... bored... missing Jax... wondering about Iain's book and how much truth was in it.

Two guys that I recognized from posters and CD covers were standing near the refreshment table, snacking on fruit. One was tall and scrawny, with strawberry blonde hair, brown eyes, and freckles that darted across his nose and face. He was animatedly telling a story to the second guy, who was a little bit shorter, with dark skin and incredibly light eyes. He had a playful, easy grin on his face, and was shaking his head at something the first guy had said.

There was a lone leather sofa toward the back of the room, where the only girl in the group sat, looking bored—distracted even—as she sipped from her water bottle. Her feet were up on the coffee table, crossed at the ankles. I couldn't help but admire her fantastic boots. She was dressed in black, almost see-through tights, black shorts with a chunky belt, an AC/DC shirt and oddly enough, a flowing, see-through cheetah print top that went to her knees. It reminded me of a robe of some sorts, only it wasn't. She wore a fedora over her long caramel hair, and her eyes looked smoky and haunted. She watched us approaching, a wariness to her that made me wonder what her story was.

"Ladies, these are my bandmates. Cam, Marcus, and Everly. Guys, this is Jenna." Kyle paused, motioning to Jenna with a ridiculously shy grin on his face. "Harlow, and Crimson."

Everyone muttered their hellos. I felt Cam's eyes drawn to me. I met his gaze, hoping to convey that I was not interested. Cam had an air of self-entitlement about him, as if he believed he was God's gift to women. It was almost comical with his wiry hair and scrawny build. I suppose most fans didn't care which guy hit on them, so long as they could claim to have been with one.

Cam grinned, sensing a challenge, and I rolled my eyes.

"This is *so* exciting!" Crimson squealed, gripping my arm as if she needed to hang on to me to keep her balance. I smiled at her, glad that at least she and Jenna were having fun.

* * *

For my fifteenth birthday, Lauren invited me to a concert at Massey Hall. Her dad worked for a company that often gave away tickets to local shows. The concert was for Steve Earle, a man I'd never heard of prior to going to the show with Lauren. Lauren's dad let us go alone, assuming that we couldn't get into much trouble at an old country singer's concert.

He was wrong, of course. He dropped us off, watched until we got safely inside, and then drove away. The moment he was gone, Lauren and I snuck out. Her boyfriend's shop was a few blocks away, so we walked there, arms linked together and our heads thrown back in laughter. That was the same night we got the matching birds in flight tattoos on our collar bones.

That time was lighter, freer. Even after everything I'd been through at that point, I was still open. Lauren's friendship made me carefree in a way that I'd never experienced before.

Being back at Massey Hall six years later, with Lauren's body cold in the ground, was a trip. And it wasn't a pleasant one. Still, I enjoyed the concert. It was impossible not to—*Autumn Fields* was a great band. Their lyrics were great, their instrumentals were phenomenal, and before I knew it, it was over and we were backstage with the other fans who had VIP passes.

There were ten of us total. The table that had held all the refreshments and food was restocked, while another table had been set up at the far end of the room for the band to sit at.

Eager fans held out posters, CD cases, t-shirts, notebooks—anything they had—to get them signed. I saw one girl press her chest forward for Kyle. He signed it with a cheeky grin, and she squealed with excitement before moving on to Cam and Marcus. She even stopped in front of Everly, grinning.

"I'm not shy!" she declared, thrusting her chest out for Everly to sign. Everly actually laughed, impressed by this girl's gall, before her fancy signature landed just below Kyle's. "Thank you so much!" The girl started to cry and had to be led away by one of her friends.

I avoided the lineup and stood near the refreshment table, sipping from a bottle of water and watching the chaos around me while I tried my best to fight off thoughts of Lauren.

Jenna was flirting with Kyle demurely and Crimson was eagerly chatting up a few of the fans. They were both having a blast. I wish I could say the same for myself, but I just wanted to go home. I had a tension headache, and an ache in my heart from missing Lauren.

It was impossible to not think about her when I was back—back *home*. That part of my life seemed so far away…and yet, it really wasn't.

Sometimes, I felt irrationally angry for the way that Lauren's life had been cut short. The two years I'd known her hadn't seemed long enough at all.

Lauren liked to have fun. She liked to push the boundaries and spent every moment like it was her last. She taught me how to live that way, and since I'd lost her, I had forgotten how.

Lauren's family blamed me for her death. They blamed me for everything, really. She was considered a "partier," but I never saw that girl get blackout drunk. She was always in control of herself and her actions. She was always smiling. And yet, her parents acted as if *I* corrupted their sweet, innocent little girl and turned her into a harlot.

Her parents hadn't known about her secret relationship with an older guy (a tattoo artist, no less). They found out the night they went to the hospital to identify her body—and they were heartbroken and pissed. Naturally, they turned their anger to me, the survivor. In their eyes, I shouldn't have lived. Lauren may have made mistakes, but it was my boyfriend driving.

I blinked away the moisture from my eyes, trying to control my breathing. I tried to push away the memories of Lauren, which were quickly resurfacing at a staggering rate.

My phone buzzed in the clutch that I'd tucked under my arm and I quickly fished it out, welcoming the distraction from my own thoughts.

Hope you guys are having fun tonight! Miss you. Be safe.

Jax's message brought a genuine smile to my face and eased the anxious racing of my heart. I responded, telling him I missed him too and wished he was here. Things would be far more interesting if he was.

I realized just how much I cared for Jax, how I wanted to be around him. With a ferocity that startled me, I couldn't help but wish he was here, and not just because Cam's sleazy eyes wouldn't dare linger on my body leeringly if Jax was present. I just wanted to feel his arms around me.

After sending my message to Jax, the silence started to get to me. It was strange how loud and chaotic it was backstage…and yet, I felt wrapped in silence, suffocating in my loneliness. I closed my eyes, not wanting to give in to those feelings. Not here.

"Hey." The sudden appearance of someone else startled me. I glanced up, seeing that my unwanted friend was honing in for the kill. He must have finished signing breasts. He was sipping a beer, trying to appear cool and calm. In reality, he reminded me of one of the dorky kids that was always getting shoved into lockers in high school. I tilted my head, wondering if he had been one before the whole band thing. Now he exuded an arrogance that made me feel ill. It wasn't that I got bad vibes off of him—he was harmless, that I knew—

but arrogance is a gross personality trait. It makes you feel dirty and cheap.

"Hi," I said cautiously.

"So, where are you from?" Cam tried again, smiling into his beer.

"A lot of places," I responded dryly. I didn't want to be rude, but at the same time, I wasn't in the mood for small talk with a stranger that I didn't particularly want to get to know.

"Me too." He grinned, his eyes slowly dropping to my chest.

I sighed, stepping back and angling my body so that I was facing him. "Okay, buddy," I said, my no-bullshit stare in full effect. "I'm in a happy, committed relationship. I have no desire to spend the night avoiding you, which I'm going to have to do if you don't lay off on the crazy eyes."

Cam looked surprised at first, then mortified. He started to turn red with embarrassment. I couldn't help but notice that his large ears stuck out quite a bit, and they turned just as red as his face. "I was just making small talk," he argued.

"With my tits? Newsflash: they don't talk," I responded. "Look, you seem like a nice enough guy. I'm sure any one of those fans over there would be beyond ecstatic to keep you company."

Cam's mouth gaped like a fish for several seconds. "Fine, whatever," he said, sending me a dirty look before disappearing.

I leaned back against the wall, relieved to be free of him, and sighed contently.

"That was impressive." I opened my eyes, watching the speaker warily. Everly stood in front of the refreshment table, an amused smile on her thin lips. "I've never seen anyone shut Cam down like that before."

"Well, what can I say? I'm not like anyone, I guess." I shrugged, fighting a smile. I felt a kinship with this girl. Although she was one of the main stars of the show, she looked as if she didn't want to be here any more than I did.

Everly tilted her head, smiling. "No, I can't say you are. It's refreshing. So many people trip over their feet to scream in our faces. I don't think I've had an actual conversation with a fan in months. Usually, they just run up to us and start screaming '*Oh my God I love you guys so much can I have your autograph oh my God, oh my God, can we take a picture!*'" Everly's voice changed a fraction, mimicking a lot of the fans that had done the exact same thing at the signing. "It gets kind of old. Rarely do we actually get to *talk* to the fans, to find out who they are and why they like our music, or what their dreams are...you know?"

"That must suck." I didn't know how she—or anyone, really—handled it. I would hate having people rush up to me and scream in my face. I'd probably punch them. I said as much to Everly, and she chuckled.

"It gets tempting sometimes," she whispered, winking. There was a lull in our conversation. "So...are you a fan? You don't seem ecstatic to be here."

"I am not really the 'fan' type. I enjoy your music, I have several songs on my playlist, and I enjoyed the concert. But...I'm not going to ask you to sign my tits or anything," I responded honestly. "As for the lack of enthusiasm? That's just my personality."

Everly laughed, smiling again. Her eyes drifted over to where Kyle and Jenna were standing. They were desperately trying to get a moment alone together, but the other fans lingering were making it difficult.

"Are you and Kyle a thing?" I asked, following her gaze.

She looked at me sadly. "No, we aren't. And we never were," she replied earnestly. She leaned forward a little. "The record label likes to pretend, though. The fans apparently love it. Anything for the fans, right?"

"Right," I felt a little sad for her. She was carrying something; it was evident in the haunted, sad look behind her pale green eyes and in the way she held herself. I wondered if it had anything to do with Kyle. "Are you into him?"

"No." Everly shook her head venomously. "I can assure you that I am most certainly *not* into Kyle Russell. He's a friend of mine, a very *good* friend. He's been a major part of my life for a while now, but we are not and never will be romantically involved. In fact, he speaks very highly of your friend. Jenna, isn't it?"

I nodded, still skeptical. "She's into him too," I responded, taking another sip of water.

"Good, he deserves happiness. She seems like a sweet girl," Everly remarked, her eyes back on them.

"Jenna's already been through hell. If he breaks her heart, I'll have to break his vocal cords." I said this seriously, my eyes focused on Kyle's flirtatious smile.

Everly's attention slowly slid back to me. Her expression was difficult to read; I couldn't tell if she was curious, angry, or amused. Perhaps all three. "Noted." she gave me the tiniest hint of a smile. Her eyes found the clock on the wall above my head, and her expression changed again. Wistful, maybe? This girl's mask was too perfect to see through. And I thought *I* built walls. "Well, it was nice talking to you," Everly said as she smiled tightly.

"Yeah, it was." I smiled back, watching as Everly slipped away from the crowd and disappeared, accompanied by another security guard.

* * *

It was nearly two o'clock in the morning when we piled into our hotel room. I was exhausted, and passed out almost immediately. Jenna and Crimson stayed up a little late talking, but fell asleep by three. We slept until nine o'clock before we all made a mad dash to get ready before check-out.

"Do you guys want to grab breakfast before we hit the road?" Jenna asked, smiling at us. She appeared lighter, happy. Her night out had done her a lot of good. I mumbled my consent and we walked down with our suitcases to grab breakfast at the hotel restaurant.

Crimson was sitting across from me, absently fiddling with her hearing aid. She'd been doing it a lot since the concert. She seemed a little pale and pinched too.

"Are you okay?" I asked after the waitress disappeared with our orders. I was more than a little concerned.

"Who, me? Oh yeah, I'm fine," Crimson said, waving away my concern. "I'm just trying to re-adjust the volume and get rid of the buzzing sound. I have a bit of a headache too, but otherwise, I'm peachy!"

"Oh, okay. Do you need anything?" I kept one eye on her while I distractedly fixed my coffee.

"No. Really, Harlow, I'm okay. This happens," Crimson said, gesturing to her hearing aids like it was no big deal. She fiddled a little more before she was satisfied enough to stop. She sat back. Jenna and I exchanged a look, and Jenna shrugged as if to say *she knows what's normal and not*. I dropped it.

"So, last night was *so much fun!*" Jenna stated, grinning.

"It really was." Crimson nodded in agreement. "That concert was amazing, and the backstage passes were so awesome! Thanks for inviting me!"

"It was our pleasure. We'll need to do it again sometime," Jenna decided. "Maybe not a concert though, since Harlow didn't seem to enjoy it…" She didn't say this cruelly; she was just making an observation.

"Sorry." I shrugged. "I enjoyed the concert part, and talking to Everly was pretty cool too."

"I saw that," Jenna said slowly, working to keep her smile in place. She appeared a little vulnerable and insecure. She dumped a packet of sugar into her green tea. "So...what did you guys talk about?" she asked as casually as she could.

"Well, she gave me props for shutting down Cam. Then we talked a bit about how crazy it gets for them, I guess. Then I asked her if she and Kyle were together."

"Harlow!" Jenna scolded, trying to appear stern. The glint in her eyes was evidence that she wasn't as mad as she wanted to seem. I knew she wanted to hear more.

"She said they weren't and that nothing was going on—and that nothing had gone on. But that the label didn't like to address it because they preferred to give the fans the impression that they were."

"Kyle said the same thing." Jenna shrugged, clearly put at ease by my words. "It makes sense, I guess."

"To a certain degree. The label is all about the dollar signs. Everly didn't seem too happy with the whole thing."

Jenna hummed, shrugging again. "Small price to pay for their level of success, I guess."

"I certainly wouldn't mind *pretending* to be in a relationship with someone as hot as Kyle," Crimson chirped, grinning.

"What about Marcus?" Jenna asked, smiling invitingly. "He was talking to you quite a bit last night."

"He has a girlfriend." Crimson's shoulders dropped. "Back home. We mainly talked about her and

–" Crimson stopped abruptly, flushing almost as deeply as her name.

"And…" I urged, arching my brows. "You didn't talk about Cole, did you?"

"A little." Crimson shrugged helplessly. "I was missing him a lot last night. Talking about it to someone helped ease it a bit, and it prevented me from going off and calling him."

The waitress reappeared with our plates of food. Jenna had ordered waffles; Crimson had ordered Eggs Benedict. I got a regular plate of sunny side up eggs, home fries and sausage with a side of bacon. I started salivating at the sight of all that grease. We were all too hungry to make much conversation, and fell into an easy silence broken only by the scraping of utensils on plates.

After we had nearly finished eating, Crimson cleared her throat. "So, I was thinking…" She pushed a lone home fry around on her plate. She looked up at Jenna and I. "Will you be looking for a new roommate, Jenna? When Harlow moves in with Jax? 'Cause…I was just wondering if I could maybe, I don't know, rent a room off you or something? My last semester is almost up and I'll have to find a new place or risk having to move home to my parent's house and I really don't want to do that. I like Ottawa. But the idea of looking for my own place is kind of terrifying so I thought maybe, well. You know…" The more Crimson spoke, the redder she got.

Jenna smiled with ease. "Of course! If Harlow's okay with that, as in…if she's actually really truly moving out, then you're welcome to take her room over."

I took my time replying, chewing the rest of the food in my mouth before I washed it down with a small sip of coffee. "I'm fine with that. Jax gets the keys on the first of March."

"Really?" Crimson's face lit up, as if she couldn't believe her luck. "I mean, you're not just saying yes because you feel like you have to? 'Cause you don't. I could probably find my own place. If I started looking now, I could—"

"Seriously, Crimson, I'd be happy to have you as a roommate," Jenna interrupted, grinning. "You're nice and funny and genuine. I doubt you'd take my clothes without asking."

I felt a little better knowing that Jenna wasn't going to be completely alone once I moved out, but I was still a little sad. I couldn't help but feel like it was the end of an era.

chapter TEN

I WAS not looking forward to my morning shift on Sunday. I knew Jamie would be there, waiting for me to return from my day off to grill me on the whole Iain thing. I wasn't looking forward to it in the slightest.

Still, I was never one to blow off work, and I wasn't about to start now. Besides, I'd be lying if I said I wasn't interested in questioning Jamie myself. Did he know that I knew Iain? Did he know our history?

When I pushed open the door to *The Bean* twenty minutes before my shift, I was greeted by the sound of coffee brewing and the oven beeping. I could hear Mark in the kitchen, whistling while he went about preparing the day's menu. I didn't see Jamie out front, so I went directly into the staff room to put my stuff in the locker.

I had to pass through the kitchen to do so and Mark was in there, just as I'd figured. He had his back to me so I ducked into the staff room quickly without saying hello. On my return, Mark was at the counter.

He looked up and caught my eye, his hands pausing over the dough he was rolling. His expression softened when he saw me. "Harlow," he said warmly.

"Hey, Mark," I said. "Where's Jamie?"

"He just went out front," Mark answered, his eyes still on me as his hands slowly kneaded the dough. I started to move toward the swinging door that separated the kitchen from the front of the café. "Wait a minute."

I halted, slowly turning to face Mark again. I crossed my arms, feeling a lot like I was about to get lectured by my boss—which was odd, because Mark wasn't one to lecture or meddle. That was more Jamie's thing.

At the thought of Jamie, my stomach sank with dread. What if he was going to fire me over this? After all, I was the reason why his brother went to jail and lost his job.

I knew Jamie cared about my well-being and wanted me to find happiness. He skirted on a thin line between boss and friend, or dare I say it...*father figure*. Jamie cared about me and so did Mark.

But they took their business seriously; they wouldn't put it in jeopardy for anything. If someone wasn't working out, they were gone—regardless of any personal attachment.

I couldn't help but worry that I was going to get fired over this. Then what would I do? I was going to need my job more than ever, especially if I moved in with Jax. There was no way I'd let him cover all the rent and bills.

I swallowed hard. Mark seemed to sense my anxiety and his dark brown eyes softened even more. He always looked like a giant, cuddly teddy bear: tall and burly, with wavy dark hair and a scruffy beard he wore tight to his face. Every time I saw him, he was wearing two hairnets—one over his head and one over his beard. "Relax, okay? You are certainly not in trouble. We love you, kid. Okay?"

"Okay," I whispered.

Mark tilted his head, sending me a patient smile. "Mind if I give you some advice?"

"Um...sure?" I was curious and a little shocked; Mark didn't usually do the whole advice thing.

"If you let it, your past can cloud your present and make you hesitate on your future. You have to let things go, release them into the universe and be content with your decisions."

"Sounds like a fortune cookie," I responded, narrowing my eyes suspiciously.

"It was." Mark chuckled. "I read it two weeks ago when we ordered Chinese for dinner. It's still true though."

I smiled and shook my head. "Okay, I'll remember that," I promised before turning back around and pushing the door open.

Jamie was putting on a pot of decaf coffee. He ripped open the bag of ground coffee beans and poured it into the filter, slid it in carefully and hit the start button. Thick brown liquid started to trickle out of the spout.

He looked up when he heard the kitchen door swing shut. "Hello, Harlow," he said. His voice was void of its usual cheerfulness, in fact...he appeared on edge.

"Hello, Jamie *Bentley*," I responded, my eyes narrowing on their own accord. *Huh, guess I was madder than I thought about this whole situation.*

Jamie winced a little. "Ah, yeah. Well. I haven't gone by my last name in years. I go by my middle name—my mom's maiden name. I thought it sounded better. Jamie Hunter. I don't know." Jamie shrugged apologetically, his light eyes seeking out mine. "Listen, Harlow...I didn't know about the whole...thing between you two. It never even occurred to me that you were...her. I didn't mean to spring Iain on you like that."

Now that I knew the truth, it was impossible to not see the similarities between Jamie and Iain. Jamie was tanner, his eyes were lighter and his nose was a little wider, but aside from that, they shared a family resemblance.

How in the hell had I missed that? Especially during all that time I had spent pining for Iain to return? Or maybe I'd been drawn to Jamie in the first place because of it. That thought unsettled me.

No, that's not it, I told myself. Jamie was warm, inviting, and the kind of person whose soul just exploded out from their bodies. I wanted to think that I had been drawn to him because of his enthusiasm for life because I'd been lacking that at the time, not because he'd reminded me of Iain.

"Well, I guess the cat's out of the bag now." I sighed. "I don't particularly want to be around for that book signing thing."

"I understand." Jamie nodded. His eyes were full of empathy and sadness. I could tell he was holding back. It appeared—for the first time since I'd met him—that Jamie was speechless.

I tilted my head, considering him. The café was still empty; none of our early bird customers had arrived yet. "I can see you have questions, or something to say. So for the next fifteen minutes before my shift starts, I'm not your employee. Let's get this out of the way," I said, raising my arms in defeat.

Jamie stared at me for a moment, and then he quietly walked around me. He locked the door to his café and flipped the sign over that read *back in five minutes*. Then he walked back behind the counter. He quickly poured us both a cup of coffee and motioned to the nearest table. We sat down across from each other.

"Iain would kill me if he knew I was talking to you about this." Jamie sighed, massaging his temple. He fixed me with a considering gaze. "But I feel like I need to."

"Yeah, I figured you'd say that. You're kind of uber invested in our lives, aren't you?" I joked, easing the sting of my words with a smile. "I like that about you. Prior to meeting you, I didn't have people like that in my life. At least, not people who were willing to push through the walls I threw up. So, I guess what I'm trying to say is that I owe you. What do you want to ask? Or say, whatever."

"I think you both need closure," Jamie said, making a face as if it pained him to say. "I know you've moved on with Jax—you are happy, you are with who you're

166

supposed to be with. But…you didn't collect all your boxes from your last relationship."

"I don't need to talk to him," I argued, my eyes narrowing at the suggestion. "I don't have anything left to say. What *could* I say?"

"No, no. That's not what I'm saying," Jamie said quickly, shaking his head. "You don't need to talk to the other person to get closure. You just need to accept your own decisions, your own part."

"What are you talking about?" I demanded, confused.

Jamie sighed, inspecting me carefully. It was as if he was trying to sift through his thoughts and all the things that he wanted to say to find the right words. "When Iain was released from jail, he moved in with Mark and me. He didn't have anywhere else to go. Our parents were appalled about…what he did. Our sister, Sarah, was busy with her new family and although she didn't blatantly show her disgust over his actions the way our parents did, she made it clear that she didn't approve. So, Iain just had…me. He never talked about you; the only thing I knew was what everyone else knew: your age, the circumstance of how you met. But I also knew that my brother—my brother that had never broken a law before in his goddamn life—was madly in love with this girl he'd lost it all for. I didn't have to understand it; that's love. You can't put pretty labels on it. The age of the girl he'd lost his heart to was almost irrelevant, and had he not been her—*your*—teacher, I doubt it would have mattered at all. But he *was* your teacher, and that shouldn't have happened."

I said nothing. My hands trembled slightly. It hurt hearing from someone that knew Iain well. It hurt.

"The other day, the look on your face when you saw Iain…it was as if you were seeing a ghost. A ghost that terrified you," Jamie continued carefully. "I thought you were scared of Iain. That pissed me off, you know?" He chuckled without humor. "I never agreed with my brother's decision to 'follow his heart' and carry on with a student. But I feel protective over you—I always have. Ever since I met you. I wanted to punch him, and I am a non-violent person."

"It wasn't like…that—like what you're thinking. I knew what I was getting myself in to. I was in a very strange place back then, although I wouldn't have admitted it to anyone. I was too stubborn to admit that I was lonely. Too stubborn to admit that losing my friend impacted my life in more ways than one. I didn't have the best relationship with my mom—probably my own fault—and I didn't have anyone else to lean on. The way Iain looked at me…it made me feel worthwhile. I felt a spark for him. I fell for him; I wanted the happy feelings he evoked in me because I was sick of feeling numb. I was naïve and selfish," I told him. "I did care about Iain, and I did until I met Jax…and even still, I care for Iain. But…I fell for Jax. Hard. In ways that are different from how I fell for Iain. *I'm* different."

"I know." Jamie's hands reached out to gently cover mine. He smiled at me; a genuine smile. "You were so closed off when you first walked in here. That boy

168

opened you up again, and that's good. That's love. So, why are you still holding back, pumpkin?"

"I feel a lot of guilt for Iain," I confessed, looking down at the table. Never before had I spoken so freely about this situation with anyone, and it was surreal that I was able to tell this to Iain's brother. "If I could go back in time and…not do the things I did, I would. He didn't deserve the jail sentence or to lose his teaching license."

"He sort of did." Jamie smiled sadly. "He knew the implications of what he decided to do, and still did it. He knew what was at stake. He didn't blame you at all—he *doesn't* blame you."

I exhaled. "It doesn't matter what he thinks. This is about how I feel, what I think. I am scared to move forward with Jax because I'm afraid of destroying his life the way I destroyed Iain's." *And Lauren's.* Although I didn't verbalize it, the words ricocheted around in my mind, cutting into my heart.

"You are absolutely right about that, it doesn't matter what he thinks. But don't let the past define you," Jamie said, his eyes earnest. "You can't treat two people like the same person. Jax is not Iain. Your relationship with him is not the same one you had with Iain. It's unfair to hold yourself back like that, not only to you but to Jax as well."

"Not what I expected you to say, actually." I tilted my head, a little amused. I was expecting Jamie to be Team Iain, if there was such a thing.

"I love my brother," Jamie clarified. "I don't agree with all his decisions but I don't have to. We are completely different people. Just so long as you were never forced in any way."

"I wasn't," I said, holding his gaze.

Jamie nodded with acceptance. "I wouldn't worry about Iain. I wouldn't waste my time feeling guilty for him. I am confident that he will find what he's searching for just as surely as I'm confident that *you've* already found it."

Jamie's words made me speechless. All I could do was nod, stunned by his admissions. The need for me to reply was cut short by the tentative knocking of our first customer. Usually, our doors were open by now. Jamie squeezed my hands before releasing me, then he stood up and went to unlock the door, effectively beginning our day.

* * *

Even after my chat with Jamie, I was still on edge. It was almost as if I was waiting for Iain to walk back into the café, but three o'clock rolled around with no sightings. I decided I needed to hit up the gym. I hadn't been since Friday morning, and after the greasy breakfast I'd had the day before with Crimson and Jenna, I needed it.

There was also a bonus to going now: Jax was working.

I spent two hours vigorously trying to make up for the days I'd missed. My work out time came to an end when I felt Jax approaching and I carefully set down the barbell I was lifting. My muscles were strained and tender.

"Good afternoon." Jax grinned, eyeing me hungrily. "Are you just about done? I'm off now."

"Yeah, I'm done. Do you mind if I have a shower first?" I asked, feeling extra sweaty and gross. Between the café, missing the last several days, and the sweat, I didn't exactly smell delicate and feminine.

Jax's eyes lit up at my question. "Go ahead, I'll grab one too. Then maybe we could go out somewhere."

"Sounds good to me." I grinned.

I didn't take my time in the shower. I showered with purpose, eager to get back to Jax and find out what he had in mind. Jax always had the best ideas for dates; he was the most creative, thoughtful person I had ever met. I used to be uneasy about surprises, but Jax made me anticipate them with excitement.

"So, where are we going?" I asked, trying not to bounce around in my seat as we drove.

"You'll see. Need to make a quick stop first." Jax smiled, winking at me. He drove up to *The Bean* and parallel parked in front of it. He leaned forward, his hand cupping around the side of my neck. He guided my lips towards his, kissing me tenderly and slowly. Each time he touched me, my body buzzed, desire coursing through my veins. My eyelids would involuntarily flutter, and I'd submit. Every time. "Stay here," he instructed, knowing I would.

He returned several beats later with a wicker basket. I arched a brow as I watched him cross the street. When Jax planned something romantic, he usually conned Mark into making food for us; Jax claimed his own cooking skills were subpar.

Jax leaned in and put the wicker basket on the back seat. A moment later, he was opening the door and climbing into the cab with fluid ease. He smirked playfully at me. "Ready?" I nodded, and he started to drive.

We drove to the industrial part of town and pulled up to what appeared to be an abandoned warehouse. He parked carelessly and pocketed his keys. Without saying a word, he stepped out of the truck and grabbed the basket and a thick plaid blanket. I followed him towards a faded red steel door, my eyes narrowing with speculation when he pulled another set of keys out of his other pocket. He unlocked the door and stepped inside, looking back at me with a delighted grin on his face. "Are you coming?"

Abandoned places made me feel uneasy, but with Jax there, I didn't feel any fear. Just a growing curiosity.

He led the way into what must have been a parts factory for vehicles. The concrete floor had lighter stains where the equipment used to be. There was nothing there now; no rows of machinery and parts, no people working. It was dusty and smelled like mildew. The ceiling was *high*. So high. It must have been sixty feet tall. Dirty windows lined the entire room; a few panels were broken from stones, but the rest were still intact.

Jax walked to the center of the cleared room, spreading the blanket out along the floor. He set the basket in the middle of the blanket.

"What is this place?" I asked.

Jax stood up to his full height and threw his arms out, gesturing to our surroundings. "You're looking at the future home of *Aconi Walker MMA!*"

I was silent for several beats, absorbing this news. "You're fucking kidding me. No way. NO WAY, JAX!" I screamed before lunging at him. He caught me effortlessly in his arms, lifting me up. I wrapped my legs around his waist, lifting my head back to meet his eyes. "That's incredible! Congratulations!" I said. Jax smiled, and I leaned forward to kiss him. His fingers pressed into my ass, squeezing me to him. We kissed for several minutes, losing track of time. The deep groan that spilled from my lips stirred Jax, and he slowly broke the kiss. He pressed his forehead against mine and gave me a wicked smile.

"We'll have to resume that later. It's pretty cold in here," he pointed out.

"True." I shivered, imagining my back against the cold concrete. Yeah, it was better to wait until we were somewhere warm. Besides, I had questions to ask. I released my grip around his waist and dropped to the ground. "So, tell me how this happened." I sat down beside the basket, facing Jax and looking up at him earnestly.

Jax sat down across from me. "Well, you know the owner of the gym, Jared Aconi?" I nodded and he continued. "I happened to mention my plans for the future...about wanting to really make that youth program grow. He told me that there's a rising interest for mixed martial arts. Then he told me he bought this warehouse last year, and it's just been sitting here. He was going to turn it into another gym, but there's already so many out there. I guess my plans got him thinking about turning it into a gym that focuses on Mixed Martial Arts. He said I could run it with his input, like a part-owner."

"That's awesome, Jax!" My heart grew with pride.

"I know." Jax shook his head, almost bewildered. "It's mind-blowing that Jared trusts me with this…it's a huge undertaking. I'll get paid in salary, and I'll be able to host that program and many others. We're drawing up the official business plans and everything. It's going to need a *lot* of renovations," Jax added, glancing around the abandoned space thoughtfully. He shook his head, bringing himself back to the present as he started digging around in the basket. He pulled out wrapped sandwiches and a thermos of hot chocolate mixed with coffee—just the way I liked it. He held a sandwich out to me.

"So, you'd potentially bring your class that you're doing at the gym over here then," I clarified, accepting the sandwich and unwrapping it.

"Yeah." Jax's grin was infectious. "I'll also hold classes for other people too, but those kids will learn for free." He was talking about the kids in the troubled youth program. "I'm hoping a few of them would be interested in volunteering too, down the road. It'd lead to employment opportunities. Jared's completely on board with my ideas. It's crazy."

"That's incredible, Jax," I remarked. "And it's really not all that crazy—you're a smart, intuitive man. Jared sees that."

"Thanks." He smiled at me. "I figured something else too," Jax said, pausing to take a huge bite of his sandwich. He chewed it slowly, and then took a leisurely sip from the thermos while I not so patiently waited. "I remember you saying a while ago that you wanted to help women who suffered from abuse. I figured, if you wanted, you could do that here. I could section off a small area for you and offer discounted self-defense classes."

My eyes widened so much, I thought they'd pop clean out of my skull. I gaped at Jax, too many words rushing me at once. "I don't even know what to say, Jax…" I finally managed. It was true: I was speechless. "But I've only taken a few psychology classes. I'm not going to be licensed to help them. I'll be getting my BA in English, remember?"

"With an emphasis on women's studies," Jax finished, winking. "Have you given any thought to continuing on to get your BA in psychology? You'll already have the emphasis on women's studies."

I snorted. Me? Be a psychologist? That was laughable. I was the most messed up person I knew. I could barely sleep, I was constantly running on anxiety and my stomach was always twisted with fear.

I paused, the amused smirk falling from my lips when I realized that lately, my stomach wasn't *always* twisted in fears. The nightmares were beginning to fade off—they weren't happening as frequently. I was by no means healed, but I was getting better. *Why?* I wondered. *Was it because I'd thrown myself into everyone else's lives?*

"I don't know, Jax." I sighed, biting my lip. I didn't want to tell him that the idea of taking out more loans was intimidating. I didn't have a fancy inheritance to fall back on.

Besides, writing was in my soul, and I sort of wanted to see if I could make an income off it…somehow.

Like Iain. The thought left a bad taste on my tongue. I took a swig from the thermos, welcoming the taste of hot chocolate and coffee. Iain wasn't my reason for wanting to write. Yeah, he was doing that now. Good for him; I was happy he was following his dreams. But before I met Iain, I loved words. Writing seemed to be the only way I could express my emotions and thoughts. Writing was the only way I didn't have to pretend to be infallible.

I'd always wanted to be a writer; I'd always *written* things, but Iain *was* the first person who made me believe that I could do it. That I could *write*, that I had a talent for it.

Professor Sharpe seemed to think I had a talent for it too.

"Well, you could host a survivor's chat once a week. Then you're just offering a support group, you know?" Jax suggested. "You're a natural, Harlow. I think it's because you genuinely get it. You've been there and you know how to react and that'll really cross over."

I thought about it for a moment, a slow smile lifting the corners of my lips up. I liked the idea of helping other women, of helping them see that they *weren't* their pasts, their circumstances. I liked the idea of making a difference, even if it was just on a volunteer basis.

"I like the idea of that," I told him.

J.C. HANNIGAN

chapter ELEVEN

JUST WHEN I thought Jax had exhausted all of his surprises for the day, he pulled out another one. After we finished eating, I cleaned up our mess while he disappeared into a tiny room off to the far left after telling me to stay put.

The tiny room had its own walls, separating it from the rest of the warehouse. It had either been an office or a staff room back when the place was functional. I felt the desire to go and explore, but Jax's eagerness kept me rooted.

Jax returned carrying a cardboard box. He set it down on the floor in front of me. "Are you ready?" he asked, a playful grin on his thick lips. He brushed his hair out of his eyes and kneeled down, pulling out a pair of rollerblades.

"We're...rollerblading?" I asked, confusion marring my face.

"Yup!" Jax smiled broadly. "I used to rollerblade all the time in Lake Cowichan."

"That was a different time," I said gravely, trying to shove the skate away. "Nobody rollerblades anymore."

"You say that like it means something." Jax cocked an eyebrow. "Since when does *Harlow Jones* give a shit

178

about what everyone's doing?" He was baiting me, challenging me. Just like he did with the ice skating.

"Fine," I said glumly. "Only it will be your fault when I end up with a concussion and can't have sex for seven months."

Jax threw his head back and laughed that deep laugh, the one that instantly brought a grin to my face. He effectively chased away my sullen mood with that laugh, replacing my scowl with a smile. "I think you're safe. I brought you a helmet, if you want." Jax lifted the helmet out from the box. "Knee pads and elbow pads too. Safety first." He winked.

"Fine. I'll rollerblade, but only if you answer some questions." I smiled at him slowly. He sensed trouble, but his expression didn't change even though he knew I was up to something.

"Ask away. I'm an open book." He set his rollerblades down beside him and started to take off his boots.

"Tell me about Lake Cowichan," I whispered.

Whatever Jax was expecting, it wasn't that. He paused pulling on one rollerblading boot, his left leg bent towards him, and stared at me. I could see all kinds of heady emotions rolling through his eyes. "What about it?"

"Just what it was like to live there?" I explained my question a little further, sounding meek. I went about the task of putting my own rollerblades on.

"You already know the gist of it," Jax said carefully. I glanced up, watching as he ran his hand through his hair, the action absent and distracted. "It's a beautiful place, but I don't have many fond memories."

"Except rollerblading," I corrected. I'd seen the smile on Jax's face when he mentioned it.

He looked at me, his eyes suspending me in time. "Yeah, except rollerblading. And fishing." He nodded solemnly.

"Who did you rollerblade with?" I was afraid to ask these questions, but I wanted to know more about Jax. I knew who he *was*, but I didn't know much about his past—excluding what he told me about his father.

"My mom," he answered softly.

The only time he had ever mentioned his mother before had been that day on our hike where he'd told me that his father had abused him and his mother had stood by, too weak to intervene.

"She wasn't always spineless." He smiled sadly, catching where my thoughts had gone. "My mother used to have stars in her eyes. Or at least…she did when she looked at me. Every time he'd come home drunk—which was all the time—she took the brunt of my dad's abuse. Each time he'd get irrationally pissed off about something—any time I was bad, or when *he* thought I was bad—he'd flip. He'd go for me, but she'd put herself between us. My grandpa helped too. He got me out of there every weekend, out of my dad's line of sight. But she stayed there, and every time I came home from fishing with Grandpa, she'd have a black eye or a busted lip, something to make me regret leaving in the first place. It was a power play by him, a way to teach me that even if I escaped, I'd pay for it."

My heart tightened with sadness as Jax spoke, telling me the secrets of his childhood that I knew he carried. Despite how heavy the subject was and how it obviously still hurt him, he seemed steady. "I'm so sorry, Jax. I just can't wrap my head around any of it..." I trailed off, frowning as I tried to work it out. I couldn't understand why Jax's mom hadn't just left with him, or why nobody did anything about Jim Walker's abusive, alcoholic behaviour. It was wrong.

Jax leaned forward, catching my chin with his fingers. He gently tipped my face so that I was staring into his deep brown eyes, the gold around his pupils flickering like a flame. "I've spent the last twenty-odd years trying to figure it out, Harlow. It's unfathomable. My grandpa was from an era where you didn't meddle; the best he could do were those fishing trips. My mom was seventeen when she got pregnant with me. She was disowned by her family and moved to British Columbia with my dad shortly before she married him. He tried to stomp her heritage out of her, isolate her so she had nobody but him. It worked. She had a fight in her, and then one day...she didn't. She stopped. She disconnected."

I was having difficulty breathing. Hearing him talk about it hurt me, and I hadn't experienced it firsthand like he had. I couldn't imagine the fear Jax must have felt as a child. My eyes welled with tears, and I tried desperately to blink them away. "How do you not hate her?" I whispered, my eyes catching his.

"I did," Jax said grimly. "For years. But time gives you a perspective you couldn't see before, and now I just feel bad for her. She was a child when she had me. She had nobody but an abusive, manipulative asshole who isolated her from everyone and everything she knew."

"And him?" I said bitterly, unable to hide my anger. "I don't get it. Your grandpa wasn't abusive."

"Not to me," Jax agreed. "But he was rough on his kids—my dad and my uncle. It was mostly the era, but he also didn't express his emotions. My dad never learned how to express his either. That coupled with the untreated mental illnesses and the alcoholism…it turned him into a pretty ugly man. I don't remember a time when he wasn't like that."

My heart ached for Jax, and at the same time, I felt guilty. I couldn't help but think about my mom, about how I was distancing myself from her for things she hadn't even done. It wasn't her fault that my dad killed himself. It wasn't her fault that her second husband was a pervert—she charged him and dumped him the moment she found out. She had never intentionally put me in harm's way. She'd been a single mother throughout my whole life. She'd made mistakes, but what parent doesn't? She loved me, and she tried.

Which was more than Jax's mom had done for him. "Ugh, this makes me so mad," I said, trying to pull away from Jax's hand. I didn't want him to see the tears I was desperately trying to keep from spilling.

The gentle expression on his face made my heart skip. He softly brushed his thumb across my cheek, catching the lone tear that had escaped. "But enough about this," he decided, a sad smile pulling his lips up.

"I didn't bring you here to talk about depressing things."

"That's true. You brought me here to torture me with another method for me to bruise my butt," I retorted, taking a shaky breath as I remembered our ice skating attempt. Jax laughed, his lips finding mine. He kissed me softly before he pulled away and helped me finish tying up my rollerblades.

Jax stood up effortlessly, looking like a natural. He held his hand out for me and helped me up. I wavered, lacking the balance to simply stay upright.

"It's just like skating," Jax reminded me, taking my other hand with his. The delighted grin was back where it belonged: on his handsome face.

"That's exactly the problem," I muttered. But Jax just smiled wider.

* * *

"He *what*!?" Jenna demanded, her eyes wide with astonishment.

"He took me to a warehouse," I repeated. I picked up my brush, running it through my long hair and brushing out the tangles the blow dryer had caused. "The owner of the gym Jax works at is going to turn it into a Mixed Martial Arts gym. Jax is going to be a part-owner and manage it and teach classes once the renovations are completed. He's also going to move his classes with troubled youth over."

"That's intense!" Jenna whistled. She was sitting on my bed, waiting patiently for me to finish getting ready so we could walk to school. Monday morning had come with a vengeance—and with Jenna stealing the bathroom for a good solid hour. The joys of having a female roommate who preferred to do her makeup in the bathroom because 'the lighting was better.' I was almost excited to move in with Jax. Hopefully he wouldn't take a ridiculously long time in the bathroom.

"I know. I can't believe it, but if anybody deserves this, it's him," I responded, picking up my liquid eyeliner. I looked past the scar on my cheek, but not before noticing that it appeared lighter. I focused on the task at hand, applying the eyeliner with a quick and steady hand. Once satisfied both eyes were equal, I set it down and grabbed my mascara.

"True." Jenna nodded with agreement as I finished doing my makeup. I stood back, inspecting myself critically. I was dressed in my basic ensemble of distressed jeans and a clingy, long boyfriend t-shirt. I tugged at the thin material of my shirt, pondering the name. It was stupid. What boyfriend would wear a shirt so feminine?

I glanced up at Jenna, noticing her thoughtful expression. A huge grin broke out on her face as she met my eyes. "That was so romantic of him to tell you like that."

"I know," I responded, my thoughts drifting back to yesterday evening. We skated on rollerblades around the warehouse for a good solid hour. We laughed, we held hands and we had a lot of fun—even though I couldn't really put the conversation we had completely behind me. It lingered there, like a low, heavy raincloud.

"You don't look so thrilled about it," Jenna frowned, catching the sadness on my face.

I bit my lip, looking at her. "He just...he told me some heartbreaking things," I answered, not wanting to reveal it all but also needing an ear. "And I kind of feel like an asshole."

"Okay, you're being *way* too vague." Jenna shook her head. "Start at the beginning."

"It's not my story to tell." I gave her an apologetic look. I wouldn't discuss Jax's business with anyone else. That just felt...wrong. "But let's just say that Jax's experience makes me feel like an asshole for how I treat my mom."

"You *should* feel like an asshole," Jenna said pointedly. "Your mom is actually really nice and caring. I don't know why you shove her away like she's contagious."

"I don't know why either." My voice was barely above a whisper.

"Is it Larry?" Jenna asked, her brow creasing with concern. She stood up, approaching me.

"No, not really." I shrugged. "It's just...me I guess."

"Well, get over yourself." Jenna gave me a small smile. "You're lucky! You've got an incredibly hot—*and totally freaking romantic*—boyfriend who loves you, and your family loves you, and *I* love you. You've got a good life, Harlow."

"I know that," I protested.

"Good. Now I really need a tea." She yawned, stretching. "I stayed up *way* too late last night."

"Doing what?" I demanded, yawning too. We grabbed our bags and left my bedroom.

"Talking to Kyle." Jenna smiled, shrugging. "They're in Detroit now, starting the US leg of their tour."

"Awesome," I replied dryly, not even bothering to feign excitement. Even though Everly had said there wasn't anything going on between the two of them, I couldn't help but wonder how Kyle behaved on tour. Each scenario that ran through my head ended the same way: with Jenna hurt.

"Don't do that," Jenna warned. "You always make that face when I mention him."

I sighed. "I'm sorry, Jenna. I'm just…hesitant about the whole thing. What are his intentions?"

"You sound like my dad." Jenna scowled as we made our way downstairs and outside.

"He knows?"

"No, but if he did he'd say the same thing," she said. I couldn't help but laugh. "I'm being careful, Harlow. I promise. I'm not deluding myself into thinking anything. Kyle hasn't made any promises to me; we just enjoy talking to each other," she added as we walked quickly down the street.

The Bean was bursting with people and we had to wait for several long minutes before we reached the front counter. Lucas was working and he looked anything but thrilled to see Jenna and me standing there.

"Hey, Lucas." Jenna smiled warmly. "Could I get a green tea?"

"Are you sure that's *really* what you want?" Lucas scowled. "Or did you maybe want something worth a little more? A Frappuccino, perhaps? Is that fancy enough for you? *Rich* enough for you?"

Jenna frowned. "What are you talking about?"

"Don't worry about it," Lucas grumbled, disappearing to make Jenna her tea. The dark expression on his face made Lucas look like a turbulent toddler who had just been denied cookies and told that it was naptime.

"Coffee, Lucas. And cut the bullshit," I demanded, my eyes narrowing.

Jamie exploded out of the kitchen with a flourish. I wasn't entirely sure how much of the conversation he heard, but the displeased look on his face spoke volumes. He glanced between Lucas, Jenna and me. "Lucas?" he questioned, arching a brow.

"I'm fine," Lucas said in an even tone. He set my coffee down harder than necessary and yanked the bill from my hand.

I pursed my lips, about to bite into Lucas. I didn't like how he was acting; I didn't like the dark, sulky looks he kept giving Jenna, and I certainly didn't appreciate having a five dollar bill torn from my hand. But Jamie caught my eye—he'd seen everything as well, and it was evident by the expression on his face that he wanted to talk to Lucas.

"Fine, whatever. Catch you later, Jamie," I said instead, rolling my eyes. Jenna and I made a quick stop off at the fixing station.

"I don't know what his deal is." Jenna glanced back to the counter. Jamie had busied himself helping Lucas fill coffee orders—likely to keep a closer eye on him so he could figure out what his problem was.

"He's acting like a brat." I shrugged. "Hipster Harry Potter is displeased."

"Harlow," Jenna scolded, nudging her elbow into my ribs. She tried to hide her smile and the quick giggle that escaped.

"That should be a meme, shouldn't it?" I grinned, pushing Jenna over the edge. She burst out laughing and quickly silenced herself when Lucas scowled in her direction. She schooled her features, trying to fight the laughter. The glare on Lucas's face and the pout to his lips had Jenna buckling over. She grabbed my wrist and dragged me out of *The Bean.* Once we were on the street, she laughed until tears started to run down her cheeks.

"I really don't know why that was so hilarious," Jenna said, finally regaining control of herself so we could continue on to the university.

"Come on, Jenna. I'm hilarious. You can't help it." I grinned.

* * *

Just as I was walking out of class, my cell phone started to vibrate with an incoming call. I slid it out of my jacket and answered after checking the caller ID. "Hey, Jamie!"

"Harlow," Jamie said, the stress evident in his voice. I knew without being there that he was likely massaging his temples. "I know that I said you could have the week off...but..."

"But what?" I sighed, fearing where this was going. Jamie was going to ask me to work during Iain's book signing.

"Lucas just quit," he rushed to explain. "I've got Crimson covering most of his shifts, but there is one I was hoping you could cover. She has an appointment that day, and I know you have a spare –"

"What day, Jamie?" I furrowed my brow.

"Wednesday," Jamie answered. Iain's book signing was supposed to start tomorrow and go until Thursday. Jamie wanted me to come in on the second day. He'd only be in the coffee shop for a couple of hours, but still. It was more time than I wanted to spend with him, and I especially didn't want to see Iain promoting his book—the one that was supposedly written about me.

But I didn't have much of a choice. Jamie wouldn't ask if he wasn't stuck. I knew he was going to be there too, and that he was expecting a lot of customers. Iain's book had apparently already drawn in a fan base, as the café had been advertising it for the last week.

"Fine." I sighed, my own fingers pressing against my temple. "But you owe me, Jamie."

"I know." Jamie exhaled with relief. "Thank you, honey. I promise you won't need to deal with him. I'll tell him not to talk to you."

I swallowed back my response: that it didn't matter if Iain didn't talk to me. Being around him was just…difficult. The confusion, the guilt, the hurt—it all overflowed whenever those tortured Caribbean blue eyes found mine. I closed my eyes briefly, envisioning Jax's face. It calmed the nervous clattering of my heart.

"I'll see you then," I told him curtly. I ended the call and shoved my phone back in my jacket pocket.

My thoughts were twisting with worry about Wednesday when someone shouted my name. I turned on impulse, my eyes narrowing when I took in the sight of Delilah strolling purposely towards me.

"Hey! How was your weekend?" Delilah asked, smiling hesitantly. Her air of self-righteous importance seemed to be gone, leaving vulnerability in its place.

"Fine…" I said, trying to gauge her intentions.

"What were you up to?" she asked, tilting her head.

"I went to a concert in Toronto," I answered.

Delilah slowly smiled as if this information didn't surprise her. "*Autumn Fields*, right?" she asked. I stared at her blankly. "I thought that was you."

"Me?" I repeated, confused. I wracked my brain, trying to think if I had seen Delilah that weekend. Nothing came to mind.

Delilah fished her phone out of her bag and fiddled with it, bringing up a photo from a gossip website. She showed it to me. I was standing against a wall with my arms crossed, holding a water bottle in one hand and looking on with disinterest at the mayhem around me. In the distance, Cam could be seen walking towards me with a look of determination on his face.

190

"Yeah, so what?" I shrugged.

"I just thought it was cool, that's all." The smile faded from Delilah's lips. "I really like that band."

"Were you there?" I asked.

"No." She smiled again, ruefully this time. "Tickets sold out months ago. I'm surprised you got VIP passes!"

"My friend has a connection…" I said awkwardly. "Look, I've got to go. I'm running late. I'll see you around."

"Oh, yeah. For sure," Delilah said, her face falling slightly.

Guilty, I walked away.

chapter TWELVE

I DECIDED to head to the gym in an attempt to force all the feelings of guilt away with a rigorous workout that made my limbs weak and shaky. I was sick of feeling guilty; so sick of it that I almost wished I could return to the numb state I'd been in after every traumatic experience I'd been through.

Sweat clung to my skin and my hair felt sticky on the back of my neck as I started towards the change room after my workout was completed, my lungs expanding and deflating rapidly. I took a sip of water with trembling hands before nearly running into Jax.

"Are you here for my first class?" Jax grinned, his eyes widening slightly with surprise.

I'd completely forgotten that Jax's first Mixed Martial Arts class for troubled youth was tonight. "Well, if you need an assistant…"

Jax watched me hungrily, his eyes caressing my body. The way Jax looked at me never set my panic off—it just made my blood turn to lava and my body scream for the sweet release I knew he offered so well. "Hmm, well, that might be a distraction to my very impressionable students," he said, eyeing the workout shorts and tight top that clung to my body. He leaned forward, his focus shifting to my lips. "Teenagers are ruled by hormones and easily distracted by their second head."

I laughed. "Men are the exact same way," I reminded him, arching my brow as my eyes slowly dropped south of the waistband of his shorts.

"I'll be at your place at nine," he told me, his eyes full of promise. He looked like he wanted to throw me over his shoulder and drag me somewhere quiet—and I knew he did. Instead, Jax shook his head to clear it. "The class actually starts in ten minutes, so I need to get ready."

"Best of luck," I told him, standing on my toes to quickly brush my lips against his. "I know you're going to change all of their lives for the better. I can't wait to hear about it later." I meant it; I almost got choked up with emotion each time I thought about the influence Jax was going to have over these kids' lives. He was going to make a difference; a positive one. That's just who he was. His caring, benevolent nature changed people for the better. It had changed me, too. He'd given me light again.

"Much later…" Jax growled. His hand brushed against my hip quickly before he jerked it back as if he forgot that we were standing in the middle of the gym. We'd gathered a bit of attention from a couple of people working out nearby, but I studiously ignored them.

"Yes, later," I agreed, smiling slowly. "I'll see you then, Jax." I continued on to the locker room, but Jax's hand shot out to gently grasp my wrist. I paused, looking over my shoulder at him.

"I love you," he said reverently.

My heart swelled in my chest, dancing with the passion evoked by our subtle exchange. I smiled. "I love you too."

* * *

My bag hit the floor with a hard thump, and I sighed as I eased my aching feet out of my shoes. Warm light filled the apartment, and the sound of Jenna's iPod drifted down the hall toward me. I could hear the familiar vocals of Kyle Russell. I rolled my eyes, sighing dramatically.

"Harlow? Is that you?" Jenna's voice called from down the hall.

"Yeah." I crossed over to the refrigerator. I opened it up, peering inside. It was mostly empty save for bottled waters, a couple containers of yogurt and questionable Chinese takeout leftovers. I sighed, grabbing a bottle of water.

"Can you come here please?" she called, her voice sounding strange to my ears. My interest piqued, I headed down the hall towards her bedroom.

Jenna was sitting on the middle of her bed with her legs crossed and her laptop in front of them. She was biting her nails, staring at the computer screen when I walked in. "What is it?"

"I found out why Lucas was being so weird today," Jenna said with disgust.

"Why?" I asked, remembering Lucas's rude behaviour at the store. Rude enough that he was no longer working at *The Bean*. Rude enough that I now had to go in on one of the days I specifically asked off.

Jenna wordlessly turned her laptop towards me. I walked in, my eyes straining to read the words on her computer screen. She had an open browser with a gossip website loaded, the same one that Delilah had shown me earlier.

Kyle Russell's picture was splayed all across the web page, and a blurry photo of Jenna and Kyle from the night of the concert was there too. They weren't doing anything explicit, but the way they were looking at each other seemed suggestive, especially with the article title blasting out in big, bold letters:

Kyle Russell invites his side dish to a Toronto concert! Longtime girlfriend and bandmate Everly is NOT IMPRESSED!

The gossip website also had photos of Everly glowering off into the distance.

"Okay, that's bullshit. I was there. Everly may have been in a bad mood, but I doubt very much that it was directed at you. Clearly, this website is full of shit. Which isn't surprising, considering it's a *gossip website*. Everybody knows that it's completely made up."

"I know that." Jenna sighed, biting her lip.

"What makes you think *that* was Lucas's problem? It doesn't mention your name and you have to really look to see you in that picture…it's too grainy." I joined Jenna at the end of her bed, my body sinking into her soft mattress.

Jenna tucked her fair hair behind her ear, her teeth sinking even lower into her lip as she worried it.

195

"Well...remember how I said that Lucas knew the band? He's known Cam for years."

"So you think Cam took these photos?"

"No." Jenna shook her head quickly, dismissing my question. "I think that Cam recognized me though. He's probably seen me in countless photos on Lucas's Facebook profile, and I think he told Lucas I was there and talking to Kyle."

"Hmm." I paused to take a sip of water, mulling over her theory. "Well, in any case...what does it matter? You don't want to be with Lucas anymore, right?"

"Right, but..." Jenna trailed off, looking hurt and confused. "He was my first actual boyfriend, you know?"

"Bullshit." I could barely keep my jaw from flapping open. "You've dated before. You had to—you were friends with Callie and Tara: resident date-aholics."

"Yeah, well. No." Jenna laughed bitterly, her eyes hardening. "I was holding out for...someone," Jenna whispered and blushed, as if the mere thought was mortifying.

"Okay, now you have to tell me who you were holding out for. And don't give me that 'the one' bullshit." I raised my hand, silencing her usual answer. I used to buy it, but in that unguarded moment, I sensed that there was something Jenna wasn't telling me.

She flushed a deeper shade of red. "Fine, but I warn you. I was young and stupid and I have matured *a lot* since then and it's embarrassing to look back on."

"Yeah, yeah. Get to the point." I smirked.

"Fine. I liked Riley." Jenna blushed, speaking about the spoiled popular guy from our English class in grade twelve. Riley had been a typical jock-type: focused on his sport (hockey), girls, drinking and throwing huge parties in his parents' house on the hills. "Well, I liked him when he didn't speak, anyway."

I snorted, nodding with agreement. Riley was good looking, but there wasn't much in the brain department. He was too conceited, too self-centered.

"Then the whole Andrew thing happened." Jenna shuddered, her expression darkening. The party that had changed Jenna's life drastically had happened at Riley's house. In fact, I'd walked into Riley's bedroom to find Andrew sexually assaulting Jenna.

"Yeah, well. You would have clued in sooner rather than later that Riley *only* had his good looks," I reminded her. "Didn't he knock up Callie?"

Jenna turned her laptop back around so she could type quickly into the search bar. "Yes, look," she finally said, turning the laptop back so I could look at the new page she had pulled up. It was Callie's Facebook. Callie's page used to be full of pictures of her and her friends partying, but now it was dedicated to the adorable newborn baby. A little boy, by the looks of it. There were a lot of pictures of Riley and Callie with their son.

"They look…" I tilted my head.

"Mostly fake, right?" Jenna laughed weakly, her shoulders sagging slightly little. I knew she wasn't thinking about her ex-best friend or her ex-crush, but her own pregnancy...her own baby. I watched as she stared at the images on screen, her jaw trembling ever so slightly.

My heart hurt for her. She'd been through so much more than anyone should ever have to experience. It was bad enough to get raped, bad enough to have your virginity taken from you and bad enough to live with that shame and embarrassment...but to get pregnant from the rapist, dealing with a pregnancy and putting a baby up for adoption too? That was beyond cruel. The reminders were everywhere for her, and as much as she tried to force a smile and live without regret, I knew she hurt over the fact that her first pregnancy—her first *child*—had been conceived in such a terrible manner. I knew she looked at photos of Callie's smiling face, holding her beautiful, wanted baby boy, and was angry, sad and broken.

The secret I carried seemed impossibly heavy, weighing me down and crushing my heart. I hated that I kept this from Jenna, but I couldn't make my jaw move. I couldn't form the words to tell her something that I knew would destroy her—or at least seriously hurt her.

I swallowed hard, trying to work up the courage to just spit it out. *But what good will that actually do? The adoption is finalized. The baby is happy and loved.*

"I know, it's stupid." Jenna sighed, finally breaking our heavy silence.

"It's really not," I argued. "It's a trigger for you. I just wish I knew what to say…"

"You could tell me to delete Callie off my Facebook," she pointed out with a tiny grin.

"Okay, you should delete Callie off your Facebook, and anybody else from that horrid town."

"Wise advice." Jenna nodded solemnly, as if my repeated words were completely my own and full of wisdom. "So…what's going on with you?" Jenna closed her laptop, keeping her eyes on my face.

"What do you mean?"

"You're home late. I'm guessing you went to the gym?" I nodded in response. "Well, usually when you head straight to the gym after class, something happened. And you had Creative Writing today, didn't you? Did Mr. Sharpe make you feel uncomfortable?"

My eyes narrowed. I resented the fact that Jenna had the perfect recollection of everything I'd ever said. *One time* I mentioned how good looking Professor Sharpe was and how all the female students in the class were obsessed with him. *One time* I told her he (or rather, his attractiveness) made me a little uncomfortable. I didn't go into detail and assured her that Mr. Sharpe was not trying to get in my pants.

Jenna's gaze was unwavering, and I knew she wouldn't stop pestering me until I told her. Sighing heavily, I gave in. "Not this time," I admitted, picking at the comforter. I realized I hadn't filled Jenna in on what had happened with Professor Sharpe a few weeks previously. "A couple classes ago…he pulled me aside to basically tell me that he loved my outline and couldn't wait to read the first draft. Then he told me I should try and get it published, blah blah blah."

I was aware how similar what Professor Sharpe said sounded to what Iain said. The entire time I'd worked out, I worried about that. Did Iain really mean what he said when he told me I had talent, or was it just his way of opening the door for something more? Did Professor Sharpe mean it, or was he looking to get extra time with me?

Even though I *knew* it was foolish and stupid, I couldn't help but wonder if maybe the details of the North Bay scandal had leaked, and Professor Sharpe had found out about it and wanted to see just how far I'd go to get good grades. It was that sneaky, evil voice of depression, lying to me and urging me straight into the spiral of anxiety. In turn, that anxiety fed the depression and it became hard to see clearly and breathe easily.

I'd coped with depression and anxiety for as long as I could remember, but separating what was real from what was in my head was getting harder and harder. I knew I needed to talk about my feelings to someone, anyone…I just didn't know *how*. I could only offer the smallest bits of myself, the smallest truths. I didn't go into details on the inner workings of my mind—I couldn't. I didn't want to revisit those memories any more than anyone around me would want to hear them. Some thoughts were better left unsaid.

Jenna was silent as she watched me. After a few moments, she gave me a small smile. "Now you're wondering if Professor Sharpe meant those things, or if

male English teachers just have a preference for you—
and not because of your writing talent?" Hearing my
muddled, complicated thoughts presented in such an
easily spoken sentence was disconcerting. I nodded
blindly and Jenna reached out to touch my arm. "You
do have talent, Harlow. I would read anything you
write, even a scary thriller novel." She said this
sincerely, her eyes wide with promise.

It was a big promise for Jenna to make; she hated
scary thriller novels. She preferred the soft, light and
fluffy romances that always had happy endings. Jenna
needed a happily ever after in her books because a
small part of her felt that she'd been robbed of *her*
happily ever after.

She'd said as much to me once. *Once.* I made sure I
stomped out that stupid notion. Jenna had a lot of life
left to live; I was certain she'd find her happily ever
after. She was too sweet not to.

"Of course I'm going to doubt myself," I confessed.
"I wish that Professor Sharpe didn't make me
uncomfortable, but he does. I'm dealing with it, just like
I'll have to deal with seeing Iain on Wednesday."

"Why would you have to deal with that?" Jenna's
confusion reminded me of the fact that I had yet to tell
her about Lucas quitting (or getting fired from) *The
Bean*.

"Lucas is no longer an employee. Jamie gave most
of his shifts to Crimson but he needs my help on
Wednesday, Crimson has an appointment. It will be the
second day of his book signing."

"Seriously? That's so not like him." Jenna's brow furrowed with concern. "He loved that job and needed it."

"Maybe he got a new one." I shrugged. "I don't really care about Lucas. Because he can't be a man about things, I now have to take over his shift on Wednesday."

Jenna was quiet for a moment, lost in thought. "Maybe nobody will show up and Iain will leave," she finally offered, trying to provide comfort.

I didn't like that possibility. Despite our complicated history, my complicated feelings for him, and my anger over the fact that he supposedly wrote a book about us, I wanted Iain to find success and happiness in his life. Anything else would just make that guilt that resides in my heart even more overwhelming and all-consuming. Because of me, Iain had lost his teaching career. I wished him nothing but the best for his writing career; he deserved it. "Or maybe nobody will show up, and he'll start talking to *me*," I pointed out instead of voicing my thoughts. "The more people there, the less chance of us being alone together."

"And what would happen if you're alone together?" Jenna asked.

I swallowed again, thinking Jenna's question over. My thoughts instantly drifted to the day Iain had showed up at the apartment shortly after Andrew's attack, and how he'd kissed me and I had responded, even for a moment. A moment was too long; I should have shoved him off me immediately, but I didn't. Now,

I could only torture myself by trying to understand why.

"I don't know," I replied honestly.

Jenna gave me a leveled look. "I don't think you give yourself enough credit," she huffed, crossing her arms. "You are completely in love with Jax. I can see it in your eyes even when I mention his name. That's real and you know it. So why are you worried about the past?"

"Technically, the past paves the way for the future, or something along those lines." I sighed, running a hand through my hair. I'd left it down after my quick shower at the gym. It was tangled from the walk home, and my fingers got caught. I tugged them out, growing aggravated and restless. I didn't do the whole *sit around and talk about feelings thing*, and when I did, I always felt like a caged animal: frantic and desperate to escape. It was bad enough I couldn't escape my own thoughts; I hated to say them aloud and make them *real*.

"I'm not going to tell you to get over it," Jenna said, her eyes serious, "but I do think you need to focus on the future and the present. You need to close the door between then and now permanently."

"I know." I pursed my lips, resisting the urge to echo her sentiments to her. They were incredibly different situations; the past that Jenna lived in couldn't be escaped and I knew that. "I am, I just feel...stuck."

Silence followed my admission. Jenna knew all about that horrible stuck feeling; it was difficult to move forward when each foot felt as if it was encased in concrete. It was a constant struggle to merely *try*.

Jenna reached out again, gripping my hand. She gave me a comforting squeeze. "I know." She sighed shakily. "I guess all we can really do is try to move forward, anyway."

"Yeah," I said, gently freeing my hand from Jenna's. I stood up. "Jax is coming over tonight. I was hoping to catch a nap before he got here."

"That's probably a good idea." Jenna smirked, humor making the dull edge of sadness fade from her eyes. "You guys don't get to sleep much when you're together."

"Ugh, please tell me you don't hear anything," I grumbled, shaking my head. These walls really were too thin.

Jenna grinned and shrugged. "It's no big deal. I bought headphones," she replied, reaching over to her end table to show me.

* * *

Later that night, I was sitting in the living room on the sofa with my legs crossed, mindlessly flipping through the channels and waiting for Jax. It was nearly ten o'clock, and I was beginning to worry. It wasn't like Jax to be late. Still, if he was late, he probably had a good reason so I tried to ignore the urge I had to pick up my cell phone from the coffee table and text him. I settled instead for watching a re-run of CSI Miami.

Jenna's gentle voice drifted down the hall, and every now and then I could hear her giggle. I knew she was likely talking to Kyle, so I left her alone.

Every couple of minutes, my eyes would dart to my phone on that blasted coffee table. Just when I was about to give in to the urge and text Jax, the sound of a heavy footfall ascending the stairs drew my attention to the door. The sound stopped in front of my door, and was followed with a sturdy rap of knuckles against wood.

I got up, crossing over to the door and opening it in one fluid, quick movement. Jax stood before me, looking apologetic and haunted. "I'm sorry I'm late," he said, distractedly running a hand over his jaw. I'd never seen Jax look so preyed upon.

Standing aside, I looked at him curiously. "Jax...what's wrong?"

"Nothing," he said curtly, coming into the apartment. I closed the door, still watching him out of the corner of my eye while he paced towards the kitchen. It certainly didn't look like nothing. Jax's entire body was rigid, as if he was ready for a fight. His eyes were a storm of so many different emotions.

"Bullshit, Jax," I told him, crossing my arms over my chest. I was deeply affected by this strange mood he was in. My anxiety was beginning to bubble up, and my throat felt as if it was constricting. Insecurities consumed me, and I couldn't help but wonder if what was eating Jax up would destroy us both.

Jax noticed my stance, and he approached me quickly, his arms going around me. He tugged me against his warm body. "Whatever you're thinking, whatever you're worrying about...that's not it. I promise."

"Why won't you just tell me?" I asked, my voice muffled against his cool jacket. I clenched the material in my fist.

His hand came up to tip my chin gently. I wanted to close my eyes, to lean in against the feel of his warm, large hand on my skin. I wanted to urge him to touch me more. Instead, I kept them open, watching as his eyes flicked across my face as he drank me in.

When we finally made eye contact, I could feel the turmoil rolling around in him. "Well, I had this whole night planned out—and it didn't really involve a lot of talking, if you know what I mean," he explained, his eyes lighting up with desire at his own suggestion. In a flash, his eyes sobered, as if hit by the reality of whatever troubled him.

"Jax...please, just tell me," I said, desperately trying to keep the pleading tone away from my voice. My heart was frantically beating in my chest as I envisioned all of the worst case scenarios, like some kind of continuous loop. Jax cheating on me, Jax no longer loving me, Jax finding out he was deadly sick. I would have laughed at the absurdity of my own thoughts if he didn't look so pale. He always glowed, between his sun-kissed skin tone and his general personality and mood.

He wasn't glowing now.

Jax released me and walked over to the small island in the kitchen. He turned to face me again, but avoided looking directly at me. He spoke to the floor. "My mom called." He sounded as if he couldn't believe the words himself. He appeared stunned. He swallowed hard, his

Adam's apple bobbing up and down. He looked up for the briefest of moments and his eyes reached into my soul, pulling me out from the shell I'd tried to hide in. "I haven't heard from her since before I left home."

He dropped his gaze, his jaw tense. I could tell he was shaken, conflicted. His fists kept clenching and releasing, the muscles straining in his forearms with the slight, distracted action. My eyes sought out Jax's, the anxiety that had been twisting at my stomach releasing with a flood of relief. This wasn't about me—about us. This was about Jax and his past...his past that I knew very little about.

I approached him without further thought, my arms wrapping around his waist. I pressed myself against him, turning my cheek to the hard muscles of his chest. His heart thudded loudly in my ear. After a moment, Jax's arms came up to embrace me and hold me even closer. His chin rested on the top of my head and he inhaled deeply, breathing me in.

"What does she want?" I whispered. I wanted to look into his eyes, to see exactly what emotions he was feeling, but I got the sense that he needed me to stay just as I was.

"Money." He chuckled without humor. "She wanted access to my inheritance."

"That's weird," I managed, hesitating. "Did she say why?"

Jax nodded, his jaw clenching and releasing. "She said dear old dad got them into serious gambling debt and she needs to pay it off before they lose the house."

"Did you…?" I let my voice trail off, the remainder of my question unspoken between us.

"I told her that if she left him, I would give her money in a heartbeat. I would help her get situated here, with her own place. I would help her clear her name and start over."

"What did she say?"

"She said that wasn't what she wanted. She wants to be with him. So, I told her to figure it out for herself. That I wasn't going to give that abusive son of a bitch a dime," Jax spat with venom.

Jax didn't usually swear; he didn't usually call people names. His parents and his upbringing always seemed to bring out that anger in him. It didn't alarm me in the slightest; I understood.

"I don't blame you, Jax," I whispered, pulling him closer. "You tried to help her. It makes no sense to enable him. You were right to say what you said."

Jax sighed heavily, some of the tension rolling off of him at my approval and understanding of his action. His hands began to roam over my body, touching and teasing. "Let's not talk about that anymore. It's done," he whispered, his fingers gliding beneath my shirt, against the skin on my ribs. "Besides…I have more important things on my mind."

"Dirty man," I joked, playfully shoving my hands against his chest. I pushed off, looking up at him. The light and humor was back in his eyes, and I knew he was seeing only me. The realization that I could make his pain fade away just as he made *mine* fade away caused my heart to stutter in my chest.

I smiled slowly, standing up on my toes so that my lips could brush against his. The kiss was soft and slow at first, and then it increased in tempo and pressure when his hands cupped my rear. He squeezed, pulling me up against his growing erection.

Heat flooded through me, and I rubbed against him, the pressure feeling just right. He picked me up so I was propped against the island. He ravaged my lips, kissing and nipping, our tongues dancing frantically, his hands exploring and touching and teasing.

"Jax," I said breathlessly, my head falling back as he moved on to that delectable spot on the side of my throat. My fingers gripped hard against him, my weak attempt at bringing myself back to the present. "We can't do that here," I whispered as his fingers went for the waistline of my yoga pants. I'd dressed for comfort tonight, knowing that my clothes likely wouldn't stay on very long anyway.

"Oh, but we could…" Jax's eyes set me on fire. He grinned playfully, nipping at my lip.

I had never had sex in risky places before. I typically kept the fornication to beds and couches. The idea of feeling Jax moving within me right then and there had me squirming, searching for a release…but my sensible side won. "Jenna could come out," I reminded him.

"This is why I can't wait for March 1st. In less than a week, I'll have my own place and I will definitely take you against any surface in that apartment, over and over again." Jax pressed his hard length against my stomach, accenting his promise with a mischievous grin.

chapter THIRTEEN

I AWOKE to the feeling of Jax's beard rubbing against my cheek as he nuzzled me. "Wake up, babe. I need to go."

"Why?" I grumbled, my voice groggy with sleep. I rolled into him, snuggling closer against his warm chest.

"I have class." He chuckled. "So do you," he reminded me.

I frowned without opening my eyes. "I'd much rather stay in bed with you."

"I'd much rather that too," Jax promised, his hands venturing along the side of my naked body. "But if we did that, we'd both fall behind and possibly fail."

"Failing sounds like a nice tradeoff." I sighed, finally opening my eyes to look at him.

Jax smiled, the warmth radiating from him. He exuded warmth like a beacon. His hair looked like a lion's mane, dark and tousled from our night of intense love making. I was sure my hair was just as tangled. I'd wanted to provide a distraction for Jax almost as much as I needed a distraction, and it had been the perfect way to escape. He seemed more centered this morning, the tormented man gone.

He leaned in to kiss me, his lips softly exploring mine. Each and every time he kissed me like that, I felt the world disappear around us. "I really need to go. I'll see you later though? Tonight?"

"Yeah," I told him, blinking sleepily. "I still have a lot of time before class so I'm just going to close my eyes for a bit longer."

"I love you, Harlow," Jax said deeply, inflicting heavy meaning behind his words. I opened my eyes again to look at him. It never ceased to amaze me just how much of an impact his words had. When I spoke, I was certain I just sounded as if I was repeating words. Jax spoke with emotion, with meaning and intent.

"I love you too," I managed, smiling. I could only hope that Jax knew the meaning behind my words, even if I wasn't very good at conveying emotion like he was.

"Get some more sleep, beautiful. You had quite the workout last night," he added with a smirk.

"Hah," I replied dryly, trying not to smile. I felt Jax leave the bed, taking the warmth with him. I could hear him moving around, dressing. He came over to my bed to kiss me deeply once more before he left.

My bed felt colder without him in it, despite zero change in the actual temperature of the room. I pulled the blankets around me, attempting to make a cocoon of sorts. It didn't work; I just couldn't fall back asleep.

Thirty minutes later, I gave up and decided to have a shower. There was no point in attempting to draw out sleep when sleep refused to visit unless I was tucked safely in Jax's arms.

Once I'd gotten ready for the day, Jenna knocked on my door. "Are you ready? I *really* need a tea and we are completely out. Don't give me that look," she added, seeing the way my nose curled at her suggestion. "Iain won't be there until this afternoon. You know that."

"Fine," I grumbled, only because she was right. The signing wasn't supposed to start until just after lunch — plenty of time to snag some caffeinated fuel before morning classes began. I finished with my makeup and joined Jenna at the door. She already had her boots on, and her jacket. She was texting on her phone, distractedly smiling. "Who are you texting?" I asked, sliding my feet into my favourite pair of shit-kicker boots. I still couldn't believe the damn boots had lasted as long as they did. I'd had them repaired a handful of times, but they still got the job done. I was reluctant to let them go.

I never used to think of myself as the sentimental type, but putting on the leather jacket that had belonged to my father, I couldn't help but wonder if *maybe* I was. I couldn't seem to let go of the past, as much as I pretended I could. The damn boots and the jacket were proof of that. The lingering feelings I had for Iain…the inability to see him or trust myself around him despite my strong, undeniable feelings for Jax…that was also proof.

"No one," she muttered, quickly shoving her phone into her pocket.

I arched a brow and zipped my jacket up, giving her a disbelieving look. "I don't know why you bother lying about it. I know you talk to Kyle."

213

"I don't know." Jenna shuffled on her feet and adjusted her bag strap across her shoulders. She looked everywhere but directly at me. "I guess I just feel like you don't approve."

"It's not that I don't approve." I frowned, stepping around her to open our door. We left the apartment and I locked up before turning to face her. "I'm just worried about you. You know that."

"And I'm worried about *you*," Jenna fired back. "But we are both going to do what we're going to do, right?"

"Right…" I sighed. Jenna had a point, as much as I hated to admit it. I chewed over her words, digesting them. I suppose it was true: we each worried about the other, but that wouldn't prevent us from continuing on the same way we were. Between my blatant refusal to see Dr. Philips and Jenna's attempts at escapism with Kyle, neither one of us were in any position to tell the other what to do.

We were both broken, both desperately trying to pick up the pieces and move on in the only way we knew how.

"Besides," Jenna continued, sparing me a quick look, "for the most part, I am happy. I know you are too…we'll probably always have to deal with triggers."

I huffed in response; Jenna was right. Triggers would always be there, our reactions to them could change slightly, but probably not by much. We both needed to learn how to move forward regardless. We both had to try—just as Jenna had said last night.

I watched as Jenna pushed the door to *The Bean* open and walked inside. "I guess," I grumbled, dropping my eyes to the floor. I walked right into Jenna's back, not realizing that she'd come to a sudden stop.

She was frozen, standing just inside the door and staring straight ahead. I peered around her, wondering what the holdup was. I figured that the lineup was just nearly out the door, which wasn't completely atypical for a Tuesday morning.

But no, there wasn't a lineup of people preventing us from moving forward. In fact, there wasn't anybody in the lineup at all, except for a few people at the counter.

My heart clenched in my chest painfully. I'd know that dirty blonde hair, carelessly mussed anywhere. I'd run my hands through it countless times. But Jenna wasn't staring at Iain Bentley. Jenna was staring at the little girl in his arms. Jamie was behind the counter, playfully tickling the little girl's feet. She had blonde pigtails, a cheeky, dimpled smile, and Jenna's cornflower blue eyes.

I knew that Jenna hadn't opened up any of the updates from the adoption agency, I knew that she'd never looked at a photograph of the baby girl she'd given up for adoption, but it was impossible to deny who the little girl was. She looked identical to Jenna. The dimples in her cheeks, the eyes, the way she wrinkled her little nose in concentration—all of those were traits of Jenna's. It didn't take a rocket scientist to figure it out, and I knew from the strangled choking sound that came from Jenna that she knew.

I put my hand on Jenna's arm and opened my mouth, about to say something. She spun to look at me, confusion and pain in her eyes. Seeing the unsurprised look in mine, something in her broke. Tears welled up in her eyes as she pushed past me, barreling out the door. I turned and followed her, my blood frozen in my veins. She stormed off in the direction of the university.

"Jenna, wait!" I called out. She was several paces ahead of me, her shoulders hunched forward.

She paused, whirling on me. "Who is that little girl with Iain and Jamie, and why do I feel like I already know the answer? You didn't act surprised at all back there," she accused, her voice trembling.

I came to a stop in front of her. "Jenna...I didn't know, at first. When you chose Sarah...I didn't know who she was."

"And who is she?" Jenna whispered, tears streaming down her face.

"Iain's sister. Jamie's too, apparently." I sighed. "I wanted to tell you, but even getting the letter updates upset you. You can't look at babies without it hurting you...I didn't want to bring it up or add to that pain." I raised my hands as I spoke, hoping to convey apology in a way that words simply wouldn't. It didn't feel like enough, and gauging by the look on her face, it wasn't. My hands dropped uselessly to my sides.

Jenna's eyes flashed with anger. "So you kept this from me. Don't you think it was something I needed to know? Regardless of how hard it would be to hear?"

"I'm sorry, Jenna." And I was. I didn't want Jenna to find out like this. I knew I needed to tell her, and I had every intention of doing it that week. But I should have told her sooner, and I regretted holding off.

"Were you ever going to tell me?" Jenna asked, tears brimming in her eyes.

"Yes," I said forcefully. "I was going to tell you. I just –"

"I can't deal with this right now," Jenna decided, brushing away the tears. "I need to go. I need to be alone." She gave me another wounded look before taking off back down the street, back towards our apartment.

My stomach was twisted with nerves. It felt impossibly empty, and not just because I hadn't eaten yet today. I didn't want to follow Jenna back to our apartment when I knew that I was the last person she wanted to see, but I also didn't want her to be alone. I pulled out my cell phone, sending Crimson a quick text message, asking her if she could go to my apartment and check up on her.

"I thought I saw you."

I froze, slowly sliding my phone back into my coat pocket. My throat suddenly felt impossibly dry. I turned my body towards the sound of his voice. Iain Bentley stood a good meter away from me, his hands in his jacket pockets. His hair was carelessly messy, his ocean blue eyes vibrant and alive as he looked at me. "Now really isn't a good time."

"It never is." He nodded, his eyes never leaving my face. He gave me a small, sad smile. His words had a

217

deeper meaning behind them, and I knew he wasn't just referring to my refusal to talk to him. He cleared his throat. "I saw Jenna too…she looked upset."

"No shit, Sherlock." I folded my arms protectively across my chest, my heart thudding loudly. My body was buzzing with the adrenaline from chasing Jenna and having her lash out at me. The knowledge that this secret I'd kept from my friend to protect her would likely severely damage our friendship, weighed heavily on my mind. Iain was the last person I wanted to see in that moment and I knew he knew it. "She didn't know that you were dear old Uncle Iain. Can't say she's happy about it."

"Ah." Iain nodded, pursing his lips.

The way that he easily accepted my anger just made me even more enraged. I hated that he acted like he deserved it, like he'd shoulder it just to make me feel better. It infuriated me because I knew he *would*. He would take anything I threw at him.

"She probably thinks the same thing *I* think: that you arranged this purposely so your sister could adopt the baby. How convenient of me to appear on your doorstep with the proverbial solution for your sister's struggles and woes."

"You couldn't possibly believe that, Harlow." Iain was flabbergasted by my outburst. He took a step towards me, his eyes filling with desperation as he willed me to listen to him, to understand.

Okay, so maybe not anything *I throw at him,* I thought. He was getting too close to me; there was barely a foot left between us. Iain's eyes were alight with a burning intensity that made me stumble backwards.

"That is *not* what happened, Harlow…and you know it. I fell for *you*; it had nothing to do with Jenna's circumstances. I didn't even know my sister was the one she'd chosen to adopt her baby until closer to the birth. Then what was I supposed to do, Harlow? Tell my sister *'oh, I know you've been waiting years to start a family and you've finally found a child to adopt, but you can't have that one because I'm romantically involved with the baby's mother's best friend'?"*

"You could have warned me! I could have told Jenna so that she could make an informed decision! I doubt she feels confident with her choice now, considering she thinks of you as a predator!" I shouted. I didn't care that we weren't completely alone, that there were several people walking the streets and driving by. I was angry, I was hurt and I was out for blood.

Iain winced at my angry words as they hit their mark. I watched the colour fade from his face, and felt the sinking sensation of guilt in the pit of my stomach. Iain turned around and started to walk away.

I rushed forward, grabbing his arm and forcing him to turn back. "Iain, I didn't mean…you're not a predator. I don't see you that way," I hurriedly said, my eyes full of apology. I was angry, but I hadn't meant *those* words. Not like that. He had to know that.

Iain's eyes dropped down to my hand still on his arm. He slowly brought them back up to my face, the saddest, most hollow look in his eyes. It was as if I'd sucked the hope, the light and the life right out of him. "What I did was wrong, I know that. It didn't matter how strongly I felt for you, I should have fought it. I should have never given you any signs. I should have turned you away when you came to me, but I didn't. I'm to blame for that. Maybe that does make me a predator, a monster."

"No." I venomously shook my head. "You are a good man, Iain. You didn't take advantage of me. I *knew* what I was getting myself into."

"Did you, Harlow?" Iain asked, his eyes pinning me. My hand was still on his arm; I couldn't move it. "Did you know what you were getting yourself into? Did you understand the gravity of what we were doing?" As Iain spoke, he stepped toward me, backing me against the wall. My hand dropped from his arm and my palms pressed against the cold brick of the building he had cornered me against. His hands went up on either side of my head. I could feel his warm breath against my lips. "Because I did. I knew, and I didn't care. You were worth the risk then, and you're worth the risk now."

He was looking at me in the same coveted way he'd always looked at me. I clenched my fingers into my palm, my nails digging into the skin. "Iain...I'm with someone. I—I'm in love with him."

My shaky words stirred Iain back to the present. He pushed off the wall and away from me, giving me the distance I both craved and—deep down inside— resented. "It doesn't matter." Iain shook his head, his jaw clenching with aggravation. "At the end of the day, we shouldn't have happened. I'm sorry for hurting you, for breaking your heart. I'm glad that you've moved on, Harlow. You should. You deserve to be happy."

I said nothing, watching as he turned away from me and walked back towards the café.

* * *

Focusing was impossible. I sat through each of my classes with a numb mind. I longed to retreat back to the apartment and check on Jenna, but Crimson had gone by before her shift and she'd texted me to tell me that Jenna just needed space.

Usually when I wanted to skip class but didn't want to go home, I headed to *The Bean* for a coffee. I couldn't do that, not with Iain's book signing happening...not after our exchange that morning.

So, I sat through each of my classes and when the final class of the day was over, I headed to the only other place I could think of: the gym.

I changed into my workout clothes and pulled my hair back into a high pony tail before hitting the floor. I did resistance training, listening to my music, repeating the motions and working my muscles without giving any of it any thought at all.

Usually, I could lose myself in this distraction. I could focus on the straining of each muscle group and the effort it took tended to occupy my thoughts.

Not today. Today, I was robotic, going through the motions but unable to truly focus. I kept thinking about Jenna's face when she learned the truth; the hurt and the betrayal. I kept thinking about Iain's hands on either side of my head, my body pressed against the cold stone, his breath warm against my lips while he told me I was worth the risk then and now. I thought about the way my heart had stuttered and clenched, the way my body remembered what it felt like to be with him.

And I thought of Jax, too. How that very morning, we'd lain together in my bed and I felt like *nothing* could beat that feeling of being with him.

I exhaled, my brow furrowing. Nothing *could* beat the feeling of being with Jax. Nothing could diminish how hard I'd fallen for him.

And yet…that part of me that felt for Iain—that part of me that I had convinced myself no longer existed—still lived on. I closed my eyes, trying to steady my breathing. I didn't *want* to act on those lingering feelings; I didn't *want* to be with Iain again. I wanted Jax, I wanted to be with him. I was with him and I was happy.

So why was I giving Iain any thought?

Jax. I picked my phone back up, scrolling to the messages and quickly typed one out, asking him to meet me somewhere, anywhere. I needed to feel his arms on me; I needed his lips to erase it all. I needed to fall into him.

He replied almost instantly, asking me where I was. I told him and he responded with *meet you out front in fifteen.*

I hurried to the locker room to grab a quick shower and change. Jax was just pulling up as I walked outside.

I opened the door to his truck and climbed inside, not giving him any time at all to even greet me before I scooted closer. I put my arms around his neck and pressed my lips against his.

Jax smiled against my mouth before kissing me back, his tongue edging my lips, seeking entrance. I gave it to him, kissing him with everything I had until everything else melted away, leaving just the two of us alone in his truck. Our breathing became heavier, weighted with desire. His arousal was evident beneath my hand.

The sound of someone impatiently honking startled us both. Jax had parked out front of the gym, on the road, and was apparently blocking traffic. He rolled down the window and waved at the driver, motioning for him to just go around. He looked at me again as he rolled his window back up, assessing my flushed cheeks and wide eyes.

"Harlow," Jax said, his voice gravelly with want. "Not that I'm complaining...but what's going on?"

"I just need you," I told him. "Please?"

"Well we can't do it here." Jax grinned with amusement, his eyes heating at the suggestion. He started to drive towards my apartment.

"No, not there," I hurried to tell him. "Could we go back to your...place?"

Jax sent me a surprised look. I hadn't been to his room since the whole Andrew thing went down. "Why?"

"Jenna's mad at me. I don't want to talk about it right now, but we will later. I just need…" I was unable to finish my line of thought.

Jax's hand reached across the seat to gently rest on my upper thigh. His fingers dug into the denim of my jeans just enough for me to feel the pressure. "Okay," he said simply.

He drove to his place, his brows slightly furrowed as if he was concentrating hard on something. He parked out front and we both got out of the truck. Jax's hand reached for mine as we walked up the front steps.

My heart was thudding loudly in my chest. I pushed away the panic, telling myself that Andrew no longer lived there. He was gone, incarcerated, without any possible chance of posting bail. Jax's hand squeezed gently, and he looked at me with concern. "I'm fine," I told him, tugging him up the stairs towards his room. I avoided looking at the door that used to be Andrew's as Jax produced a key for his.

His room had changed since the last time I'd been in it. The posters of MMA fighters and trophies and other personal items were gone, and boxes lined his desk. Jax was prepared to move already, even though he still had two weeks left here.

I exhaled and turned to face him. Jax kept his eyes on me the whole time as he closed his door and locked it. Time seemed to move in slow motion as I stepped towards him, taking my jacket off as I went. He copied me, tilting his head with concentrated precision. He swallowed hard, his eyes searching mine. I knew he could read that there was more going on with me than just an insatiable need to have him in me, although that was definitely there too.

Our lips crashed together, our hands tangling in clothes in a desperate attempt to shed them. My shirt came off over my head, and Jax's followed. His fingers brushed against the taunt muscles of my abdomen as he unbuttoned my jeans. I shimmied out of them while Jax took his own jeans off. Soon, we were just in our underwear, our lips meeting and crashing again. His large hands came up to tangle in my hair, gently tugging my head back so he could deepen the kiss. His lips moved from mine to my neck. A moan escaped my lips, and I felt him smile against my skin as he walked me backwards to the bed.

* * *

For the first time since Jax had left me that morning, I felt at peace. I lay in his arms, the blankets pulled around our naked bodies, and felt the tension rolling away from me, replaced by the after-high that sex with Jax provided.

My left leg was hooked across Jax's body. His fingers played with my hair, twirling it around while his other hand rested against my upper thigh. I almost felt as if I would start purring.

"So, do you feel like telling me what's going on?" Jax finally questioned, lifting his head to better look into my eyes.

"I wanted you," I answered honestly, meeting his gaze. "I had a shitty day, and I needed to be with you."

"Why did you have a shitty day?" Jax asked, arching a brow. He smiled though, as if my answer had pleased him.

I sighed, my lips falling into a rigid line. "Jenna found out. About the baby being adopted by…Iain's sister," I struggled to say Iain's name. It felt wrong to say while lying in bed with Jax. I watched his eyes harden slightly, just as I knew they would at the mention of my ex-boyfriend.

"You told her?"

"No." I bit my lip, looking down at Jax's. I couldn't take the look in his eyes right now. "We went to get coffee this morning, and…he was there. But he had…her." I shook my head, aggravated at my inability to just *say* it.

Jax exhaled loudly. "So, she guessed."

"The little girl looks identical to Jenna. I've seen pictures of Jenna when she was that age—it's undeniable. Jenna's very…mad at me."

Jax said nothing, his hands still stroking and touching me. We both knew that Jenna had every right to be angry, but the whole situation was so fucked up. Was there even a right way to have handled things? I didn't know. Telling Jenna as soon as I found out might have damaged our friendship sooner, and she might have changed her mind about the Fetchers adopting the baby—Jayden. Then what?

"That's not all…" I sighed again. "I guess Iain saw Jenna fleeing, and me going after her. He came outside."

Jax's hands stilled and his body tensed. "Oh?"

I lifted my head up, staring at Jax solemnly. He had every right to be upset about Iain being around me, especially after the kiss, but it still pissed me off. Maybe because I didn't trust myself either. "I didn't kiss him or anything, if that's what you're worried about."

"What happened then?" I could see apprehension, fear and pain behind Jax's gentle eyes. He was waiting for me to drop another bomb on him. My heart squeezed painfully in my chest.

"I...accused him of things," I said, willing myself not to cry. "I accused him of...using me to get his sister a baby. I called him a predator."

Jax's eyes widened with surprise and he appeared torn between smiling and frowning. He wisely chose to frown. "What did he say?"

"He got upset, and he agreed with me. I tried to rephrase it...I didn't mean to call him a predator. I knew what I was getting myself into, but..." I shrugged helplessly.

"Why do I feel like there are things you aren't telling me?" Jax's frown deepened, the hurt apparent on his face.

"Because there are." I closed my eyes for a moment before I looked at him. "He backed me up against the wall. He asked me if I had really known what I was getting myself into, if I had really known the gravity of it. Then he told me I was worth the risk, then and now." Anger flashed in Jax's eyes, and I put my hand on his chest to keep him down. "He didn't touch me, Jax, and I didn't touch him. I told him I was with you, that I loved you."

"What did he say then?" I could tell that Jax was fighting hard to control his reaction, to remain calm and level headed.

"He basically said that none of the things he said mattered and that he was happy I'd found someone and that I was happy, and then he walked away. That's...everything."

"Is it?" Jax questioned, his eyes searching mine.

I looked at him and smiled. "Jax, I'm in love with you. I chose you, over and over again. Even if there is a tiny part of myself that still has the slightest, lingering feeling for him, it's nowhere near to what I feel for you..." I trailed off, my smile fading slightly as the realization dawned on me. "I think that because he was the first person I connected with like that, I'll always feel a little something for him, but it is *nothing* compared to what I feel for you. You consume me in the best way possible. You bring me back to life, you make me want to live and feel. You center me, you ground me, and you help me fly. You're everything I never knew I wanted and more. The thought of losing you scares me more than anything I've ever been through. More than a hunting knife on my neck, more than a truck running me down, more than—" I stopped myself and looked at him again. His eyes were full of warmth and love, the most perfect smile on his lips.

His hand came up to frame my face. "You mean everything to me Harlow," he told me. "I love you in all those ways and more. I fell for you the moment I saw you walk into that lecture hall late. I want to spend the rest of my life with you. I want to wake up with you in

228

my arms; I want to come home to you. I want you, in every possible way."

I smiled, the tears I'd struggled to hold back finally spilling over. I lowered my lips to Jax's, kissing him despite the salty tears. He kissed me back slowly, as if savoring the taste of me.

"I can't wait until March," he added, grinning mischievously.

"Me either," I said, smiling wider. "I can't wait to wake up next to you..." My smile faded as I thought about Jenna. "But first, I need to fix things with Jenna."

"I understand," Jax told me sincerely. "And I'm here for you, Harlow. If you need to talk about any of it—even..." He took a deep breath. "Just know that I'm here for you, and I will do anything in my power to keep you safe and happy."

"The same goes for you," I said, nudging him with my knee. "I'm here for you too, Jax. If you want to talk about your mom and stuff."

Jax's expression darkened for a moment before he smiled and kissed me on the nose. "I know."

chapter FOURTEEN

JAX DROVE me home later that night. As much as I wanted him to spend the night with me, we both decided it would be better if I went alone.

I opened the apartment door to find the living room lamp still on. Two empty bottles of wine sat on the coffee table in front of Jenna, along with the shoe box that she'd put each and every update letter from the adoption agency in.

Despite the empty bottles, Jenna looked alert and awake. She glanced up at me as I locked the door behind me. Her eyes welled with tears and she drew in a shaky breath. A letter lay open across her lap and she clenched what appeared to be a photograph in her right hand. Her left hand held a half-full glass of wine.

"You opened them?" I asked, referring to the letters. I cautiously took off my jacket and dropped my bag, waiting for her to reply.

Her eyes dropped back down to the photo in her hand. "Yeah, I did."

I crossed over to the couch, and she shuffled over to make room for me. We were silent for several minutes. I was wracking my brain searching for something to say; I could only guess where Jenna's thoughts were.

"Look, Jenna," I said at the same time she said, "Harlow, I –"

We both paused, waiting for the other to speak. "You go first," I told her, motioning with my hand. I felt weak, hollowed out. I knew that whatever Jenna said would determine the course of our friendship.

"I've thought a lot about what you did today." Jenna sniffled, using the back of her hand to wipe away the moisture from her cheeks. "I'm still angry at you, Harlow. I don't know how long I'm going to be angry at you. But I understand why you didn't...why you couldn't tell me. I get that. I just..." Her shoulders went up in a half-assed shrug, as if she didn't have the energy to complete the motion. She didn't look at me; she chose to keep her eyes on the letter on her lap. I didn't know if she was reading it again, or if she was even seeing the words.

"I understand that you're angry, and I expect you will be for some time," I said, the words scratching my raw throat. "I never meant to hurt you, Jenna. You have to know that."

"I do." Jenna finally looked at me with wide, glassy eyes. "I do know that. I know that you not telling me came from a good place."

"It did," I agreed. "I just–" I paused, sighing deeply as I picked at my nails. "I didn't want you to rethink your decision. Regardless of what happened between Iain and me, regardless of his relationship with the birth mother you chose...when I saw Sarah holding the baby in the hospital, I just *knew* she was destined for this, you know?"

Fresh tears spilled from Jenna's eyes, and she nodded. "I know," she whispered. "I felt the same way. Sarah was—*is*—right for this. For Jayden." It looked as though it caused her agony to speak her daughter's adoptive name.

I glanced down at the photo in Jenna's hand, seeing the chubby-cheeked girl from the café that Iain had been holding. "She's happy, Jenna. She is loved."

Jenna nodded again, heaving a heavy sigh of her own. "I know. I know I made the right choice. It still hurts, it'll always hurt...and no offense, Harlow, but I can't help but wonder if this was planned. Not by you, you would never—" she uttered, closing her eyes.

"I've wondered that too," I whispered, my eyes dry and itching. I had no tears left. "I said as much today when he...when he came out after us."

"Iain came out after us?" Jenna frowned as she looked at me.

"Yeah." I sighed. I really didn't want to go into this whole thing for the second time today, but I needed to fill Jenna in a little bit. "I accused him of setting it up and he assured me he didn't. He said he couldn't tell Sarah that she couldn't adopt the baby because he was...involved with me."

"I still don't get why he didn't tell you." Jenna's voice was angry again.

"I don't either," I whispered. I hesitated before asking the question I needed to ask. "Does this change anything? For the baby...for Jayden?"

"What can I do?" Jenna demanded, her eyes flashing. "Ask for the baby back? I can't be a mother.

Not to her…not…" she said, the hurt apparent in her tone and the way her shoulders hung. "Besides, the adoption is final. I've read through all the updates a billion times and she's happy. I just worry about Iain."

"Don't," I assured her. "Iain's not a monster or a predator." It hurt to say that word—the same word I'd tossed so carelessly at him. "It was…"

"A once in a lifetime thing?" Jenna snorted. "How do we know that? How do we know that as soon as she gets a little older, he won't do what he did to you?"

"Because I asked for it," I said sharply. "Because I pursued him. I showed up at his door."

"He didn't say no," Jenna retorted, her eyes narrowing. She set the glass down harder than intended, and the wine sloshed over the rim and onto the coffee table. Neither one of us acknowledged the spill.

"It's a different circumstance," I told her. "Besides, Jenna…we can't control things like that. Who's to say that if you demanded they place her in another home, she could end up in a family where there *was* a predator? Who's to say that she wouldn't be stuck in foster care forever? How do you know? I know in my heart that the Fetchers would *never* let anything happen to Jayden."

Jenna watched me for a moment, considering my argument. Another tear escaped, but she made no move to wipe it. "You're right," she finally said, dropping her gaze to her lap. "I wouldn't know. I'd never know. Look at what happened to us."

"I honestly feel as if the Fetchers will give Jayden all of the skills she needs to survive in this world, don't you?" I asked, thinking back to the first time I saw Sarah hold Jayden.

Jenna nodded, taking a deep, shaky breath. "Yes," she exhaled.

"You can be mad at me, Jenna, I understand that. But know that I love you, and I wanted and still want what's best for you. Know that even if you're mad at me, even if you can't stand the sight of me, I will *always* be here for you."

Jenna started sobbing hysterically and I did the only thing I could think of doing: I wrapped my arms around her shoulders and cried with her.

* * *

The last thing that I wanted to do was go in for my shift the next day. I didn't want to see Iain; I didn't want to revisit the past again. But I'd given Jamie my word, and I couldn't bail on him. Besides, I knew I couldn't hide from Iain forever. I'd made my choice, and that choice was Jax. I had no doubt about his love for me, or my love for him. It was pure, it was real, and it was *now*—in the present.

I told myself all that before I walked into *The Bean*. On the left side of the café, the comfortable chairs had been cleared away. A table with a clean white linen sheet was set up, along with a stack of books. There was a banner to the left of the table that said *Iain Bentley: Circumstance*, along with the cover of the book.

234

It was my first time actually *seeing* Iain's book. I wanted to go up to the table, pick up the book and maybe read it, but that was counterproductive to my plan to avoid visiting the past. I wasn't ready to read it. I wasn't even ready to gaze upon the cover.

Still, my eyes were drawn to it. A girl with long, dark hair was walking away down a twisted, windy dark pathway. The surrounding landscape was dark and sad. The cover was both ominous and regretful. It was beautiful, and it made my heart ache.

I forced myself to look away and headed into the staff room to get rid of my coat and purse. Jamie was waiting for me out front when I returned. He eyed me critically. "Are you okay?"

I wasn't sure if Iain had told Jamie about Jenna's connection to them, or if he'd just told Jamie about my angry words on the street. I suppose it didn't matter, although my heart ached each time I thought about my angry words, about how they'd twisted the knife I'd put in Iain's heart, damaging him even more than his disappearance had damaged me. I'd called a man that I once loved a predator. I insinuated that he'd preyed upon me when that wasn't the case. I was just as guilty of our mutual actions.

I pushed those thoughts away and pasted on a smile. "Yeah, I'm fine."

Jamie tilted his head, trying to piece it all together. "Okay, well. The signing will start in half an hour. Iain's supposed to arrive any minute."

I nodded, resisting the urge to purse my lips. "How did yesterday go?"

"Very good!" The pride was evident on Jamie's face as he smiled. "Lots of people showed up to buy the book and got it signed. Today is kind of a big deal." Jamie paused, studying me again. "The local news station is coming in to take pictures and interview Iain."

I whistled, my eyes widening. "How did he manage that?"

"His agent." Jamie shrugged. "I don't really understand all that crap, all I know is that we will definitely be mentioned in the paper. It'll be great for our business and for Iain too."

"Good," I said. My voice sounded hollow. Jamie looked as if he wanted to ask me again if I was okay, but something in my expression made him stop.

"Right then." Jamie nodded curtly. "I'm going to go see how Mark's doing in the kitchen." He left me out front to tend to the customers.

I focused on serving the lineup in front of me. When the last person received their coffee and a quick smile from me, I glanced up towards the table and noticed Iain was there. He was standing near the table, speaking to a woman I didn't recognize. He gave her the tiniest fraction of a smile and she touched his arm, nodding at him while she spoke soft words I couldn't hear. She was beautiful with caramel skin and dark hair, and eyes that seemed to only see him.

I ignored the small part of me that felt jealous by this sight, and instead focused on making another pot of coffee.

Within ten minutes, the café was bustling with people there for Iain's signing. I could see him out of the corner of my eye; each time he wasn't engaged with someone, he would look at me.

Halfway through my shift, I glanced up to see Jax weaving his way through the bodies to get to the counter. His smile eased my frazzled nerves.

I had mentioned to Jax that I had to work today, during Iain's book signing. I didn't think for a moment that he was staking his claim though; from the gentle way his eyes assessed me, he was just checking in to make sure I was okay.

"Hello, beautiful." He smiled, his thick lips spreading into that wide grin that did unspeakable things to my heart.

"Hey, handsome. What brings you here?" I asked, arching a brow.

"Mostly you, but also coffee." Jax grinned. I smiled in response, reaching for a paper cup. "I need to head to the garage for a bit, and then I'll swing by your place…if Jenna's okay with that?"

"She should be." My smile faded slightly as I thought about Jenna. I knew forgiveness was a stretch, but at least she didn't hate my guts for my actions. After our heart to heart, after we had cried together last night on the couch, she went to bed. She was gone before I woke up this morning.

Thinking about Jenna made me think about Iain. I glanced toward the table, meeting Iain's eyes for the briefest of moments before I broke away to pour Jax's coffee. Iain had a sad look in his eyes, and his jaw was clenched. My hands were trembling, and I knew Jax noticed. I held his coffee out to him and his hand covered mine for a moment. I looked at him, feeling the instant warmth radiating from him, covering me like a blanket.

"I love you," he said, giving me a crooked smile.

"I love you too," I told him. Jax grinned, his entire face lighting up. I didn't think he'd ever get tired of hearing me say that.

He glanced at the clock over my head. "I've got to go." He sighed regretfully. "I'll see you tonight."

I watched with a smile as he weaved his way back through the crowd. He glanced towards the table, his jaw clenched. Iain was watching him too, and I saw Jax's left hand ball up into a fist. But Jax wasn't one to give in to male displays of testosterone—neither was Iain—and Jax walked out of the café without further incident. Iain and I both watched the door close before turning to look at each other.

I busied myself wiping down the counter and Iain went back to signing books and posing for pictures. For the rest of my shift, I tried not to think about how Iain was achieving great things because of a book that I'd inspired.

Iain's signing ended shortly before my shift. I tried to grab my stuff quickly, but I ran into him anyway. He was waiting for me by the door.

"Do you mind if I walk you home?" he asked, giving me a wistful smile.

"That depends," I replied, my brow furrowing as I contemplated him. "What's your angle?"

"I don't have one." Iain shrugged, shoving his hands in his pockets.

"I don't know." I sighed. "It's not a good idea."

"Why? Don't trust yourself alone with me?" Iain challenged. He knew how much I detested turning down an opportunity to prove someone wrong.

My eyes narrowed. "I think we've said all we need to say to one another," I corrected, my spine straightening. I needed to feel taller.

"I think you're wrong about that," Iain said softly, his eyes dropping to my lips.

I looked him straight in the eye to drive my point home. "I don't, Iain," I said before I walked around him and headed for the door. It pained me to walk away from him, but I didn't know how many times I had to say it.

Until you believe it, a tiny voice in my head whispered as I pushed open the door and stepped outside.

* * *

Over the next two weeks, my inability to sleep increased. With things still awkward between Jenna and me and the nightmares, I found that any time I *did* fall asleep, I felt as if I was losing my mind.

It got to the point where I felt like I could use an outsider's opinion, someone who wouldn't judge me or get mad at me for my decisions. Which is exactly why I'd finally gone back to see Dr. Philips.

I walked to the bus stop a few blocks away from Dr. Philips' office, thinking about the appointment. I'd finally opened up the floodgates. I'd finally told her every stinking thing there was to tell about myself; so much crap that our hour had run over and then some, and she didn't stop me. It was as if she'd known that by stopping me, she'd never hear the rest of it. So, she let me talk.

"Think of it this way," she'd said, once my steady flow of words had finally trickled off into nothing. She was sitting across from me in a winged back leather chair, her notebook balanced on her knees. She pushed her square rimmed glasses further up on her nose and gave me a gentle smile. "All the secrets are weeds in the gardens of your relationships with other people. You need to talk about them, and that action is pulling the weeds out of the garden. Sometimes, the weeds are deeper than they appear. You really have to work at it to get them out. But, once you've tugged out their stubborn roots, your garden will be free of weeds."

I still didn't know *exactly* what she meant, but I got the gist of it: honesty was important. Lies and secrets were weeds and they needed to be pulled.

Her words turned over in my mind as I took the bus to my house. The bus stop was several houses down from our place. I was surprised to see Jax's truck out front, along with a moving trailer that he was casually leaning against.

February was a short month, and with so much of it gone to drama, anxiety, and the weirdness between Jenna and me, it had flown by. It was the twenty-seventh, two days before Jax was supposed to move in. He'd called me last night with the news that our landlord, Richard was allowing him to move in two days early, given that all the work with renovations he'd been doing were finally completed.

I knew what this meant for us, and while I was excited to move forward with Jax, I didn't want to leave things with Jenna the way they were. I didn't want Jenna to think that I was walking away from our troubles—from our friendship. Even though things were complicated *right now*, I held on to the hope that they would improve.

"Hey, babe. How was your appointment?" Jax asked. I'd told him that in the morning I had an appointment with Dr. Philips. He hadn't flinched or pressed for answers; he just accepted it for what it was.

"It was good," I murmured, looking up at the Victorian house. I could see the kitchen window. "Is Jenna home?"

"I don't know, I just got here," Jax confessed. I nodded, accepting his answer. He reached out, gently tugging my hand, pulling me towards him. His large, strong arms wrapped around my body, holding me close. I rested my head against his jacket, inhaling his scent and melting into him. He held me for several minutes, and I nestled in closer to him. "So...I've pretty much brought up all of the boxes. All that's left is my bedroom stuff. Think you could help me carry that up the stairs, or should I call for backup?"

"Who would you call for back up?" I asked, intrigued. Upon first glance, Jax seemed to be friends with just about everyone…and I suppose he was. He got along with everyone, he was the life of wherever he went, but he didn't have many people that were close to him. He didn't seem to have a best friend, or someone he hung out with all the time. Granted, Jax didn't get a whole lot of spare time and he spent what time he did get with me.

"Either Stephen or Keith," Jax answered. I snorted. Stephen worked at the gym and nearly wet himself whenever he was around me (probably because I glowered at him), and Keith was Jax's other boss—the one that owned the mechanics garage. He was forty and seemed nice enough, but I definitely didn't want either Stephen or Keith crashing in on the only alone time Jax and I had managed to carve out for each other all week.

"I can do it," I scoffed. "It's only two flights of stairs."

"That's my girl." Jax grinned. His arm came up to encase my waist, and he pulled me closer.

"Well, let's do this," I said, trying to free myself from Jax's heavy arms.

"Don't you want to come up and see it first?" he asked, amused.

"Well, duh. I want to see how badly you butchered the renos," I joked, smirking at him.

Jax threw his head back and laughed. "It didn't need much. It mostly really needed to be painted. There was this god-awful burnt orange in the bedroom, like the colour of those thick shag carpets from the 70s. It wasn't pretty."

"You really think that *I* would have cared?" Eyebrows arched, I looked at Jax as if he had sprouted an extra head. "Maybe Jenna, but I'm practically colour *and* design blind." Mentioning Jenna stung. I swallowed hard, forcing the smile to stay on my lips.

"That may be true," Jax allowed, pushing open the door that lead to the house. "But it would have bothered me."

"You're so particular." I chuckled, shaking my head. "Mind if we stop in at my place for a minute? I want to check in," I added as we came to the second floor landing. Jax nodded and I pushed open the door.

I didn't notice that anything was off. The apartment was just as clean as it'd been for the last two weeks. After her falling out with me, Jenna had taken her frustrations out on the house. Angry cleaning, as I called it.

"Jenna!" I called out rather timidly, standing in the doorway with Jax. I knew she was home; she didn't work and only volunteered at the woman's help line on Tuesdays and Thursdays, and it was Friday. I figured she was likely in her room, doing homework and continuing to ignore my existence.

Jax nudged me, gesturing to the floor to the left of the door where a pair of unfamiliar shoes sat neatly on the mat...a pair of Air Jordan's I'd never seen before. They were unfamiliar shoes, *male* unfamiliar shoes.

Panic bubbled in my chest, and I flew down the hallway without thinking. Had I thought about it a little more, I would have realized that an attacker wouldn't have carefully placed his expensive, almost brand new looking shoes on the mat by the door.

Jax tried to stop me by reaching out, but I was quicker. He called after me, but I ignored him as I raced down the hall. Many things were going through my mind at this particular moment. There were memories of that party all those years ago in high school, where I walked in on Andrew Cooper raping Jenna, along with memories of Andrew attacking me several months ago in this very apartment. My adrenaline was so high; I couldn't hear a damn thing but my own panic.

I pushed open Jenna's door hard and it smacked against the door stopper. Jenna let out a terrified yelp.

"Jenna! Are you okay?" I demanded, trying to get my eyes to adjust to her dark bedroom. Impatient, I flicked on the overhead light.

"Jesus, Harlow!" Jenna screamed angrily, pulling her blankets up over her head. Her bed seemed a little lumpy, but there wasn't anybody holding a knife to her neck. "I'm fine!"

"Who the hell's fancy shoes are in the hallway? You gave me a goddamn heart attack!" I felt disoriented and a little faint on my feet. The adrenaline rush I'd flown in on disappeared just as quickly as it had come, draining me.

Jenna snorted with laughter beneath the blanket, and I realized that she wasn't alone in her bed. "Um, I have a friend in from out of town this weekend…" Jenna's voice was muffled.

"Right, okay. Well. I'm glad you're not getting attacked or anything. Maybe next time let me know if you have company so…right. Anyway, I'm going to head up to Jax's place now…so…yeah." I flicked the light off again, my face a deep shade of red.

"Fine, great. Bye," came Jenna's muffled, short reply. She sighed, and I heard the low murmur of a voice I definitely didn't recognize.

Jax broke out in laughter when he saw the look on my face as I approached him. "I tried to warn you." He shrugged helplessly.

"Whatever, let's just go," I muttered, aggravated and stunned. That kind of behaviour just wasn't Jenna. Jax seemed amused though, and he laughed again before leading the way up the final set of stairs to his new apartment. There was a small landing at the top of the stairs that was big enough for just the two of us to stand on while he unlocked the door.

"Welcome to the love shack." Jax grinned, playfully opening the door with a flourish. I whistled while I looked around. The apartment *was* incredible. The door opened up to the open concept living area, similar to my apartment with Jenna. It had beautiful, dark hardwood floors throughout. Jax's living space was a little smaller than ours, the recently updated tiny galley kitchen was half the size of ours, and he didn't have an island.

I stepped inside, my gaze continuing to sweep around the room. The far wall was made up entirely of white built-in shelves that went from the ceiling to the floor. Across from the galley kitchen was a dining area, and the shelves on that half of the room were closer together. The lower half of the wall had cabinets. On the other side of the room, the built-in shelves had enough space between them to fit a decent sized flat screen TV.

"Holy shit. Were those here before?" I demanded, gesturing to the shelves.

"Nope," Jax answered. "I added them. This apartment does lack in storage space, so I improvised."

"You didn't tell me you were a wood worker too." I eyed him suspiciously.

"I'm a man of many talents." He winked. "Come check out the bedroom." He wiggled his eyebrows playfully at me and I laughed, shaking my head as I followed him.

There were two doors on the far side of the apartment and both of them were closed. Jax approached the first door and opened it. "This is the bathroom," he explained while I peeked inside.

I expected to see a tiny, cramped bathroom, but I saw just the opposite. The bathroom had a large claw foot tub and shower combination, a toilet, and a sink with more than enough counter space to leave a curling iron. It was clean and neat, new white tiles glistening on the floor.

"You scored a claw foot tub too?" I asked, astonished.

"That's not even the best part," Jax promised, taking my hand. He led me back out of the bathroom to the last door—the bedroom. He opened the door and stood aside, letting me in first.

"Wow." I whistled again, looking around. The bedroom was a lot bigger than I expected it to be; even the sloped roof didn't take away from the vastness of it. "I thought you said that this place was small."

"It is small," Jax answered. "Well, compared to some of the other places I was looking at." I hummed, my finger brushing against the freshly painted walls.

Jax's room in the student house he used to live in had been white and sparse. He'd painted the walls of his apartment various shades of earth tones, each room a slightly different colour but each complimenting the last. His bedroom was an inviting, warm milk chocolate colour. It reminded me of his eyes. It was him. I loved it.

"This is probably my most favourite part," Jax said, motioning to a door on the left side of the room. He opened it, revealing a tiny rooftop patio that faced the backyard. It was roughly the same size as his bathroom, small enough for a bistro patio set and a barbeque.

"Wow, Jax!" My eyes widened with astonishment. This apartment was a labyrinth of surprises. I couldn't believe that I'd lived in the same house since moving to Ottawa, and I'd never known this place had a patio. I suppose I wouldn't have; the patio was on the east side of the house, and I had no access to it.

I stepped outside, taking in the view of houses and treetops around me. Jax came to stand behind me, his arms wrapping around my waist and pulling me toward him.

"There's a fire escape too. A ladder that slides down," Jax explained. "It's pretty cool. One of the reasons why I readily grabbed this place up."

I hummed my approval again and closed my eyes for a moment, feeling Jax's warmth as he held me while I envisioned what it would be like to live with him.

I wanted to move in with him then and there, but I couldn't leave with my friendship in shambles. I stiffened in his arms, swallowing hard.

"Hey, don't act so excited," Jax joked, nipping lightly at my earlobe. I could feel his smile against my skin, and I shivered with desire and pulled away from his embrace so I could turn to face him.

"Well, let's go bring your bedroom furniture up. What are you going to do about the living room?" I asked, purposely changing the subject. I didn't want to get distracted from the task at hand: moving Jax in.

"I was hoping you'd help me with that." Jax grinned. "Tomorrow we'll hit up IKEA, if you're up for it."

"IKEA, huh?"

"Hey, I'm not completely made of money." Jax shrugged. "I just need somewhere to park my ass on occasion."

chapter FIFTEEN

"JESUS, JAX. This thing is heavier than it looks." I grunted, trying to keep my hold on the heavy dresser we were struggling to get up the stairs. He was at the bottom, carrying most of the weight and gently instructing me on how to lead it.

I was failing miserably at this job. I made a mental note to add more *arm days* to my gym schedule.

"You've got to lift with your legs and your arms. You're lifting with your back," Jax answered, his voice straining. "Here, set it down for a minute."

I obeyed, carefully setting it down. We weren't even at the second floor landing yet, and I was dripping with sweat and huffing like I'd run a marathon.

The deceivingly heavy dresser was the last thing to get upstairs, and naturally, it was the hardest. I'd already helped Jax carry up his dismantled bed, his desk, his night stands and his box spring and mattress without any issue.

Jax grinned at me, keeping his hand on the top of the dresser to prevent it from sliding back down the stairs. "Are you ready?" he asked.

"Yeah." I huffed, getting back into position again. My hands were clammy, and it felt as if I was already losing my grip. "Wait, no. Can we put it down for a minute?"

"Yup," Jax exhaled, lowering the dresser again.

The door to my apartment swung open and Jenna stepped into the hallway. She had her black leather leggings on and a fancy top; she looked like she was headed out for some drinks at the bar. Her head was turned and she was speaking to someone behind her. My jaw almost hit the floor when I saw who.

"Oh, you're the owner of the fancy ass shoes," I said matter-of-factly, as if this made all the sense in the world. Only, it didn't, because Kyle Russell was not someone you expected to see waltzing out of your apartment. He was blocked in by the massive dresser that Jax and I were struggling to get up the stairs. Or rather, the dresser that *Jax* was struggling to carry up the stairs, as I'd proven myself pretty much useless.

"Hey, yeah. I guess that's me: fancy ass shoes." Kyle smiled his megawatt, charming boy next door smile that had graced several magazine covers and gossip websites and made the better half of the female population swoon. He was dressed in his usual getup of designer jeans, a plain white t-shirt and a brown jacket. "Do you need help with that?" he added, looking between Jax and me.

"Do you mind?" Jax asked. "I think Harlow's pretty much tapped out." I glowered at him and he winked at me. "Save your energy, darling," he added meaningfully. I rolled my eyes, attempting to hide the smile.

"Sure thing," Kyle said, nodding to me as he took my position. I stood out of the way, quietly watching as they maneuvered the dresser up the last remaining flight of stairs.

"Do you want to come up and see it?" I asked Jenna. She stood in the doorway of our apartment, clutching her purse in her hand and looking at me warily. It was obvious that she hadn't completely forgiven me yet.

I could see the indecisiveness warring in her eyes. On the one hand, I knew she was every bit as curious about Jax's new place as I had been. On the other, she was still *very* mad at me and didn't exactly know how to process that anger. "I don't know. We were going to go out for dinner…"

"It'll just take a minute," I pleaded, feeling like an idiot. I was wearing my need for Jenna to forgive me like a goddamn cloak and she knew it. "I miss you," I added, my voice barely above a whisper.

She sighed, looking sad and resigned. "Fine. But just for a minute." She glanced towards the stairs. Jax and Kyle were already gone. It had taken them less than two minutes to carry the dresser the rest of the way up the stairs to Jax's apartment, and there certainly wasn't a lot of effort behind it, either.

"Okay," I exhaled, unaware that I'd been holding my breath. I started walking up the stairs, hearing Jenna on my heels. Jax's door was open, so Jenna and I went straight inside.

"Nice little place you got here," Kyle was saying to Jax. Jax had offered him a beer, and the two of them were standing in the empty dining room, assessing the place.

"Thanks." Jax grinned. "Beats renting a room from a house," he added, winking at me.

"Yeah, that can't be fun." Kyle shuffled from foot to foot, seeming a little uncomfortable. I watched him carefully, trying to get a read on him.

I'd entertained Jenna's quirky online friendship with Kyle Russell because I honestly hadn't expected anything like *this* to happen. Not even after watching them flirt with one another at the concert, not even after knowing Jenna spoke to Kyle quite often on the phone. I just assumed that Kyle was toying with her.

I was curious, and I was skeptical. Jenna was my best friend and I had watched her go through hell and back, and recently…I pushed her right back to hell. The last thing I wanted was to see some celebrity with an inflated ego rip her tender heart out and stomp on it.

I knew I was the last one to talk about ripping Jenna's heart out, but hypocrisy is a funny thing.

"I'm sure living on a tour bus isn't any fun either," Jax pointed out.

Kyle saw the frosty look I was giving him, and promptly turned back to Jax. He was uncomfortable, and I wanted to know why. Was he uncomfortable because I knew his game?

"Yeah, it can be. Luckily, they're pretty easy people to travel with. I grew up with them." Kyle shrugged, his discomfort growing.

"Knock it off," Jenna grumbled in a low voice, elbowing me. She gave me a warning look that clearly told me to stop pestering Kyle with my dagger eyes.

I smiled innocently at her before I turned my attention back to Kyle. "So, what brings you back to Ottawa? I thought you guys were touring in the States."

"We are," Kyle answered, forcing a tight-lipped smile. I got the impression he didn't like me very much. It probably had something to do with the mega bitch vibes I was throwing out at him. "We had a week off, so...most of us came back home."

"Where were you guys from again?" I tilted my head innocently. "You're all from the same town, right?"

"Newcastle." Kyle shoved his hands into his jacket pocket.

"Why don't you show me around, Harlow?" Jenna demanded, gripping my arm a little harder than necessary. "We'll let them finish their beers."

"Alright, fine." I sighed, tugging my arm free. I put on a show for her, giving her the most monotone tour in the history of tours. "This is the living room, the kitchen, and here's the bathroom." I pushed opened the door and flicked on the light.

"Oh my GOD. He has a claw foot tub?" Jenna exclaimed, forgetting for a moment that she was extremely angry with me. Her eyes widened as she looked at it. "What a lucky bastard! Why don't *we* have a claw foot tub?" she added, almost whining.

I felt a spark of hope in my chest, hope that Jenna and I could put this whole thing behind us and move forward. "Just wait," I murmured, knowing she'd be just as envious of the patio. I led her into Jax's bedroom. The bed was pushed against the far wall. We made our way around it to the patio door and I pushed it open. With the sun fading fast, it was difficult to make out the entire view, but I gathered from Jenna's sharp intake of breath that she was just as impressed with it.

"So, when are you moving then?" Jenna asked, the bewilderment falling away and leaving her discontent with me in its place.

"I didn't want to move until we figure things out with us," I answered. To be honest, I wasn't entirely sure if she even *remembered* our conversation on the couch. She'd had a lot of wine.

Jenna stared at me, a thousand thoughts expressed on her face at once. She sighed, dropping her gaze. "I know you didn't mean any harm, Harlow. But that doesn't erase the fact that you caused harm. You hurt me. You kept something *huge* from me, for rather selfish reasons. You're my best friend…I wasn't expecting to ever feel betrayed by you and that hurts."

"I'm sorry—" I attempted to speak, but Jenna cut me off by lifting her hand, and I fell silent, my heart gripped with fear and anxiety. I didn't know what I would do if Jenna couldn't forgive me.

"I'm angry with you, and I'll probably be angry with you for a while. But that doesn't mean I'm going to cut you out of my life for it. I just need time to process."

"Okay," I whispered, trying to blink away the pesky water droplets forming in the corners of my eyes.

Jenna considered me for a moment before her face scrunched up with unshed tears of her own. She sniffled and stepped forward to wrap her arms around me. "Don't cry. You *never* cry. If you cry now, I'll just feel guilty for being mad and I don't want to feel guilty for being mad."

I laughed, shaking my head as I put my arms around her. "I'm sorry. I just... I never wanted you to hurt about it. I know you think you would have told me if the roles were reversed but, it's easier in theory to think that. If you watched me fall to pieces at each letter, if you watched me quietly shed tears when I thought no one was looking—you'd feel a little differently about telling me something that could shatter me."

Jenna's tears were beginning to soak my shirt. I patted her back awkwardly; I hadn't meant to make her cry again.

"I know, okay?" she hiccupped, pulling away from me. She wiped the tears from her eyes, careful to avoid messing up her makeup. Her eyes seemed darker, heavy with sorrow. She straightened her shoulders and drew in a deep breath.

"We should probably stop crying now," I managed, wiping my own eyes.

"Yeah." Jenna snorted. "I have a date with a celebrity. I can't look like Dawson for it."

"Who knows, maybe he's into Dawson. With that hairstyle...I wonder," I joked. Jenna tried to give me a stern glance, but she ended up snorting. We fell into a fit of laughter, and I felt for the first time in weeks that things might end up being okay between us.

* * *

It was nearly ten by the time we took a break from setting up Jax's bedroom furniture to eat pizza. We'd pushed his bed against the far wall between the two windows and shoved his dresser against the opposite wall.

"I don't think it's going to fit in here," Jax finally said, grabbing another slice of pizza from the box on the floor between us while he glared at the desk. We'd spent the better part of an hour trying to figure out a place for it. It was currently sitting in the middle of the living room, while Jax and I sat on the floor against the wall that separated his bedroom from the living room. "I forgot how big my bed was."

"And yet, it still feels like a single bed when we're both in it," I joked. "Why don't you put the desk in the dining room?"

Jax rubbed his fingers along his jawline, looking at me sheepishly. "I wanted to get a table and chairs."

"Okay...what about here, in the living room?"

"Once I get a decent sofa in here, that'll basically be all the space," Jax pointed out. "I've never had my own place before—a *real* place. I've rented rooms before but... maybe I'm going a bit overboard with things."

I froze with my slice of pizza halfway to my mouth. Jax hadn't been tight-lipped about his past, but he also wasn't an open book in that regard. I got the feeling he worried I couldn't handle whatever he had to tell me.

What I did know about Jax was that he'd had a rough childhood, and as soon as he could get away, he did. He travelled for a bit, spending time in hostels in Europe and working on a work visa. When he came to Ontario, he moved into a room in a house for university students and started school.

"Well, screw the desk then. You mainly needed it at your last place to do homework and eat on, and you'll be getting a table so..." I trailed off.

"That's true." Jax said. "What would I do without you?"

I shrugged. "You would have figured it out."

"Doubtful." Jax grinned. "I didn't really picture myself staying around in Ottawa after I graduate." He said this factually before taking a huge bite of pizza.

"What do you mean?" I questioned. Jax was lounging with his back against the wall while I sat cross-legged across from him. His knees were drawn up and loose, and his left hand rested on his left knee. He appeared comfortable and at ease.

Jax finished off his pizza and took a swig of his beer before answering. "I wasn't going to stick around." he shrugged, his eyes drinking in my face. He looked at me with unrestrained desire and depth, hiding nothing.

"What were you going to do?"

"I still wanted to open that program for troubled youth, but I wanted to do a little more travelling. I didn't know where I wanted to settle down."

J.C. HANNIGAN

"Why did you change your mind?" I asked. He was setting me on fire with his eyes.

His tongue ran across his lips quickly, his eyes focused on my lips. He slowly raised them to meet my gaze. "Because I found something worth changing it for," he replied simply. His eyes were endless pools of intensity. I could fall away into those eyes, into *him*.

My heart skipped a beat in my chest, and I inhaled slowly. "So, you're staying here because of me?"

"Yes, and no," Jax answered. "I will be running a gym soon."

"That's true." I laughed. My voice was shaky and my palms were sweaty. Jax often told me about the depth of his feelings for me, but I still wasn't used to it. "I'd just hate to think that you felt you needed to stay here because of me," I added. *I* wasn't even sure where I wanted to go after graduation.

He scooted forward so that his knees were on either side of me, and we were close enough to kiss. His hands cupped the sides of my neck, the pads of his thumbs brushing across my jaw. "It feels right, being here. It feels like home now, and it has since I met you. I have a feeling it has less to do with the location and more to do with you, but for now...Ottawa works."

"What about travelling?" I whispered. My heart was pounding so frantically, I was sure Jax could feel it.

Jax smiled. "I can still travel—but I want to travel *with you*."

Jax kissed me then, his lips and tongue turning the burning lingering beneath my veins into lava. The minutes slipped away as Jax's fingers tangled pleasantly in my thick hair. He broke away for a moment, looking at me with a mischievous glint in his eyes. "Do you want to break in my new place?" he asked.

"Like you even have to ask," I murmured.

* * *

"That's kind of ugly," I remarked, my nose wrinkling at the sight before me. Jax was eyeing a glass table set from IKEA.

"Really?" His head shot up, surprise lining his expression almost comically. "I thought chicks liked glass stuff."

"Maybe Cinderella." I smirked. "But I can see you dummying this thing in under a week."

"That may be so." Jax pointed a finger at me, the corner of his lip lifting up. I knew exactly where his thoughts had gone. "Okay, you pick."

"It's your place!" I raised my hand defensively. I shouldn't have said anything about the glass table; it was his decision to make.

"It'll be yours too," Jax brought to my attention. "Unless you've changed your mind about moving in with me."

"I haven't," I said quickly. Waking up in his arms, in the apartment that he wanted me to move into, had been incredible. I had lain in his arms while he still slept and watched the sunbeams dance across the floorboards as I imagined it, hoped for it. But I couldn't move in just yet…not until I knew things would be okay between Jenna and me. "But it's your money."

"It is. I should totally get the glass table." Jax winked, but he turned away from the glass monstrosity and started eyeing up a solid birch table. It came with three chairs along one side, and a bench side along the other. "This one looks sturdier," he remarked, leaning on it a little. I wisely kept my mouth shut, letting Jax figure out what he wanted.

While he was busy trying to decide between the gray sectional couch and the fake leather three-seater, I found myself staring at a carpet, thinking that it'd look great in the living room. I ran my fingers across the material and shook my head, smirking. I *never* used to think like that; to run my hands over a rug and picture it in a place I wanted to live with a man I'd let myself fall so completely for.

I never let myself *imagine* a future with a guy. Even Iain. When I was with him, thinking about the future was just…painful. I couldn't see it. There was no way we could come out of the shadows without him risking his job. His morals would have been questioned if we came forward with our relationship, even if we hadn't been caught.

Jax came up behind me, wrapping his arms around my waist. I closed my eyes and leaned back into him, loving the feel of his arms around me. When Jax held me like that, the world seemed right, even if most of it sucked.

I still had problems; I still thought about them. I stressed about the Iain thing, about having to possibly see him more. He *was* my boss' brother, after all. I was still at odds with my best friend, still isolating myself from my mother. I was still carrying the fear from the attack, but it all seemed a little more manageable with Jax. I felt like I could face anything with him by my side. It was alarming, but it was also somehow freeing.

I never thought that needing someone would be freeing, but needing Jax…that was freeing, that was natural. That was right.

"What are you thinking about?" he murmured, his lips pressing a tender kiss to the back of my head.

"Just things," I said, smiling. I tilted my head and Jax nuzzled my neck.

"What kinds of things?" he asked, his lips vibrating against my skin. I could feel him smile.

"That this carpet would look good in your living room." I shrugged.

Jax lifted his head, studying it. "It would," he agreed. "Let's get it."

The causal usage of *'let's'* made my heart thump erratically in my chest, but it wasn't unpleasant. It excited me because I wanted it. I wanted the "us" with Jax. I smiled and nodded in agreement, allowing him to grab it off the shelf.

Four hours and two trips home later, we were staring at the huge pile of purchases spread out on the living room floor. He'd bought the solid birch table, chairs and bench, as well as a dark gray sectional couch and several kitchen supplies: pots, pans, dishes, cups—the works. He hadn't had any of those items at the house he rented from, as the common areas were already furnished.

"Oh, I forgot about this part," I tittered gleefully, rubbing my hands together as I looked at the chaos on the floor. "IKEA instructions are notorious for being complicated. I'm so glad Jenna and I skipped this part. Secondhand IKEA furniture comes already put together."

"I can build a shelving unit without instructions," Jax pointed out, kneeling on the ground and organizing the boxes. "I'm pretty sure this will be easy."

I smirked, kneeling down beside him so that I could help. Every guy said something like that when it came to furniture assembly.

And naturally, Jax broke the mold for that too. He swore a little, and had to improvise a few times, but it only took two hours to set up the sofa and the dining room table.

We stood back to admire our handy work. I'd swept and cleaned up while he finished with the table, and the apartment was looking more like a home. The shelves were still empty and void of personalization, but it was getting there.

Jax wordlessly slid his arm around my waist, resting his hand against my hip. He pulled me closer to him and kissed the top of my head. "Thanks for all your help. You make this place feel like a home."

I couldn't help but duck my head and smile. The effect Jax's words had on me was ridiculous. Not that I was surprised; the man had my heart.

"Well, thanks for distracting me," I responded. The last few weeks were hard on me. Hard enough for me to reconsider seeing a psychiatrist; hard enough for me to feel weighed down with the decisions I'd made. All the damage I'd caused inadvertently while trying to protect the ones I cared about—and myself.

Jax was a welcoming respite from all the bad shit that chased me around every conscious moment of the day—and most subconscious moments as well. After the shit went down with Jenna, my nightmares came back. Only these nightmares were not memories forcefully replaying in my mind. These nightmares were about Jenna being in danger, and me unable to save her.

They were a perfect metaphor for me breaking Jenna's heart. I'd wanted to protect her, not cause unnecessary damage by telling her something that may not even matter. In the end, the hardest pill for Jenna to swallow had been my silence.

Jax's fingers gently squeezed my hip, urging me to return to him. "I'll be a distraction for you any day," he murmured, using his arm to guide me so that I was standing right before him. His hands cupped my face, tipping my chin back so he could claim my lips.

chapter SIXTEEN

IT WAS Monday morning, and I was doing a non-traditional walk of shame down the stairs to the second floor. I'd spent the night at Jax's again, and needed to stop off at home so I could get ready for the day. I needed a shower, a change of clothes, and my toothbrush. Stat.

I slid my key into the lock of our apartment, hesitating for a moment. Although Jenna and I had briefly spoken at Jax's the other day, I wasn't entirely sure how she was going to receive me. I'd spent the weekend helping Jax get set up in his new place, and Jenna hadn't been home often either. She'd been busy with Kyle. When I did stop by the apartment for a change of clothes, it was vacant.

At this hour, Jenna should be getting ready for class. I could hear the distant sound of music playing. I took a deep breath and twisted the key, unlocking the door. I pushed it open and walked inside, closing it behind me. Music wafted down the hallway, spilling out from Jenna's partially opened door and joined with the sound of her blow dryer.

I walked down the hall and cautiously peered in. Jenna was running product through her short tresses, styling her hair. Her makeup was already perfectly applied, and she dressed in her typical manner: jeans and a baggy yet dressy top that hugged her narrow waist.

She glanced towards the door, seeing me. "Hey," she said, looking back at the mirror. "How was your weekend?"

"Good...yours?"

"Great." She smiled, her eyes taking on a dreamlike quality. "Kyle is incredible."

"Wait, did you..." I felt awkward for asking the question. I wasn't sure if Jenna was still angry at me, but I was dying to know. I wasn't an idiot; I'd put two and two together. Kyle had been in Jenna's bed with her, but after our conversation all those weeks ago, I guess the possibility of them actually having sex hadn't really crossed my mind. I hadn't thought Jenna was ready for it.

She glanced at me again, biting her lip as she warred between spilling the beans and freezing me out. She decided to go with the first choice. "Yes!" she finally blurted, her cheeks flushing. "And Harlow, it was *perfect*. He was perfect! I...I actually wanted to." She looked lost, as if the admission startled her.

I stepped towards her, trying to hide my smile. Even though I wasn't certain about Kyle, even though I worried about him hurting her, I was *so thankful* that Jenna had finally been able to get past that fear when it came to intercourse. Separating yourself from sexual abuse victim to sexual being was no easy task, and I knew that Jenna still had a long way to go, but at least this encounter would give her hope that it was possible for her to still experience a sexual life without the panic. I was happy for her, happy for that relief and elation that danced across her flushed face.

"Jenna, that's great," I told her sincerely.

"You really mean that? I know you don't like Kyle..."

"Of course I mean it, and it's not that I don't like Kyle, Jenna...I'm just apprehensive about him. He's a star, or well on his way to being one anyway." I shrugged. "I'm...protective of you."

At my words, Jenna's mouth hardened. She took a deep breath, dropping her gaze. My shoulders slumped. "I know," she said simply. She bent over to pick up her book bag. "I need to go..."

"Yeah, okay. I'll see you later tonight?" I asked, stepping aside so she could leave her bedroom.

"Yeah." Jenna nodded.

"Maybe we could do Ryan Gosling and Ben & Jerry's night?" I added hopefully.

"Well...I was supposed to hang out with Crimson tonight, but maybe she could join us?" Jenna responded, pausing in the hallway.

"Yeah, no that'd be great," I said, my words rushing out and tripping over one another. I hadn't really had a chance to hang out with Crimson in a while; it'd be good to see her again. I tried to ignore the fact that the idea of sharing this ritual with Crimson made a tiny swell of jealousy rise up.

Jenna gave me a small smile and headed down the hall and out the door. The apartment was oddly quiet without her. I wasn't impervious to the fact that usually,

Jenna would have waited for me to shower and dress. She was still mad at me, but she was trying to move past it. I suppose that was all I could ask of her. I'd hurt her badly, and she needed time to get over that.

At least she was speaking to me again, and sharing a little bit of her life with me. With that thought, I sighed and glanced around the apartment. Moisture started to build on my palms, and I suddenly felt light; weak.

I hadn't allowed myself much of an opportunity to be alone in this place, not since the attack. If Jenna wasn't there, then Jax was.

I drew in another shaky breath and shook my head, trying to clear out my jumbled thoughts. I didn't want to revisit the night of the attack, and I hadn't really done so in a while—I was too distracted by the drama with Jenna and Iain.

Still, I couldn't think about having a shower until I locked the doors.

* * *

Professor Sharpe announced that towards the end of our Creative Writing class we would have a guest speaker, someone who was going to talk about the process of writing a book, publishing and marketing it. He thought we could benefit from the opinion of someone that wasn't him.

"An outsider's view," he'd explained with a smile. "And one of my personal friends from University. I'm excited for you all to meet him! We'll actually be reading his novel and then discussing it."

My interest was piqued; we hadn't yet had any authors visit our class to discuss the lengthy process. I doodled on my notebook, half listening to Professor Sharpe's lecture. I only lifted my eyes off the page when I heard the sound of the lecture hall doors opening and Professor Sharpe stop mid-sentence to greet the visitor.

"Iain! Welcome to Creative Writing. It's been awhile since you've been in this hall!"

The sensation of my stomach falling was discomforting. All I could do was blink stupidly towards the door where Iain Bentley stood. He gave Professor Sharpe a small, friendly smile. "Yeah, it's been some time, Nick."

Professor Sharpe motioned for Iain to join him at the podium. I sank down lower in my seat, frowning. In a million years, I hadn't expected Iain Bentley to be the guest speaker that Professor Sharpe had arranged. His career was just launching, after all. How much success could he have seen?

Iain walked up to the podium, exuding confidence from every pore. He was comfortable in front of a huge crowd of students; he was at ease. I watched as he shook Professor Sharpe's hand. The professor grinned and pulled him in for a hug, slapping him on the back. He muttered something that none of us could hear, and Iain nodded.

"Alright, if you're ready then?" Professor Sharpe arched a brow. Iain inclined his head and stepped up to the podium.

His eyes slowly drifted over the faces before him, and I slunk down even further in my seat. I didn't want to be seen. Thankfully, I was sitting behind a very tall, very large guy, and Iain's eyes glanced right past me.

"I'm Iain Bentley, the author of *Circumstance*. It released a few months ago, and has already been well-received. Or at least, Professor Sharpe likes to think so." He added this part playfully, like a joke. Some of the students chuckled at his attempt, and Iain raised his hand with a smile. "I know, I'm not the best at telling jokes. But I seem to know what I'm doing with this writing thing, so that's why I'm here today. That and Professor Sharpe probably didn't assemble a decent teaching outline for today." More laughter followed his statement, mainly from the female students. Most of them sat up taller in their seats. Delilah was sitting beside me, twirling her hair with a flirtatious smile. I wanted to smack her. Of course she'd be salivating all over Iain.

Iain went on to talk about the gist of his book, his journey with finding the right agency to publish him, and how traditional publishing differed from self-publishing. Professor Sharpe was an expert at self-publication, while Iain had gone the traditional route. It was interesting to hear the differences between the two methods, but I couldn't focus. My nails dug into my palms as I thought about Professor Sharpe's words. He wanted us to read, and discuss, Iain's book: the book that was written about me.

I couldn't even bring myself to read the summary on it, or any of the reviews. How was I supposed to *read* it?

"I'm really honored that Professor Sharpe has selected my book as a part of your reading list. I can't wait to hear what you all think about it." I realized with surprise that Iain was wrapping up his speech. He stepped away from the podium, leaving it to the professor.

"Don't be ridiculous, Iain. Your book is incredibly well-written and raw. I'm sure my students will enjoy it. Why don't you tell them about the Margo show?" Professor Sharpe added, grinning at Iain. Iain almost blushed at his suggestion.

"No, that's quite alright. I've said enough." Iain politely smiled.

"Fine, I'll tell them. Iain's flying out tomorrow to appear on the Margo Morning Show in sunny LA!" Professor Sharpe informed us, speaking as though he was a proud father. The class clapped for Iain, and shouted out congratulatory comments. I remained silent, all colour fading from my face.

"Are you okay?" Delilah demanded, looking at me. Her nose was wrinkled with distaste.

"Yeah, I'm fine," I muttered, dropping my head so that my hair would shield my face from her judgmental eyes. I could see her through the strands, leaning away.

"Well, you look like you're going to throw up," she said.

I ignored her, willing the class to just end. I did feel a little nauseous.

"If you throw up, don't aim it anywhere near me," she added. I rolled my eyes, my fingernails digging deeper into my skin. She was the first thing I'd aim for.

Finally, Professor Sharpe wrapped it up with a reminder to pick up a copy of Iain's book from the local bookstore, and we were free to leave.

Now the next challenge came. The challenge I wasn't looking forward to: leaving without Iain noticing me. I took a deep breath, steeling myself.

"I am going to go up and talk to him," Delilah declared. I ignored her again, beginning to make my way out of the lecture hall, following the sea of students and trying to be inconspicuous. I wanted to leave undetected, but Professor Sharpe caught sight of me.

"Ms. Jones! Come here please!" he called out, alerting Iain to my presence. Surprised to hear my last name, Iain looked up. His eyes locked with mine, and I was trapped. I couldn't ignore my professor; he knew I'd heard him. I walked down the rest of the stairs, joining my professor and Iain at the front of the class.

Delilah glowered at me with pure rage, obviously put out that Professor Sharpe hadn't asked her. Still, she lingered, waiting for her opportunity to speak to Iain.

"Ms. Jones, I wanted to introduce you to Iain Bentley personally. Iain, Harlow is my star pupil. Her work is phenomenal," Professor Sharpe said, grinning at me with great affection.

Iain seemed dazed by my presence; he couldn't take his eyes off me. "I know," he muttered distractedly.

Professor Sharpe glanced at him quickly, his eyes widening with surprise. "You know each other?" he asked, looking from me to Iain.

Iain swallowed hard, and I watched as his Adam's apple bobbed up and down. He forced a smile for Professor Sharpe. "We're...acquainted," he finally said.

"Right." Professor Sharpe's smile faded slightly and he cleared his throat. "Anyway, as I was saying...Harlow is one of my most talented pupils. I really feel that with the right encouragement, she'd be a fantastic author—if that's what she chooses to do after graduation. I've already offered to help her tackle the self-publishing sea, but figured an introduction to someone going the traditional route would be beneficial as well."

Iain pursed his lips, nodding with agreement to Professor Sharpe's explanation. He was dressed in grey dress pants and a white dress shirt, the sleeves rolled up to reveal his lean forearms, the muscles taut with tension.

"Thank you," I said sincerely, taken aback by Professor Sharpe's open praise.

"I thought she'd benefit from some guidance from you, Iain. If you aren't too busy promoting your new book that is," he joked, shoving Iain's arm playfully.

My jaw fell slack as Iain's Caribbean eyes smoldered. "I—" I couldn't think of a single response. I clamped it shut.

"I'm rather busy, unfortunately," Iain finally said, picking up on my discomfort. "But if you ever want to shoot me an email with questions, I'd be happy to answer. I'd also recommend you to my publishing agency. I can't guarantee approval, of course." He fished a business card out of his pocket and held it out to me. I took it with a trembling hand, our fingers brushing for the briefest of moments.

"Good!" Professor Sharpe's hands clasped together. "Now, how about we go for lunch, Iain? Catch up, just like old times?"

"Sounds good." Iain nodded. He gave me another look, speaking a thousand words without saying a single one. "It was nice seeing you again, Harlow," he added, humor sparking in his eyes.

"Yeah, ditto..." I said numbly. Delilah chose that moment to approach Professor Sharpe for her opportunity to speak to Iain. I left, and I could feel Iain's eyes on my back the entire time.

* * *

"What's wrong with you?" Crimson asked, tilting her head. Her curls fell over her shoulder and nearly into the glass of wine she held on her lap.

"Nothing," I muttered quickly, not wanting to divulge the complicated mess in my head.

We were watching a movie—something with Ryan Gosling in it, naturally—and hanging out. Wine was involved: Jenna's idea. I'd barely touched mine while both Jenna and Crimson were on their second glass.

I'd mostly been quiet, leaving the talking up to Crimson and Jenna. I sort of felt out of place, and my mind was still twisted over the strange encounter in my

Creative Writing class. I'd listened quietly while Jenna talked about her incredible weekend with Kyle, Crimson eating up the details like a starving child. Crimson was every bit as obsessed with *Autumn Fields* as Jenna. I couldn't help but feel a little jealous over their easy companionship.

"No, Crimson is right. Something's up with you. What is it?" Jenna said, siding with Crimson. They both stared at me, waiting for me to speak.

"Really? You're teaming up on me now?" I sighed, rolling my eyes. Jenna and Crimson exchanged a look with each other, grinning. "Fine. I had to see Iain again today."

"Where?" Jenna demanded, her expression hardening.

"In my Creative Writing class. I guess my professor is friends with Iain and invited him in to talk to us about his book—*which we have to read*, by the way." I glowered, crossing my arms across my chest sullenly. I still wasn't excited about our latest project.

"You're kidding," Jenna said, sounding anything but amused.

"Nope." I frowned, shaking my head. "I *have* to read his book to participate in the discussion."

"What's wrong with reading his book?" Crimson looked momentarily confused.

"Because it's about Harlow, and she doesn't want to revisit the past," Jenna responded automatically, giving me a comforting look. As angry as she still was about the whole secret thing, she knew how much this was affecting me too. She knew I hurt too.

"Oh," Crimson said. "Well, can't you just tell your professor that you don't want to read the book?"

"If I don't participate, I don't get the grade and I am *not* ruining my average over him," I declared stubbornly.

"Did he notice you?" Jenna asked, taking a sip of wine. It was like she needed something to do with her hands. She wrinkled her nose, as if the wine left a bitter aftertaste. I knew that wasn't the wine. *Iain* left a bitter aftertaste. The subject definitely wasn't an easy one between us, especially not anymore.

"Not until the very end of class when I tried to sneak out and Professor Sharpe called me over to introduce us."

Jenna winced, imagining the massive amount of discomfort I'd been in. "So you had to deal with Professor Suave *and* Iain. Nice." She shook her head. "Why is he stalking you?"

"I don't think he is," I rushed to explain. "Iain looked shocked to see me there."

"Doesn't he always?" Jenna mumbled quietly. I could barely hear her, and I knew Crimson definitely didn't. I rolled my eyes at her and she pursed her lips.

"Does Jax know?" Crimson questioned, peering up at me with wide, innocent eyes.

"About Iain? Yes. That I saw him again today and have to read his book? No." I pulled my hair behind my neck, feeling flushed. "I'll tell him when I see him next. But that's not even the craziest part."

"What's the craziest part?" Jenna set her now empty wine glass down, fixing me with a penetrating gaze. I think she expected me to confess my undying love for Iain.

That was *not* going to happen. While I still had a small amount of love for Iain, it wasn't like *that*...not anymore. It was just an affection of sorts; I honestly wished him well. I honestly wished him happiness and success. I didn't want harm to come to him, and I didn't want to be at odds with him.

"Professor Sharpe wanted Iain to be my mentor." I snorted as if I found the whole thing absurd. And I did. "He wanted Iain to mentor me in the ways of getting traditionally published or something."

"That is weird." Jenna frowned. "And you're sure this wasn't...prearranged?" she added, carefully filling up her glass again.

I thought back to the look of surprise on Iain's face. "Definitely not. Besides, Iain basically said he couldn't. He's apparently flying out to LA to appear on the Margo Morning Show."

"Holy shit, that's *huge!*" Crimson declared, her eyes going wide. "She only interviews people who are going to make it *big!* She has an eye for that, you know."

"It's true." Jenna nodded thoughtfully, her eyes glazing over with pride. "She interviewed *Autumn Fields*, and they are skyrocketing right now."

"It doesn't matter. I'm happy he's found success. I just didn't want to read the book, and now I have to." I sighed. "But I'd rather not talk about it—or him—anymore. What's going on with you, Crimson? How are things with Cole?"

"Non-existent," Crimson replied sadly. "I think we're over. I can't wait forever..." She took a shaky breath. "He won't even talk to me."

"I'm sorry to hear that, but if Cole can't see past his own troubles to see how incredible you are, someone else definitely will," I told her, and Jenna nodded.

Crimson gave a tiny smile, distractedly picking at her sweater. "Yeah, I guess..." she said without conviction. "I just...I want someone that makes me feel..." she trailed off, flushing a deep shade of red.

"Makes you feel what?" Jenna pressed gently, giving her an encouraging smile.

"Wanted, I guess." Crimson blushed deeper. "Everyone around me has someone they can't get enough of and someone that can't get enough of them...then there's me. I feel like I'm trapped in a terrible eighties movie."

"Molly Ringwald always got the guy," I pointed out.

Crimson laughed. "I guess that's true, but I haven't even met anybody..."

"You will," Jenna said with confidence.

"Yeah." Crimson still didn't sound convinced. Her smile wavered on her lips, and she tucked her hair behind her ears. I watched her touch the hearing aid, her smile fading even more.

"Okay, it's time for Ben & Jerry to make an appearance," Jenna declared, pushing up from the couch. She disappeared into the kitchen to grab the carton, three bowls and spoons. She returned, handing us our empty bowls.

I was more interested in the ice cream than I'd been in the wine, so I eagerly dove in. Peanut Butter Chocolate Chunk was definitely what I needed after today. We were silent for a little bit, enjoying the flavor and absently watching the movie.

"So…Harlow," Crimson finally broke the silence. "How's Jax's new place? It's so cool that he found an apartment right here in this building! I bet you'll be seeing a lot more of each other now."

"Especially once she moves out," Jenna interjected, nudging me playfully with her shoulder.

"Yeah," I said, my voice sounding hollow. "It's great…it is."

Jenna's smile faded as she assessed me. "Don't you want to move in with Jax?"

Tears welled up in my eyes, a reaction I couldn't have anticipated or prevented. I nodded, letting my hair fall in front of my face, an attempt to shield myself. Some women cry over everything; they cry when they're happy, when they're scared, when they're angry and when they're sad. Jenna was one of those people — she cried easily, and didn't bother trying to hide her tears. Not me, I rarely cried and when I did, I did my best to hide it from the world. For when someone who doesn't cry often, it's a major deal.

"Are you crying? Harlow?" I heard Jenna's bowl clink against the coffee table, and suddenly she was wrapping her arms around me. "Why are you crying?"

"It's nothing." I sniffled, fighting for control. My brow furrowed with concentration as I forced the tears to ebb.

"It doesn't seem like nothing," Jenna said. "I thought you wanted to move in with Jax."

"I do, it's not that." My shoulders shook as I dragged in a ragged breath. "I guess I'm just...scared. It's scary."

I felt so stupid for admitting it. Crimson and Jenna were silent, listening to me. "Of course it's scary. It's a big step," Jenna told me, her hand massaging my back. "If you aren't ready for it, you don't have to move. There's no time limit."

"But Crimson wants out of student housing," I said.

"Oh please." Crimson waved her hand, brushing off my words. "I can stay at student housing for a bit. No big deal. I'm not forcing you out of your room. If worse comes to worse, I could just find a different apartment. Or maybe *I'll* move in with Jax," she joked, winking at me.

I snorted with laughter, remembering Crimson's comment the first day that we'd met. She'd joined me under a tree on Tabaret Lawn, when Jax had come up to us and I'd asked him to stop stalking me. She'd stared at him in a daze and said "You can stalk me" aloud.

"I want to move in with Jax," I said. "I just...I don't want to move when things between us aren't...right," I added, looking at Jenna.

She bit her lip. "Things with us are fine, Harlow," she insisted. "I love you, you're my best friend...the closest thing to a sister I've ever had. Sisters get mad at each other, don't they?"

"I don't know, I don't have any siblings," I pointed out with a small smile.

"I do, and yes…they *definitely do*." Crimson's eyes were wide. "Like, all the time."

"See? So it's fine. We're fine. I promise. With that said, if you truly aren't ready, don't move out. I'm serious, Harlow. You don't want to jump the gun. Besides, have you even told your mom you're thinking about it?"

"No." I frowned. "Why would I?"

"Because it's a big deal." Jenna shrugged. "Maybe they won't even want you to do it."

"Frankly, I don't care what they want," I responded, crossing my arms again. "I'm a big girl; I can make my own decisions."

Jenna smirked, amused. "So make them, and don't worry about us—or about Crimson. We'll figure that out!"

chapter SEVENTEEN

MY BAG felt a thousand times heavier with Iain's book inside, and I felt the weight the entire time I walked home from the bookstore. I headed to my bedroom, thankful that the apartment was vacant. Jenna was out somewhere; she'd messaged me, saying she wouldn't be home until later.

Pulling the door closed behind me, I set my bag down on my messy bed, staring at it as if it contained a poisonous snake.

What if it's not harmless? I thought. *What if it's the opposite of harmless? What if it destroys me all over again?*

Sighing, trying to push my own thoughts away. The book certainly wasn't going to read itself, as much as I wished it would. I needed this grade, and I'd put off reading it for as long as I could. Mr. Sharpe had given us three weeks to read the book and compile some notes on it for our class discussion, and I had four days left.

I opened my bag, pulling the book out. My hands glided across the glossy cover, my eyes focusing on the dark haired girl walking off to an unknown future. I swallowed hard, steeling myself. I wisely decided to skip the acknowledgements, diving straight in to the first chapter. I lowered myself onto my bed, my eyes never breaking from the page, my heart thudding in my chest to a nervous tempo of anticipation.

I didn't know what I expected. Maybe that Iain would paint the student as a harlot that endlessly persuaded the teacher until his will was worn completely down, but that wasn't what I got.

I was sucked in from the first word; I saw things from Iain's perspective—even if he'd written this book as a fictional novel. I could hear him in it; I could see him in the character of the teacher. There was no denying that I was the student. She was every bit as broken, lonely and stubborn as I'd been. Convinced she knew what she wanted, what she needed.

I read until the light faded from my bedroom, and then continued to read once my arm absently shot out to turn on my bedside lamp. I read until my eyes were strained and sore, absorbing each and every word and scene and twist. I'd never read anything so quickly before; and I was an avid reader.

I didn't know if the ease of the words came from knowing them in my heart – from having *lived* this story – or talent. It was clear that Iain had plenty of talent.

When my fingers turned the last page and I read the last words, I held the book and blinked back tears. Reading it caused me to revisit the past, and those old feelings I'd felt so strongly once for him. Reading it tore my heart out and placed it in front of me to assess.

Iain had given his characters a happier ending. The teacher never went to jail, but he didn't end up with the girl. She'd walked off into the sunset, sent away by him to find out what she truly wanted. In the epilogue, they met again years down the line. They had the same intense chemistry that they possessed all those years before. It was one of those open-ended books, up to the reader to decide what happened.

I heard the sound of the apartment door opening and closing, and I frantically wiped away my tears. Footfalls sounded as Jenna made her way down the hallway. She paused by my bedroom door, seeing the light spill from the cracks.

"Harlow? Are you still up?" she whispered. I closed my eyes, feigning sleep, my heart and mind too numb to talk to anybody. She opened my bedroom door and saw me lying in bed with my eyes closed. She walked over quietly to turn off my lamp and disappeared, closing the door softly behind her.

I remained where I was for several hours, thinking about the book and my relationship with Iain. I thought about the part of me that missed being with him — because I'd be lying if I said there wasn't. There was, and I wasn't sure how long that would linger. As I'd told Jax, Iain was the first person I allowed myself to form a connection like that with.

My connection to Jax was different, deeper. More stable. I'd chosen Jax, and I didn't regret that decision in the slightest. I *wanted* to be with Jax; I wanted to have a future with him. What future could I have had with Iain? Our relationship had been formed in secrecy. Our relationship was forbidden and yes, exciting. But once the forbidden factor was removed, I wasn't entirely sure a functional relationship was possible.

I *knew* it was possible with Jax. I knew it was possible because I lived it. He fit into my life now; that was the important part.

Now I just had to figure out how to move on with the present and the future, when the past still kept knocking, demanding to be heard.

* * *

For the first time since the term began, I dreaded Creative Writing. I dreaded sitting in class, discussing and possibly dissecting Iain's novel. Still, I showed up, my notes clutched in my hands. I sat between two people I didn't know, hoping to avoid having to be near Delilah. Still, she managed to snag a seat in front of me.

Before the lecture began, she turned around to face me, giving me one of her malevolent smiles. The vulnerability I'd seen in her expression several days before was gone, replaced with a calculating coldness that instantly chilled my blood.

"You know, Harlow…the character in this book, Leah? She reminded me an awful lot of you," Delilah said, her hazel eyes fixed on me, watching my reaction. I willed myself to be impassive, but I could still feel the colour draining from my face. "Everything from how her physical appearance is described, to how she behaves…"

My eyes narrowed. "I think your obsession with me is rather unsettling. Do you spend a lot of time following me around and comparing me to fictional characters, Delilah?" I inquired, tilting my head and returning her stony gaze. The students around us were watching the exchange with interested eyes.

Delilah smirked. "I just thought it was very interesting, considering you seem to know Iain Bentley a little...*too well*, shall we say?"

"Just what are you insinuating?" I hissed at her, my anger flaring. My heart thudded in my chest, and I could feel the heat of my boiling blood beneath my skin. I felt hot and trapped.

"Don't play coy, Harlow. Anybody with half-decent research skills and access to the Internet can find out exactly what I'm 'insinuating'." Delilah's eyes were almost slits, and the corners of her lips were curled up in a sneer.

I knew my instinct about her was right. She was a bitch; a petty one at that. I opened my mouth, about to light into her. My reply was cut short by the appearance of Professor Sharpe.

Delilah gave me another calculating look before she turned around to face the front. I resisted the urge to knock her upside the head with my hardback copy of Iain's book as Professor Sharpe entered the room and approached the podium with his usual confident demeanor.

"Good afternoon, class," he greeted us, setting Iain's book on top of the podium stand. "I trust you all read and completed the notes on Iain Bentley's *Circumstance*?" The room buzzed with the murmurings of students' answers, all of them yes. "We'll be doing a class discussion today. In the last twenty minutes of class, Iain Bentley will be here to answer any questions

you may have. I encourage you to not go easy on him—
even if this is his first novel. You are here to learn, to
question. You'll get extra points towards credit for
participation in the discussion, and the question
segment as well."

The colour once again drained from my face as
Delilah glanced at me over her shoulder. She winked,
her lips snaking upwards in a deliberate smile.

I wasn't counting on Iain being here today. Hell, I
wasn't counting on Delilah being a nosy little bitch and
finding out about the events of North Bay either, and I
had no doubt that she did know. She wouldn't have
made comments if she didn't know, and she was right.
Although Larry had worked hard to protect my name,
it wasn't difficult for people to draw the same
conclusion after facing the facts.

Iain Bentley wrote a book about a student teacher
relationship after serving time in jail for one. Delilah
knew that we knew each other—she'd been there the
day Professor Sharpe had introduced us. She'd seen
Iain's reaction to me, and likely, my reaction to him.
And she had read the book. She was right, the student
in the novel could easily be interpreted as me.

I couldn't focus on the discussion. I couldn't even
participate. My mouth felt sewn shut; my tongue was
impossibly dry. I wanted to escape, to run away, but I
was sandwiched between several students and there
was no way for me to leave without drawing attention
to myself.

All I could do was sit through the class, my fingers
digging in to the armrests on either side of me, my

body rigid. I watched the clock with a growing sense of dread as the hands ticked closer and closer to the time Iain was scheduled to arrive.

When I heard the familiar creak of the doors as they swung open, my eyes flew in their direction. Iain stood there, with that same woman he'd been with at his book signing. Iain was dressed to impress again, looking every bit the part of a successful author. He stood by the doors with his female companion, waiting for the discussion to wrap up. I could see him looking around the room, searching for me.

His gaze drifted over to where I was and we locked eyes, and I know he saw the panic and dread on my face. The small smile on his face faded to a frown, his brows creasing. He looked away.

Once upon a time, Iain was fairly good at reading me. Not as good as Jax, but good enough to detect danger on the horizon. Now…not so much. He folded his arms and stared stonily towards the front.

Professor Sharpe glanced towards the door, seeing Iain and the woman. "Welcome, Iain! I see you've brought your agent."

Iain nodded, his arms dropping to his sides as he approached Professor Sharpe at the front of the classroom. They shook hands. "I'm going to open up the floor to questions now, if you're alright with that?" Professor Sharpe asked him.

Iain smiled tightly, unaware of the dire situation before us. Then again, he didn't know Delilah. I closed my eyes, praying she'd keep her mouth shut and that I was panicking for nothing. "Of course. I'd be happy to answer any questions."

Professor Sharpe nodded and slapped Iain on the back in a cordial manner before he stepped back and headed over to the doors, where the woman Iain had walked in with was observing.

I assumed Delilah would be frothing at the mouth to spill her knowledge, but she remained still in her seat. Several other students asked Iain about his process—both the written one and the publishing one. Some asked about how it had felt to go on the *Margo Morning Show*. Others wanted to know if he had any more books planned for the future.

I started to relax, thinking that maybe Delilah would keep her mouth shut after all. Towards the end of Iain's twenty minutes, Delilah's hand shot up, dashing my hopes.

Iain looked up, catching the movement. "Yes?" He smiled at her encouragingly.

Delilah stood up. "Mr. Bentley, I adored *Circumstance*. It was beautifully written, very descriptive and raw." Her tone seemed friendly and star-struck. Innocent.

"Thank you." Iain smiled at her praise, and Delilah cast a glance at me and smirked before continuing.

"I was just wondering, Mr. Bentley…if this novel was based on a true story?" Delilah asked loftily. There was an edge to her words; she was making it clear that she knew it was.

Iain studied her for a moment, considering her and her question. He didn't seem surprised by it at all.

"Most writers ingrain a lot of truth in their novels, be it the emotional aspects or characteristic traits."

"So…this is the story behind what happened in North Bay?" Delilah's voice held a note of challenging contempt. The room was so silent, you could hear a pin drop. Nobody knew what Delilah was talking about. Nobody but Iain and me.

Iain clenched his jaw, the only outward sign of his aggravation. "Readers often find connections between stories and the real world. After all, most stories are based on events that could really take place. The beauty is that everyone finds something different in it and connects it with their own personal experiences."

"Yes, I agree. However…you—" Delilah began, but Iain's eyes hardened and he raised his hand, silencing her.

"I see that you are familiar with certain facts or truths that pertain to me and my story. However, this venue is not the place to discuss such matters and I'd rather limit discussion to the book itself. If you would like to discuss your obvious issues with me afterwards, you may do so."

Delilah bowed her head as if thoroughly chided and sat back down in her seat. Silence fell upon the lecture hall for several moments before the whispers erupted.

"And that's a wrap. Class, you are free to go." Professor Sharpe's voice was stern, cutting through the whispers and tension like a knife. He approached Iain with a frown, followed by the woman. She looked absolutely livid.

Students started to leave their seats and the lecture hall. Most were confused about what had transpired. I was vibrating with anger. I tried to leave, because I *knew* if I had to face Delilah, it was not going to end well.

She followed me though, catching up to me as I neared the bottom of the stairs. Her hand shot out, grabbing my arm and forcing me to turn and face her.

"What the hell, Delilah?" I demanded, my eyes narrowing in on Delilah's smug face. She looked quite happy with herself. I yanked my arm out of her grasp, almost shaking.

"I guess that answers our question, doesn't it? You were definitely the muse for this book. Did you actually sleep with your English teacher?" Delilah inquired, smirking. She waited a beat, watching my face as the colour drained. "Judging by the look on your face, I'd say yes. Are you sleeping with Professor Sharpe, too? Is that why you're his 'prized pupil' this year?"

Delilah's words were harsh, full of bitter resentment and jealousy. Her voice carried with ease throughout the lecture hall. The remaining students stopped in their quest to leave and stared at the altercation happening near the bottom of the stairs.

I looked behind me helplessly. Professor Sharpe, Iain and the woman were less than five feet away, and it was obvious by the looks on their faces that they had heard every word Delilah had said. Iain's jaw was tense, and Professor Sharpe looked appalled. Iain went to step towards us, but the woman shot her hand out, gripping his arm tightly. She shook her head at him.

"Delilah Moreno." Professor Sharpe's voice rang out like a whip, and Delilah's head shot up. I could tell by the surprise on her features that she hadn't intended for *him* to overhear her accusations.

Delilah straightened, lifting her chin up. "Yes, Professor Sharpe?"

"What is the meaning of this?" he demanded, looking from Delilah to me and to Iain.

"Why don't you ask your old university buddy?" Delilah suggested sweetly. "Or maybe your 'prized pupil', perhaps?"

I opened my mouth, searching for something to say, anything. Nothing came out. I was in a state of complete and total shock.

"Miss. Moreno, I've had about enough of you running your mouth. The accusations you are throwing around are serious and frankly, I don't appreciate them." I'd never seen Professor Sharpe so angry before. "You're both going to need to accompany me to the Dean's office—now."

"I'm not accusing anyone of anything," Delilah said calmly, thrusting her chin upward. "It's public knowledge that Iain Bentley served time for an inappropriate relationship with one of his high school students. Your 'prized pupil' happens to be that very high school student."

"That may be so," Iain said, stepping forward with angry determination. He ignored the woman's attempts at stopping him. "I served time for my crime, and I've moved on with my life, as has she. Now, you're tossing serious accusations around at your professor. That's slander, Miss. Moreno. I trust you know that slander is illegal?"

Delilah paled at his words. "I didn't mean to accuse Professor Sharpe of anything. I—"

"But you did accuse me, and that's slander." Professor Sharpe's lips were in a thin line. "Dean's office. Now." His words left no room for argument.

* * *

My hands were trembling as I sat in the wooden chair before the dean of the university. Delilah sat beside me, sullen and pale, while Professor Sharpe stood behind us looking very grave.

I hadn't seen Iain Bentley, or the woman who I now knew was his agent since Professor Sharpe walked Delilah and me out of the lecture hall to the dean's office.

I had been in the office for the last three hours, in a separate room from Delilah and Professor Sharpe. Professor Sharpe spoke first, and then I had to recount the situation with Iain in North Bay before the dean and two other staff members. Then it was Delilah's turn to share her side of the story, and now we were all together, about to hear the verdict.

I felt emotionally drained, as if someone had scooped out everything inside of me. I knew I wasn't in any trouble—after all, I hadn't slept with Professor Sharpe—but I still couldn't ignore the anxiety that rolled through me like a cobra, coiled and ready to strike as I waited for the dean to speak.

"It looks like what we have here is a jealous, petty individual throwing accusations around out of spite," the dean said, fixing his cold eyes upon Delilah's face. She lowered her head, tears streaming down her cheeks. I didn't have it in me to pity her—she was reaping what she'd sown. I didn't understand what I'd done to evoke such needless cruelty from this individual, and I certainly didn't have to pity her for making my life hell. "However, due to the severity of the accusations, and despite the fact that Ms. Moreno confessed to these feelings of petty jealousy, our university procedure still dictates that we launch a full investigation," he added, glancing at Professor Sharpe apologetically.

I followed his gaze, looking at Professor Sharpe. His face was grim, but we had nothing to hide—we'd done nothing wrong. "What does that entail?" I said, finding my voice finally.

"Unfortunately, Professor Sharpe is going to be suspended while we investigate these allegations. We will have to bring in all the other students in your class for individual questioning," the dean replied, sitting back in his chair. He massaged his temple. "We're also going to have to look into your grades to make sure that there wasn't an exchange of…an inappropriate nature to receive them."

The blood rushed from my head and I swayed in my seat.

"Don't be alarmed, Ms. Jones. I'm certain we'll find nothing of concern. As I said, it's just a procedure we must follow."

"I'm really sorry, Professor Sharpe," Delilah said, never raising her head. "And Harlow...I'm sorry too. I shouldn't have behaved the way I did. It was childish."

I couldn't reply. I'd lost the ability to speak and I wasn't sure I wanted to accept her apology either. She'd caused a bunch of heartache and stress with her careless words. I was so angry at her, I could barely see straight.

"Ms. Jones, you're free to go."

I stood up on shaky legs, grabbing my messenger bag before fleeing the office. I couldn't look at Professor Sharpe or Delilah. I kept my gaze focused on the floor in front of me as I threw open the door and let it slam behind me.

I couldn't believe I was in this situation again. My grades were going to be reviewed, I was going to be judged and scrutinized by the board of yet another educational institution, and this time, I hadn't even done anything.

My eyes started to burn, but I willed myself to keep it together for just a little longer. The last thing I needed right now was to break down and cry.

My phone started to vibrate in my pocket, and I fished it out with trembling hands. I had ten missed phone calls. Two were from Jamie, likely wondering where I was and why I hadn't shown up for my shift. I'd missed half of it already. One was from Jenna, one from Crimson and the rest were from Jax—save for one, a number I didn't recognize.

Jax was calling again. I answered it, my voice sounding hoarse as if I'd been crying. It was remarkable that I hadn't yet burst into tears, but my voice betrayed the emotion.

"Harlow, what's wrong?" he demanded. "Jenna's called me three times looking for you. Jamie said you didn't show up at work. Where are you?"

"At the university. I'm walking home now. I—" I paused, my voice trembling. I had no idea where to begin.

"I'm picking you up. Wait for me out front," Jax told me. "I'll be there in ten minutes."

"Okay," I whispered, finally allowing the tears to flow free. I hung up, swiftly changing directions so that I could wait for Jax in front of the university.

I walked over to the curb, needing somewhere to sit down. My legs felt impossibly weak. I collapsed there, dropping my head into my hands.

My head was swirling with a thousand thoughts and emotions. I couldn't sift through a single one of them to categorize or make sense of it. My heart was pounding, and I was shaking.

True to Jax's word, he was pulling up to the curb within ten minutes. I heard his truck door slam as he jumped out and jogged around the rear length of his truck to reach me. I looked up, tears streaming down my face.

"What happened?" Jax squatted before me, his eyes full of tension and concern. He had known about the book discussion today.

I opened my mouth and tried to speak, but it wasn't cooperating. All I could do was let out a strangled cry. I was beginning to hyperventilate and I felt like a weak fool.

Jax picked me up with one fluid motion and carried me over to his truck, opening the passenger door. He set me inside on the seat, my legs still hanging out the door on either side of his body. His eyes bore into mine. "Tell me what happened."

I was fighting to breathe, and I stared into Jax's warm brown eyes as I tried to regain my composure and untangle my tongue. I opened my mouth, about to force words through my windpipe.

"Harlow!" Jax's head and mine both turned to the sound of my name being called. Iain was jogging over, his brow creased with worry. Jax stiffened in front of me, and I squeezed his muscles and shook my head to try and express that Iain was not the cause of this, but Jax wasn't looking at me. He was glowering at Iain. Iain slowed his pace, eyeing Jax warily before looking at me. "I just wanted to check up on you after...everything..."

Suddenly, Jax was gone from in front of me. He had a fist full of Iain's jacket and a savage look on his face. "What did you do to her?" he demanded, his voice menacing. "Ever since you started showing your good for nothing face around here, she's been a mess. Give me one good reason why I shouldn't break you!" Jax said deliberately, each of his words searing into the air around us. I knew he meant every word.

"Jax! Stop!" I cried, jumping out of his truck. I propelled my body towards him, grabbing his arm. "It wasn't Iain," I said, almost shouting it.

Jax released his grip on Iain, although the hellish look didn't leave his eyes. He didn't believe me. "Then what happened?"

"Delilah. Delilah happened," I responded, my throat raw and sore.

"Delilah?" Jax looked confused for a moment. "Delilah Moreno?" I nodded, trying to breathe through the racing of my heart. He knew who Delilah was—he trained her at the gym, but I hadn't mentioned my recent issues with her for fear of sounding insecure and foolish. "What does she have to do with any of this?" Jax demanded, gesturing to Iain and me.

"She's in my Creative Writing class." I exhaled, my legs trembling. I swayed on my feet, the panic, the anxiety, and the events of the day all completely taking their toll on me. Blood rushed to my head.

My vision was beginning to fade and I felt faint. Jax's expression changed from lethal to alarmed, and I heard his voice and Iain's at a distance, as if I were underwater. Jax stepped towards me, catching me in his arms just before I fell.

Jax held me in his strong, capable arms and placed his lips near my ear. "Breathe, Harlow," he said.

I focused on the sound of his voice, instructing me on how to breathe, and did what he said. I inhaled slowly, then exhaled slowly and repeated the process until the darkness receded from my vision and I felt more stable on my feet.

"You know, I'm getting really sick of fainting," I mumbled, feeling embarrassed. Jax chuckled without humor, his expression still troubled from my near-fainting incident. He was still vibrating with anger. I knew it wasn't towards me, but it was still intimidating. Not because I was worried he would hurt me, but because I knew he could easily inflict pain on Iain. Despite everything, I didn't want Iain to suffer any more than he already had.

I blinked, my focus returning to me a little more, and glanced at Iain. He was still standing there, his hands in his pockets and a ruptured look on his face. When I looked at him, he schooled his features into a tight smile that didn't reach his eyes.

"There was a student in Harlow's class today that caused some problems during and after the question segment," Iain explained, noting that I had yet to find my voice. He wasn't afraid to meet Jax's angry gaze. I had a feeling that Iain would welcome any physical pain Jax wanted to unleash.

"What kind of problems?" Jax was fighting to control his reaction to Iain. The desire to rearrange Iain's face was still strong, but he was holding the majority of my weight in his arms still, the little fainting spell had brought him back to his rational self.

"She knew about what happened in North Bay and accused Harlow of sleeping with her current professor to get in his good favor in front of several other students. The professor, my agent, the other students and me all heard her accusation. Professor Sharpe had to report the entire incident to the dean." Iain explained this with a detached voice, as if he was relaying an incident that didn't really concern him. The only detection of his true emotion was in his fragmented eyes. "I just wanted to check in on Harlow after that incident, and when I saw you carrying her limply to the truck..." Iain trailed off, implying that he was worried without actually saying it.

The tension between the two of them was thick and heavy. Iain's words were careful. I knew he didn't want to say the wrong thing and make the situation worse for me. It would suck to have another boyfriend of mine end up in jail. If Jax got into a fight on university property, there was no telling what would happen.

I took a deep breath, steadying myself. I moved a little ways away from Jax, just to stand on my own feet; just to regain some control and some composure. "Now my grades are being reviewed, and Professor Sharpe is suspended and they're going to question all of the other students in our class—even though Delilah admitted she said those things out of jealousy and spite."

"It's just a procedure, Harlow. You aren't in any danger and neither is Professor Sharpe," Iain assured me.

"How do you know?" I whirled on him angrily. Out of the corner of my eye, I watched as Jax backed away a little to lean against the front side of his truck. He was watching me with furrowed brows. "With my track record, it doesn't look good. One or several of the other students will attest the praise he's given me, and the time he asked to see me after class."

Iain smiled patiently. "Yes, but I know Nick. Let's just say...you aren't his type." I frowned, not understanding what Iain was implying. "Nick is gay;

he used to date Jamie when we were in university. Like I said, you aren't his type."

"Still," I muttered, shock momentarily washing over me. I allowed Iain's words to calm me a little. At least I didn't have to worry about Professor Sharpe losing his job and serving jail time. I'd seen how the entire town and the school board crucified Iain. Even if the so-called charges had been true, all the 'female victims' that came forth certainly weren't. It had turned into a damn witch hunt. Male educators had a difficult time proving their innocence once accused.

My hands clenched into fists and released with the tension and aggravation I was feeling about the entire situation. There was still the fact that my grades were going to be reviewed, and that thought had me in a tailspin panic.

"I wouldn't worry about that," Iain insisted, knowing where my thoughts had gone. His jaw locked, as if the memory was bitter for him as well. I knew it was.

"No, instead I get to worry about this following me everywhere I go, about this always being the under note. 'Does Harlow have talent, or does she just sleep with people to get ahead?' will be the question that follows me everywhere," I ranted angrily. My head was throbbing and I was so sick of the past constantly coming back.

Iain paled at my words and swallowed hard. He stepped towards me, his eyes focused on only my face. Jax stood up straighter, ready to intervene if needed, ever watchful. His usually gentle brown eyes flashed with barely controlled rage. "Yeah, Harlow…this might follow us. You don't think I get questioned about it still? You don't think I don't relive my mistakes every day? I do. You're not the only one who's paid for it."

My mouth opened and closed as I thought desperately for something to say. Iain was right, and he'd suffered more than I had. He'd lost his job, his career, his home and a lot of his friends. He'd gone to jail.

It appeared that we'd reached an impasse. "Thank you for checking up on me, Iain," I said, my voice strained. "But I think we need to go our separate ways now." It hurt to say those words to him, especially with the way he was looking at me. It hurt to inflict more pain, but being around each other wasn't helping. It was just reminding him of what he'd lost. I'd moved on. I was with Jax, and I was happy with him. Seeing Iain just made me live in guilt and regret; it just reminded me of what I'd cost him. Everything. I had cost him everything.

Iain's eyes locked with mine. "You're right. I'm sorry all this happened, Harlow. I'm sorry for any stress or anxiety today has caused you," he said sincerely. "You'll be okay. This will blow over," he added, glancing at Jax. He clenched his jaw and nodded once before turning and walking away.

I let out a sigh of relief. I looked back at Jax apologetically and he had a perplexed look on his face. "I'm sorry," I muttered, my eyes dropping to the ground with shame.

"Harlow, don't be sorry." Jax sighed. He closed the distance between us and raised his hand to stroke my face. "You've had a really shitty day. I understand that. You didn't do anything wrong."

"But I did. I keep letting my past affect things," I replied, closing my eyes against his touch. I could feel a tear escape and trail down my cheek. He moved closer to me, using the pad of his thumb to brush away the lone tear.

"You're talking to someone who understands completely how the past can boomerang to your present and fuck everything up," Jax reminded me gently.

I snorted with disbelief. "Your past never seems to knock you down. You are easygoing and affectionate and…stable. You're stable, Jax. You're the most stable person I know, despite what you've been through."

Jax smiled sorrowfully at me, his finger brushing against my jaw as he looked deep into my eyes. The gold that edged his pupils seemed more intense than it ever had before. "My past knocks me down, Harlow. I just get back up again. I'm good at concealing it because that's all I've ever done, but I'm not unaffected by it and it does still pain me. Every day. Even more before I found you. Now, I have more good to focus on…more light. There's more value in my life, all because of you. You may not see it this way, Harlow, but you saved me. I was drowning in myself, a smile in place to curtain it. Now I'm not drowning because I have you. Now when I smile, it's real…because of you."

"How is that possible when I make everything harder?" I whispered, my heart breaking and expanding at his beautiful words.

He swallowed hard. "Nothing in life is easy, Harlow, and I never said this would be easy. I just said you were worth it. And you are—you are completely, undeniably worth it," he added. My heart swelled at his words, and I smiled. I felt his lips brush against mine in a tender kiss. His hand rose to the nape of my neck, his fingers twisting gently in my hair as he deepened the kiss.

chapter EIGHTEEN

RUMORS SWIRLED around the school about the scandal in North Bay and the allegations Delilah made about Professor Sharpe and me. Our next Creative Writing class after the incident was canceled so that each and every one of the students could be questioned individually. The process took several weeks, and it was incredibly difficult for me.

Finally, the board decided that Delilah's allegations were just that: allegations of a petty and jealous individual. Professor Sharpe returned to teaching, and things returned to normal. The university atmosphere was constantly in motion, with new scandals replacing the old ones almost weekly.

The weeks flew by. I attended my classes and got my work done. I worked on my novel, still due at the end of the term. I didn't see Delilah around, and for that, I was thankful. I wasn't sure where she'd gone, nor did I care. I was more focused on collecting the pieces of my life and rearranging them so that they made more sense. I was focused on the good.

It was surprisingly easy to focus on the good. I'd added an additional routine to my daily regimen: meditation. I wasn't the best at it at first, but I was getting better. It helped me to center my thoughts before I started each day.

I had also started to spend more time at the gym again, helping Jax demonstrate different moves for his students. It proved to be a good distraction. I liked helping teach the students something positive.

"Just think, Harlow: in a couple of months, you'll be doing your own thing at the other gym. That evening support group," Jax reminded me, stepping up behind me and wrapping his arms around my damp waist. We'd just finished cleaning up after that evening's Mixed Martial Arts class for troubled youth.

Despite feeling sticky and gross, I didn't push Jax away. I leaned into his embrace and smiled. "And just think, you'll be able to do this more, give kids more reasons to stay out of trouble." Renovations for the gym were nearly completed, and it was set to officially open at the end of the summer. Jax would be managing it and teaching several classes. He'd even gotten me on the schedule, with my monthly support group meeting for women. Women who attended the support group meeting would get extremely discounted memberships and be able to take the self-defense classes for free. Jax's vision was beautiful, and I was happy that he wanted me to be a part of it.

"Yup," Jax said in agreement, pressing his lips to the side of my neck. I could feel his smile. "What did Professor Sharpe say when you submitted your final project?"

"That it was incredible, of course." I rolled my eyes, my smile widening. Professor Sharpe hadn't *just* sung praise for my finished manuscript; he'd had a lot of constructive criticism for me, but the important thing was that I'd aced the project and had his complete recommendation for anything I wished to pursue in the future. He'd even given me several job leads.

"Are you going to try and get it published?" Jax asked.

I turned around to face him, looping my arms around his neck. "I don't know. I can't think about that right now," I answered, plopping a quick kiss on his lips before dancing out of his embrace. I wanted to hit the showers. I had a lot to do that evening.

"Why?" Jax tilted his head, confusion on his face.

"Well, I have to finish packing—Crimson starts moving in this weekend," I reminded him, arching a brow. "And I need to finish a couple of applications." I was surprised at how quickly my three years at university had flown by. June was nearing, and with it... graduation and the completion of my Bachelor of Arts in English (with an emphasis on women's studies, of course). I had to find a job in the real world and prove to my mom and Larry that it was definitely possible to get a job in my field with my credentials.

I wasn't being picky about my job hunt. Any chance I could put my degree to use, I intended on doing so. I'd already applied to work at the library and I'd sent a resume in for a job as an editor for a small local paper. But my eyes were really focused on local publishing houses. I'd sent out my resume—and Professor Sharpe's letter of recommendation—to every publishing house I could think of, hoping to land a job as a literary agent.

"That's right. We're going to be roomies soon," Jax joked, his hands shooting out and gripping my waist gently. He tugged me towards him, a playful glint in his eyes.

"Yes we are." I smiled. We practically *were* roommates; I spent nearly every night over at Jax's place. I just needed to commit by bringing everything I owned up that flight of stairs, then it would be official. "Seriously though, I need to shower. Meet you out front?" I tilted my head, grinning.

"Of course." Jax smiled, his fingers gently squeezing before he released me. I shook my head, glancing at him once before I left the training room and made my way into the woman's change rooms.

I showered quickly, wrapping a towel around my body as I exited the shower. I felt light and happy; content. Things had come full circle, and for the first time in a long time, my life made sense. Sure, it was still hectic and dramatic at times and I certainly still stressed about the hazy future, but I loved the people in my life.

Not only did I have Jax's stable, loving presence giving me everything I didn't know I needed and more, but I had Jenna, Crimson, Jamie and Mark. I still considered Jamie and Mark to be close friends of mine, even after everything that happened between Iain and me. Jamie wouldn't hear of me cutting ties. He was sad that I was looking for work elsewhere, but he completely understood.

I also had Mom and Larry. I was still working to repair my relationship with my mom and step-dad, but things were better. I made it a point to call her at least once a week and fill her in on things, and that action alone changed the dynamic of things—not just between us but for her as well. She worried less and she wasn't so overbearing. She was able to relax more and do her own thing.

I smiled to myself while I dried my hair. The girl in the mirror didn't look so unrecognizable anymore. I was getting to know her still, but at least I could meet the emerald eyes looking back at me and not sneer when my gaze dropped to the faded scar on my cheek. I had to give myself credit; I'd been through a lot and I was still kicking, still fighting.

I set the dryer down on the counter and made my way toward the locker where my clothes were. Rounding the corner, I came to a stop when I saw a dark haired girl tying up the laces of her shoes.

Delilah Moreno looked up, seeing me in the doorway between the locker room and shower area. "Oh, hi," she said, straightening up.

My eyes narrowed. Residual anger boiled in my blood. "Really? That's all you're going to say? 'Oh, hi'?"

Delilah's shoulders slumped. "I see you still haven't forgiven me."

My eyebrows practically shot up to my hairline. "Forgive you? You caused unnecessary drama and almost cost Professor Sharpe his job."

"You can't blame me for drawing that conclusion," Delilah argued. "Anyone else would have thought the same thing. I shouldn't have said it, but still."

If I wasn't standing with only a towel wrapped around my body, I would have flung myself at her and punched her in her pompous nose. "You are seriously messed up," I said, shaking my head. I strode past her, towards my locker to grab my clothes. I looked back at her; she was still staring at me. "Seriously, why are you still here?"

Delilah's lip trembled, making me feel a little guilty for the way I was treating her. Then I reminded myself all of the damage she'd needlessly caused. "I just wanted to say that I *am* sorry. It's…hard for me to admit that I was wrong, and…well…I was wrong. I'm sorry."

"Noted," I responded.

Delilah pursed her lips and nodded. She went to leave, then stopped by the doorway. "You know, I'd hoped that we could be friends…" she remarked.

"You need to work on your friendship skills. Trying to destroy someone's academic credibility is *not* going to earn you any friends around here," I snapped, glaring at her. Delilah bit her lip and nodded, her eyes welling. She left before my guilt could win out and before I could retract my coldness.

The encounter unsettled me a little, but I did my best to shove it aside as I finished getting dressed and met Jax outside.

"Guess who I ran into," I told him after I climbed into his truck and slammed the door. He looked at me, arching his brow in question. "Delilah."

"Huh. Haven't seen her in a while," Jax remarked. After the incident with Professor Sharpe and Iain, Jax had made it perfectly clear to his boss and Delilah that he would no longer train her. One of the other personal trainers at the gym took over, but even still, Delilah hadn't been seen in a while.

"I feel a little bad for being so bitchy, but after what she did, I didn't exactly want to roll out the friendship carpet."

"Don't blame you." Jax shrugged. "You can forgive someone, but you don't have to forget what they did — and you certainly don't have to bring them back into the folds of your life."

I knew Jax was talking about more than just Delilah. He was talking about his mom too. In the past several months, her phone calls had become so frequent that Jax had to block the number. All she wanted was to plead for forgiveness and ask for money to pay off the debt his father had accumulated.

It made me sick, but it also made me appreciate my mother more—as imperfect as she was.

* * *

I hadn't seen Iain since the day of Delilah's allegations; since he walked away in the parking lot. I still heard about him sometimes. He was on several local talk shows and his book was on the New York Times Bestsellers list. Sometimes, Jamie would forget about all the things between Iain and me and proudly relay information about Iain's life. During one of my shifts, he'd happily reported that Iain was about to publish another novel; a psychological thriller. Mark had given him a warning look and Jamie stopped mid-sentence.

I didn't mind hearing about Iain. Secretly, hearing that he had found success made me feel better. It made me feel like I could be happy. I was thankful for him, thankful that he was flourishing in his new career and not rotting away in a jail cell, twisted and angry over the way things had happened.

Almost a month after graduation, I was sitting on the sofa in the apartment I no longer called home, having a girls' night with Crimson and Jenna. We had ice cream, a rom-com, and nail polish. I was more invested in the tub of Double Chocolate Delight than I was the nail polish or the rom-com, but still content to be there among my friends.

It was still a little strange, not living there with Jenna anymore, but it still sort of felt like home. Jenna made sure I came over once a week for these silly girls' nights. The old me would have scoffed at the notion, but I found that now, I appreciated it.

Part of me had worried that things between us would change for the worse when I moved in with Jax, *especially* after Jenna found out the secret I'd kept from her. Things between us had been rocky for a bit, and sometimes still were, but we persevered through it. I think it helped that we both knew exactly what would trigger turbulence: Iain.

"So, how's work been?" I asked, looking at Crimson. My mouth was full of ice cream, and my words weren't exactly clear but she somehow managed to understand my meaning.

"Incredible!" Crimson gushed, stars in her eyes. Not long before graduation, Crimson had applied to work at a hospital as a Social Worker after earning her diploma in Child and Youth Work. She wasn't expecting to land such a position so quickly after earning her degree, but she rocked the interview and got hired on the spot. It was her second week working there. "I still can't believe I got the job! I'm not going to lie...it can be hard, so hard," she added, her starry eyes misting. "But I know I'm making a difference, and I love it."

"It's so awesome." Jenna grinned in agreement. "Wish I could get that excited about my job," she added, her smile fading slightly. Jenna's father had scored her an entry level job as a certified financial planner at his friend's business. Jenna didn't have stars in her eyes when she spoke about her work, but she didn't hate it. I'd find it difficult to get excited about that job too. Then again, numbers had never been my strong suit.

I was still applying. I hadn't heard back from any of the places I'd applied to, except for the editor job— which had already been filled. Presently, I was still at the café feeling like a major failure.

"Don't worry, Harlow," Crimson said, giving me a sympathetic smile. "The right job will come along!"

"I know," I muttered, my brow furrowing. I hadn't meant for my friends to pick up on my strange mood, but that was the thing with people that cared about you. They picked up on your moods and emotions. They learned to read you even when you didn't want anyone to see.

I was learning that that wasn't always a *bad* thing, either.

"I still think you should try and get your book published," Jenna said, arching her brow at me with a challenging twinkle in her eyes. I'd only let three people aside from Professor Sharpe read my novel: Jenna, Crimson, and Jax. The idea of letting anyone else read it intimidated me. It was too personal, too poignant.

"I don't know," I muttered, my eyes dropping to the chip on the coffee table. It felt weird to talk about my book, the novel I'd written for my Creative Writing class. I'd been proud of my grade, naturally, but since Professor Sharpe returned it with his notes and suggestions, it sat in the top drawer of the night stand I shared with Jax, untouched.

My book wasn't about Iain and me...that would have been too easy, and besides, Iain had already done it. My book was about what happened *before*. I created a fictional character and gave her my experiences, more to give myself closure and also to tell my story in my own way. Iain had been right: the best stories came from true experiences and people, from situations that could (and, in this case, did) happen.

I'd finally opened up about what had happened to me *before* I set foot in Iain's classroom. I didn't write about my childhood or even the incident with Cole and the basketball team; those were stories for another time, another book. The book was mostly about my remarkable friendship with Lauren, and about her death and how it affected me. This book was for

Lauren. A way to keep her memory alive, a way to lament that painful part of my life.

It was deeply personal to me, and I wasn't sure that I could share it with anybody aside from the few I'd already let read it.

"Harlow, I definitely have to side with Jenna. I mean, so many young teens lose friends in tragic ways. So many of them ache over it and don't know how to move forward in constructive ways. I honestly think it'd help them to read your book," Crimson added.

Her words struck a chord with me. The moment she mentioned helping aching souls was the moment I realized that my book wasn't meant to sit in the top drawer of a nightstand. This story wasn't just mine; it wasn't just about Lauren and me. My story was many other peoples' stories and Crimson was right: it could potentially help another grieving individual.

How could she live on in dusty pages read by no one?

The wheels started to turn in my mind, and I knew I had to find a way to share her story…

About the Author

J.C. Hannigan lives in Ontario, Canada with her husband, their two sons and their dog.
She writes contemporary new adult romance and suspense. Her novels focus on relationships, mental health, social issues, and other life challenges.

Facebook: www.facebook.com/jcahannigan
Twitter: www.twiter.com/jcahannigan
Website: www.jchannigan.com

Other Books by J.C. Hannigan

Collide Series
Collide
Consumed
Collateral

Damaged Series
Damaged Goods
Reckless Abandon

Rebel Series
Rebel Soul

www.ingramcontent.com/pod-product-compliance
Lightning Source LLC
Chambersburg PA
CBHW021205250626
47155CB00008B/2676